T4-AHG-000

TWO CLASSIC WESTERNS
FOR A FRACTION OF THE COST!

NORTH TO POWDER RIVER

"Somebody shootin'!"

"Get out, man!"

Buck had carefully scouted his hiding area. Rabbits and other wild creatures had made a faint path along the side of the hill, a path that wound through high buckbrush.

He ran ten feet to his right. He screamed, "Shoot the hell outa the bastards! Follow an' kill 'em boys! They meant to kill you! Wipe the ambushers off'n the face of the earth!"

THE GRINGO

Cliff had seen Shorty in action before, but never had he seen the small man move with such machine-like precision. The blocks were just right, his forearms took Martinez' mauling blows. Those his forearms missed, he took with his shoulders. He knocked Martinez across a table, spilling it with crashing dishes. Martinez got to his feet, fighting hard. Shorty's right almost lifted Martinez, despite his bulk. His left smashed the man, turning him slightly. The right came again.

NORTH TO POWDER RIVER/ THE GRINGO

LEE FLOREN

LEISURE BOOKS ⏚ NEW YORK CITY

A LEISURE BOOK®

November 1990

Published by

Dorchester Publishing Co., Inc.
276 Fifth Avenue
New York, NY 10001

NORTH TO POWDER RIVER Copyright©MCMLXXXIII by Lee Floren
THE GRINGO Copyright©MCMLXXV by Lee Thomas, a nom de plume
of Lee Floren

All rights reserved. No part of this book may be reproduced or transmitted
in any form or by any electronic or mechanical means, including photo-
copying, recording, or by any information storage and retrieval system,
without the written permission of the Publisher, except where permitted
by law.

The name ''Leisure Books'' and the stylized ''L'' with design are trademarks
of Dorchester Publishing Co., Inc.

Printed in the United States of America.

NORTH TO POWDER RIVER

ONE

The Rio Grande sun was warm that late April of 1899 when two strong young men circled each other, fists raised and ready, there in the backyard of Charlie's Place, a saloon in Old Mesilla, Territory of New Mexico.

One was the lanky Texan, Buckshot McKee, who was a full foot taller than his big bellied opponent, Charlie, the saloon's proprietor.

Charlie panted, "You're slow blockin' my left, McKee! An' you're not counter-punchin' fast enough—or hard enough!"

Eight years before Charlie had been slated to fight for the world's heavyweight title but in training his tough fists had killed a sparring partner and then and there he had hung up his gloves.

He'd gone west and bought this border saloon deep in the high *chamisal*. Within a short time he had grown fat from wild booze and wilder women. His sagging belly covered even his wide Mexican belt buckle, but he still remembered the old fight patterns.

"Show me," Buck challenged.

Charlie panted, "My left comes in. You raise your right. You block it. Then in comes my right. Like this, Buck."

Buck blocked the left. He didn't see the right come in. He remembered flying backwards.

When he came to he sat with his back against the wall, his wavering vision finally focusing on a lovely dark-skinned girl who bent over him, concern on her Spanish face.

She wore only a small brassiere and smaller panties.
"You are coming out of it, my love?"

Buck shook his head gingerly, eyes finally achieving full and natural power. Tortilla Joe, his long-time Mexican partner, was now sparring with Charlie, their boots scuffling the dust, their fists raised.

"My love?" Buck asked.

"Yes, you are my love, Buckshots. My true love, too. We go inside an' you buy me a drink, *no es verdad*?"

"Drink, hell. I've not got a *centavo* to my name, Guadalupe."

A lovely frown. "You keed me, Buckshots."

Buck dragged his wallet from his hind pocket. He was wrong—it contained a Mexican *peso*, worth fifty *gringo* cents. "I beg your pardon," he said.

When Guadalupe stood up love slid from her sleek shoulders. "I go back into the saloon. I let you three crazy fools keel each other."

"We were in love, remember?"

"I remember nothing." She spat unladylike and entered the saloon's back door, hips swaying.

Buck reluctantly put his eyes back on Charlie and Tortilla Joe who were circling each other, fists up and ready.

"You knocked my pardner silly," Tortilla Joe panted. "But I'll see to it you don't punch my ticket and—"

Tortilla Joe never finished his sentence. Later he reported seeing Charlie's left come in ... but not Charlie's right.

He sailed backwards to land on his wide rump, back to the stone wall. Buck stumbled upright and lurched toward a bucket sitting beside the saloon's back door.

The bucket was half-full of lukewarm Rio Grande water. He threw the water into Tortilla Joe's wide face.

A few minutes later Buckshot McKee and Tortilla Joe stood at the bar with Charlie setting up the booze. "But just one time aroun'," Charlie said.

"You ain't set 'em up free for a long time," Buck reminded. "What's the occasion now?

"I've met fools before," Charlie informed, "but never

two as big as you two, so you get a free shot—but one only. How come you ain't buyin' for Lupe, Buckshot?"

"Only got one single Mexican *peso* in my wallet. How about you, Tortilla?"

"Got you beat. I got two *pesos* Mex."

Charlie looked from one to the other. His eyes had suddenly become small and unfriendly.

"Credit?" Buck asked.

"One buck, an' one only."

"Not *mucho*," Tortilla Joe reminded.

"I don't grubstake fools," Charlie said. "Two weeks ago you two old friends of mine rode in with six months of wages from the Rafter S north of Silver City, an' you pooped it all off, which shows to me you are fools."

"*Gracias*," Tortilla Joe said.

Buckshot McKee said, "I thank you, Charlie."

"I've even given you free boxin' lessons, remember?"

"I remember," Buck said.

"So do I," Tortilla Joe said and added, "An' I crave no more."

"What're you goin' do?" Charlie asked.

Buck dug a telegram from his pocket. He'd not carried it long, for it was clean and crisp. He handed it to Charlie. "Read this, *friend*."

Charlie read aloud:

Buck and Tortilla: 32 head of Brahman bulls in Dumas, Texas. Head them north to Powder River City, Wyoming. When you wire back *yes* I wire you one hundred dollars each.

Pothook Malone.

Charlie handed back the paper. "Who's Pothook Malone?"

"It ain't none of your business," Buck coldly reminded, "but Pothook a few years back owned one of Texas' biggest spread, The Pothook M, out of Amarillo, up in the Texas Panhandle."

"I know my geography," Charlie spoke sarcastically.

Buck overlooked Charlie's surly tone. "Sodbusters ran

Pothook outa the Panhandle. They brought in bobwire, ploughs, windmills. Pothook sold out all his cattle except about three thousand head an' he trailed them into the Powder River country up north in Wyomin'."

"Why'd he buy these Brahman bulls?" Charlie asked.

"Breed up his cows here, I guess." Buck looked down at squat Tortilla Joe. "We'll ride over to Las Cruces." Las Cruces was a bigger town a few miles to the northeast along the Rio Grande. "We can wire Pothook collect from there. Then we'll have *dinero* to take us up north."

"You think he'll wire you money?" Charlie asked.

"Pothook's word is good as Black Hill gold," Buck said. "You seem awful interested in us two now that we're gettin' some cash."

"Don't rub me, Buck." Charlie grinned. "You know damn' well I was jus' a-funnin' you when I said no credit. You got credit here anytime you want it."

"As long as we got money comin' in for sure," Buck said.

"I don't like your attitude," Charlie said.

"We're even up on that point," Buck assured.

Buck glanced at full-breasted Guadalupe who now sat listening at a table drinking with a stray cowpuncher. The word *dinero* had jerked up Guadalupe's dark eyes. Now she smiled sweetly at Buckshot McKee.

Buck didn't return the smile.

Suddenly Tortilla Joe laughed.

"What's so funny?" Buck wanted to know.

"Charlie. Now he thinks we'll have some money. We could make a big fool of him—leave him holdin' the potato sack—"

Charlie studied Tortilla Joe.

"How?" Buck asked.

"Drink some more booze on credit. Run up a big bill an' then ride out—an' never come back."

"You're a bastard," Charlie told Tortilla Joe.

"An' I aim to stay that way," Tortilla Joe assured.

Buckshot McKee gingerly touched his jaw. The remembrance of Charlie cold-cocking him still irritated.

"Come out from behin' the bar," Buck told Charlie. "I

wanna show you somethin' you never learned about fist-fightin'."

Charlie studied the long Texan. "Want me to send you into Sleep Land again, McKee? Onct wasn't one time too much?"

"I'd like to block thet blow afore I leave," Buck said.

Charlie grinned. He took off his white apron. He moved his massive bulk around the end of the bar.

Buck glanced at Guadalupe. Her dark eyes glowed with interest. Buck figured she and Charlie shared the same bed nights. Not that it cut a difference with him. But they acted so puritan by day . . . Calling each other *sir* and *senorita* and all that crap.

Charlie spread out his thick legs. Buck put his left hand against Charlie's huge right shoulder. "Now gimme your other hand," Buck said.

Suspicion rimmed Charlie's bloodshot eyes. "I don't savvy this," he said.

"Give me your hand," Buck said.

Charlie did. Buck instantly whirled. He laid Charlie's arm across his right shoulder. He ran forward three steps, then stopped suddenly. Charlie sailed over Buck's shoulder and crashed on his back on the concrete floor.

Buck stepped back. "Good deal," Tortilla Joe said. "Ol' Jake Smith learned you thet at San Juan Hill, didn't he?"

"He sure did," Buck said. "Right afore you an' me an' Bucky O'Neill an' the rest of the Rough Riders stormed the Hill."

Charlie groaned in pain. "My back—Jeezus, it's busted. Man, you might've kilt me—"

"You'll live," Buck said.

Tortilla Joe said, "Watch out, Buck!"

Guadalupe had left the table. She sprang for Buck, long fingernails poised. "You—son of a bitch! You killed him—He ees mi *esposo*, my husband—!"

Buck jumped backwards. Tortilla Joe got the enraged female with an ankle in each big paw. He lifted her upside down. Her dress fell around her head. She wore nothing under the dress but Guadalupe.

Unceremoniously, Tortilla Joe leaned forward, dropping her head-first behind the bar. The partners heard the crackle of bottles and a screaming Mexican curse. The cowpuncher Guadalupe had been drinking with had already made his hurried exit. You could hear his bronc hurriedly putting hoofs down in retreat.

Buck and Tortilla bowlegged outside to their broncs. Buck swung up on Rusty, Tortilla Joe doing likewise on Midnight.

Spurs hit horseflesh. Dust rose behind digging shod hoofs. They loped toward Las Cruces with Tortilla Joe hollering, "They ain't legally married, of course. You sleep with one of those gals a few nights an' she calls you her husband."

"That good or bad?"

Tortilla Joe had no answer.

TWO

The huge Brahman bull stared upward at Buckshot McKee standing on the other side of the corral. Buck stared down at the bull.

"Jeezus, he's a big sonofabitch," Buck said.

"He likes you," Tortilla Joe said.

"Likes me? You gone completely loco? One of these damn' things don't like nobody, not even a cow in heat! They jus' work a hot cow over outa sheer habit!"

Buck spoke truth. Tortilla Joe knew it. Both had tried to ride Brahmans in various rodeos and stampedes. Tortilla Joe had stayed with five for a full ten seconds. Now the Mexican said, "A cow sure must be blind. What in the hell could a healthy-minded cow see in an ugly bull?"

"Maybe there ain't no cows with healthy minds," Buck reminded.

The thirty-two bulls stood on the opposite side of the railing and looked at Buck and Tortilla Joe who in turn looked at the bulls. Both partners suffered from huge hangovers. Both had dry mouths crusted with the stinking residue of rotgut whiskey and stale beer.

The road up from the telegraph office in Las Cruces to here in Dumas, Texas, had been anything but arid.

True to his promise Pothook Malone had wired each partner one hundred dollars at Las Cruces. The partners had then loaded Rusty and Midnight and themselves into a boxcar headed for Amarillo, Texas.

"Hope Pothook has some dough waitin' for us in Dumas," Buck had said. "The way my luck's runnin'—"

13

He tossed his draw poker hand into the discard and glared at the few silver dollars he still possessed.

"I ain't cuttin' no gigantic swath, either," Tortilla Joe said.

Three others—railroad hands—were in the boxcar game. They were the two brakemen and the conductor. They'd dropped into the boxcar from the railing and had started a poker game, dealer's choice.

They'd loaded up with whiskey and beer at a siding. Within two hours all were rather tipsy. And Buck and Tortilla Joe lost steadily. Buck knew why. Three against two. The old skin-mule game. He knew he and Tortilla Joe were fools to get in the game. But they'd been fools before and never learned not to repeat.

"You jaw good English for a spic." The words came from a squat, heavy-set redheaded man, the head brakeman. They were directed sarcastically toward Tortilla Joe.

Evidently and plainly the brakeman didn't like Mexicans. The word *spic* was what struck. A spic was a worthless Mexican.

Tortilla Joe wisely had no reply. Buck secretly nudged his partner's flank. The nudge told the story. Two in fists against three and the three with hardwood clubs used to pound bums off boxcars.

So Tortilla Joe let the word ride. Still, it rankled him. He and Buck were on their last tens when Amarillo arrived. Both were pretty drunk. The day had been hot. The close boxcar—freighting the two sweaty horses— had been hotter.

The freight switched onto the siding. "Well, here we is," the redhead said. "End of the line, greaser."

The word *greaser* was a bigger insult to a Mexican than *spic*. And actually Tortilla Joe, while of Mexican descent, was not a Mexican. He and Buck had been born a few months apart in Laredo, Texas, where each had gone to the eighth grade before simultaneous wanderlust had struck both and given them itchy boots.

But, again, Tortilla Joe let it ride. And, again, it rankled.

14

The redhead was rather angry. The last hour he'd lost steadily even with the aid of the other two railroad hands. Buck was now the possessor of fifty dollars odd and Tortilla Joe a hundred.

"God damned Mexican," the redhead said.

That was too much for Tortilla Joe. Despite his better wisdom, he swung. His right sent the redhead tumbling down the right-of-way grade. The other brakeman jumped on him. The conductor slammed into Buck.

The railroad shacks didn't use fists. They used billys. When it was over Buck and Tortilla Joe lay knocked cold in the ditch. When they came to they'd been robbed. A scrawled note lay on Buck's chest.

'Two bucks each in your saddle-bags, bastards. Get outa town by tomorrow mornin' or it's the jug.'

"I'm gonna kill me a railroad hand," Tortilla Joe said.

"No you ain't, *compadre*. Them three are prob'ly well established here. They know the cops an' lawmen. You an' me get on Rusty an' Midnight an' drag ass out headin' north for them Dumas bulls."

"Aroun' forty odd miles, Buck."

"Ride'll do us good. Settle our heads, if we got any heads left."

Tortilla Joe considered. "Reckon you're right, pal. We was foolish to get into thet skinflint game."

"Not the first time we was foolish."

Neither again spoke of the railroad men. Each knew the other through long trial and acquaintance. They'd driven trailherds from this area—a number of times. Undoubtedly next year they'd go up north with another herd. The railroad men could wait, both knew.

"I'm kinda worried," Buck said.

"About what?"

"Them Brahmans been in Dumas quite a few days now. They might have a feed bill against them. An' we ain't got much *dinero* atween us, *compadre*."

"We'll cross thet bridge when we come to it," Tortilla Joe said.

So now they stood there. They gazed at the bulls and the bulls gazed back, long tails lazily switching flies, long ears flopping back and forth.

"What'd you know about these damn' India cattle?" Buck asked.

"Only thet it takes a real bronc-kicker to sit one of the bastards for ten seconds. What'd you know?"

"Well, Texas ticks won't bother them. That's why cowmen are breedin' their she-stock to Brahmans down around south Texas where they's lots of ticks. Their get is tick-proof, too."

"Wyomin' ain't got no ticks," Buck pointed out. "So why would ol' Pothook want these sacred cattle up in the Powder River country?"

"More than that to it."

Buck licked a Durham cigarette into shape. "Okay, like what, for instance?"

Tortilla Joe had read in a stockman's magazine that when a Brahman bull bred a Hereford cow the calf needed about one-third as much grass as would a calf thrown by a Hereford bull.

"I doubt that."

"Well, that's what the article said."

Buck looked at Rusty. The big sorrel pointed his ears north. Buck turned and looked that direction. About a hundred yards away was a shed.

A huge man dressed in overalls and a straw hat had just left the shed's wide door. He was headed toward the partners. He walked like a rolling stud-horse, he was so big.

Huge boots ground dust. He toted a rifle under one arm. Buck scratched his head and scowled. For some reason this big bastard didn't look too hospitable.

"No horse livin' could hold him up," Tortilla Joe said.

The human dray-horse stopped in front of them. "I'm Tank Willard," the deep voice intoned. "Who, might I ask, is you two drifters?"

Buck didn't like the word drifter any more than Tortilla Joe had cottoned to spic and greaser but he let that pass. He gave Tank Willard their names and said, "We come after these Pothook Malone bulls."

"Which bulls? I got pens and pens full of bulls. Be

pacific, McGee."

Buck spoke to Tortilla Joe. "This man has a command of the English language."

"Sure has."

Tank Willard's narrowed eyes moved from one to the other. "What's so damn' funny?"

"Not a thing," Buckshot McKee assured. "I mentioned the Pothook Malone bulls, Mr Willard."

"I dunno this Pothook gent. Got to look it up in the manifest, I guess."

Buck explained.

"Oh, them damn' India bulls! Hell, they been here about ten days longer than the manifest said. I got a nice feed bill ag'in 'em. They consume hay like they ain't no tomorrow."

"Feed bill," Buck said.

"Feed bill," Tortilla Joe chimed.

"Yep, runs into two figgers, men."

Evidently Pothook had figured the hundred bucks he'd given each in Las Cruces would have taken the bulls from Dumas into Wyoming, but Pothook had reckoned without taking the railroad-poker-game into consideration.

"You got any papers tellin' me you can legally take over these bulls?" Tank Willard asked. "Manifest says nothin' about two strangers comin' in an' claimin' this valuable property."

Buck produced Pothook's telegram. Willard read it with lips moving slowly. "Now you two got any personal identification?"

This was getting involved, Buck quickly noticed. He had a hunch his birth had not even been filed in the church records in Laredo, and the same undoubtedly stood for Tortilla Joe.

Then, he remembered. He had a letter from the sheriff's office in Pecos, Texas, stating that he, the bearer, one Buckshot McKee, would be jugged immediately upon re-entering the town of Pecos.

Tortilla Joe had a similar letter.

They showed these letters to Tank Willard who again

17

read slowly with moving lips. The huge lips then grinned and the ox-like eyes rolled up and again moved over the battered and cut and swollen faces of the partners.

"You boys has been in more trouble since this letters was writ," Tank Willard said.

"Let's skip that," Buck said. "How about shiftin' attention to these bulls, Mr Willard?"

One bull—an enormous dun—stood and watched through the corral bars as though he understood each word said. Buck noticed his long ears switched back and forth mechanically and silently dubbed the bull with the name of Flapears.

"Let's go to the office an' look up the feed bill," Tank Willard said.

Buck and Tortilla Joe dutifully followed the bovine back. The office consisted of an old desk, old chairs, and old newspapers everywhere you looked. Tank Willard dug into a pile of newspapers and his big hands finally came up with a sheet of paper which he consulted carefully, lips moving as he read.

"Thirty six dollars an' eighty cents," he finally said. "Wait a minute. That doesn't include today's charge of one dollar and twenty cents."

Buck looked at Tortilla Joe. The Mexican slowly shook his head. Buck spoke to Tank Willard. "Beyond our financial limits. Me an' my pard need to have a conference."

"Then hold the conflab outside." Tank Willard's tone was sharp.

"You ain't very hospitable," Buck said.

"Two things break through my morose nature," Tank Willard said. "One is the clink of gold coins. The other is the flash of green. An' from here it looks like you two drifters ain't got neither."

Outside Tortilla Joe said, "We got to get a wire to ol' Pothook, but have we got enough cash to send it?"

They counted their fortunes. The fortunes were deplorably low. "Maybe we can send it collect," Buck said.

"Let's go to the depot an' see," Tortilla Joe said.

The depot agent was smaller than Tank Willard but just as morose. "No telegrams go out collect. Company orders. Railroad been stuck too many times by drifters sendin' out collect an' the thing bein' refused at the other end. Cash or no send, boys."

"What's the tariff?" Buck asked.

The agent grumbled his reply. The partners had the necessary sum with a few pennies—but damned few—over. "Leave us nothin' to eat on until we get Pothook's reply," Tortilla Joe said. Then, to the agent, "when will an answer an' cash come back?"

"How would I know? I'm not God."

"I figgered you were," Buck said.

The telegram was sent. The partners hied themselves to the Dumas Downs, the biggest local saloon. They began on the free lunch. They didn't want to waste their limited capital on beer, a fact the owner soon noticed.

"You boys ain't bought no drinks. Free lunch is for customers only."

Tortilla Joe pointed out that he and Buck were potential customers. The proprietor pointed out the world was full of potentials but he needed and wanted active customers.

Buck then related their problem.

"You boys got anythin' to pawn? You both pack good-lookin' side-arms. Seen you ride into town, too. Them hosses you straddled are worth a few *pesos gringo*."

"Not our guns," Buck hurriedly said. "An' not our mounts, either. You know where Hinsdale, Montana, is?"

"Nope, an' don't care to know."

"Well, we run them two horses out of the Larb Hills south of Hinsdale an' close to the Missouri, the Big Muddy."

"Not interested, boys. Dig up somethin' to pawn—an' if I like it—"

"An' if it's sol' cheap enough," Buck finished.

Next day they haunted the railroad depot. No wire came. Next day, no wire. Third day, no wire.

They lay on their blankets on the north edge of town.

19

Mosquitos kept the partners' arms waving.

"Can't understand this," Tortilla Joe said.

Buck summed up. "Each bull's worth at least three hundred bucks, mebbeso more. But we'll say three hundred a head."

"Uh huh."

"Three hundred times thirty two in my summin' makes nine thousan' an' six hundred iron men."

"That's more than I got on me."

"Me, too. At the present, that is," Buck joked, thinking that maybe in his lifetime he'd never made nine thousand six hundred. "An' ol' Pothook ain't gonna throw thet much away."

"Maybe he never got our telegram. Him bein' out on his ranch, like that. Six miles from Powder River City, somebody onct told me."

Neither had seen Pothook Malone's Wyoming spread although their advice had caused the old cowman to trail his Texas herd into the Powder River areas. That had been five or six—or maybe just four years ago—Time went so fast Buck had a hard time keeping track of the months, let alone the years . . .

"Maybe we oughta send him another wire," Tortilla Joe suggested.

"What'll we use for money?"

"Let's dig deeper into this," Tortilla Joe said. "We got almost ten thousan' bucks down in thet corral. What else you got to say?"

"I got a feelin' somethin's gone haywire up in Wyomin'. Or we'd have had a reply. But no matter which way the cards fall, I ain't leavin' them bulls here for this fat bastard of a Willard."

Tortilla Joe batted at a mosquito. "You can't steal them bulls. Hell, they're slow a-foot, pard. Sheriff an' his gang of legal thieves would haul us an' them down within a few miles. Now, if they was horses—"

"But they ain't."

"We're right back where we started, Buck."

"Somebody's comin', Tortilla."

A boy of about ten materialized out of the growing

Texas dusk. He carried a bucket and some kitchen utensils. "Pa sent this grub out to you," he said, setting down his load.

"Your pa?" Buck asked.

"We own the Dumas Downs saloon. Pa heard about the trouble you boys is havin' with them bulls an' that damn' Tank Willard."

"A boy your age ain't suppose to swear," Tortilla Joe said.

"A man your age ain't supposed to use the word ain't, either," the boy replied. "I'll come back later for the bucket."

The bucket contained boiled beef and french-fried spuds and a salad for each. Both tied in. Between hunks of grub Buck said, "Something like this restores my faith in humanity."

"But just for a short while. I then think of things like Willard. You know, Buck, I've got a sudden idea."

"Better hang on to it. Might be your first and last. But what is?"

"We take the bulls—and with 'em, we take Tank."

"Kidnap the bastard?"

"He's got five hands takin' care of his corrals. He won't be missed for a few days. He's feedin' them bulls half-rations to skin them down so they can't walk very far in a day. He figgers we aims to highsteal them bulls."

"I won't dispute that. When will this happen?"

"Let's wait one more day. Then, if tomorrow brings no wire, we jump him at the day's end when his help has gone home."

"Only thing we can do," Buck said.

No wire arrived next day.

The terrible heat had driven even the blowflies into the shade. The bulls suffered. They had no shade. Buck was angry. So was Tortilla Joe. About three a stranger again hove into view—and this was not the saloon-keeper's son.

This man was somewhere around thirty, the partners judged. He was a full two inches taller than tall Buck McKee who signed in at about six foot three.

He'd been to the corral before in the last two days. He

had sauntered about, apparently just looking around. A chambray shirt covered his wide shoulders and he had the slightly bowed legs of a cowboy. He wore old levis and he packed a .45 in an old holster.

"Still waitin' to get your bulls out, eh?" he asked.

Buck studied him. "How come you know about us an' them Brahmans?"

The stranger rolled a Bull Durham cigarette, Buck noticed his cigarette paper was brown wheat straw. That meant he was a south Texas cowboy. All cowpokes there used brown paper. Up north cowboys rolled Durham in white cigarette papers. The man got his smoke going, handed the makings to Tortilla Joe, who hurriedly began to twist a smoke into shape. He and Buck had been so broke they'd been bumming the straw and paper.

"Kinda common talk around town," the stranger said. He inhaled and said, "Them India cows are worth quite a bit of money. I know a cowman up in Montana—right in the corner of Wyomin' an' thet state—who'd pay at least a hundred bucks a head for them."

Buck's ears went up. He wasn't giving up on these Brahmans. They were going north come hell or high water. And if not to Wyoming—if perchance old Pothook didn't want them—or had suddenly died of old age—well, these bulls were going to belong to two people, one named Tortilla Joe and the other Buckshot McKee.

"I know Montana kinda well," Buck said. "About every summer we go up there an' punch cows for ol' Dad Sturdivant's Circle Diamon'. Dad runs north of Malta which is on the Milk River."

"I've heard of him."

The man got to his feet and walked off without another word. Buck looked at Tortilla Joe and Tortilla Joe looked at Buck.

"Who the hell is that gink?" the Mexican asked.

Buck McKee shrugged. "Damned if I know. I don't get his drift, *compadre*."

"When we goin' move against Tank?"

"Let's wait until it gets deep dusk."

"He might leave afore then."

22

"If he does, we jump him."

Soon a kerosene lamp glowed in the corral's office. Through the window you could see immense Tank Willard hunkered in a chair over his desk evidently doing some paper work.

The partners had planned carefully. They entered together. Tank Willard looked up, plainly angry at their appearance.

"What'd you two drifters want? Cain't you see I'm workin' on the books? Spiel an' drag ass."

Buck said, "You're goin' with us, mister."

Ox-big eyes studied the tall Texan. "You goddamned fools—I catch your drift. You drag me along with you. You've heard about me goin' on week-long drunks an' never showin' up here an' you think with you makin' me prisoner everybody'll think I'm holed up somewhere with some woman on a drunk, eh?"

Buck's Colt .44 was out. "You hit the nail on the head."

Tank Willard came up like a giant uncoiling spring. He had terrible agility for such a massive man.

Writing equipment and ledgers sprang upward as the big desk erupted. Buck jumped to his right. The desk missed him but hit Tortilla Joe. The desk drove Tortilla Joe to the wall. He went down out of sight as Tank Willard dived for Buckshot McKee.

Dismay hit Buck. Things had happened too fast. He'd planned to buffalo the giant over the skull if needs be— and it appeared this was needed and needed right now.

Tank charged Buck. Buck slammed his gun down. He aimed to hit the big man behind the ear. He'd knocked out men before with a pistol barrel. But Tank Willard moved too fast.

Buck's heavy weapon missed the man's head. It hammered down hard on Willard's massive right shoulder. It bounced harmlessly upward. Buck had not planned to shoot the man. But he might have to do so to keep Willard from killing him.

Tank Willard stood with his back to the door. Without warning a gun-barrel appeared raised behind him. Buck caught himself in surprise, trigger finger freezing, pistol unfired.

The barrel belonged to a Winchester rifle. It came sharply down. It caught Tank Willard full on the top of his cranium and he slid flat on his face against the office floor, an unmoving mass of human meat.

Buck gawked at the man holding the rifle. He was taller than Buck and he said, "Listen, you two bastards. You get them damn' bulls outa here, savvy? Head them north, and *pronto*."

"Who t'hell are you?" Buck's words were forced.

"Makes no difference who I am. I'll take care of this big hunk of slobbering Texas jerky. I tol' you to move. Now move."

"You're the guy who was talkin' to us today," Tortilla Joe uselessly said. "The tall stranger . . ."

The tall man disregarded the Mexican. "I tol' you to move. I won't tell you again."

The stunned partners moved—and fast.

THREE

The Powder River begins southwest of Hell's Half Acre in middle Wyoming. It then twists its way northeast for about ninety miles until it meets the Salt coming in from almost southeast.

The Salt loses its name and identity when it meets the Powder which then continues almost due north to become a dubious asset to what is now the state of Montana. Once in the Treasure State the Powder adds on a few almost always dry side-streams and finally, after some one hundred and fifty odd miles, it loses itself and its name and its sluggish and dirty current into the Yellowstone River.

The bulls were destined for Powder River City which was located at the point where the Salt entered the Powder. Here old Pothook Malone had stopped his northern trail drive—at the advice of Buckshot McKee and Tortilla Joe—and had put up his ranch buildings, his cattle roaming free and mosquito-bitten over thousands of unfenced acres—land he did not own but which belonged to Uncle Sam.

Buck and his partner figured the drive from Dumas, Texas, to Powder River City Wyoming, was, as the crow flies, a little over six hundred miles. They and the bulls left Dumas in the first week of May, 1899.

"Them critters are in poor shape," Tortilla Joe pointed out. "First week out they can't knock off more'n ten miles or so a day."

"We'll take 'em slow."

After rousting the bulls from the corral they pushed the

25

animals hard and dawn found them some fifteen miles north of Dumas with already weary bovines. They watered them at a pot-hole containing a little muddy water, the bulls eagerly drinking.

They then let the bulls scatter out up and down the draw and the animals immediately sought out what little grama grass they could find. The partners rode up the north slope and squatted on a brush-covered hill and watched their backtrail.

The backtrail was without riders. All south and west and east extended mighty Texas. The wind was ice-cold and cut through their denim brush-jumpers.

"I sure t'hell can't understand this," Tortilla Joe finally said.

Buck nodded. "Got me stumped, too."

Ever since leaving Dumas one of the partners had ridden the backtrail scouting for possible followers. None had been found. No posse followed them.

"Up ahead," Tortilla Joe said shortly. "They could've circled us in the night. Set a trap up ahead."

"You scout ahead. I'll haze 'em in the rear."

"Got to let them graze for a while. What say we drive nights and take days to rest them?"

"Good idea."

"Until we get outa Texas, of course. Then drive days an' rest nights."

Buck McKee scratched his whiskery jaw. "My figgers say it's aroun' fifty odd miles from Dumas to the Oklahoma border. Onct there we'll be safe."

"Only redskins to pester us acrost the Territory."

"Cavalry's got them under control," Buck pointed out. "But I sure can't understan' thet tall stranger. Him knowin' so much about us an' them bulls, an' him takin' Tank Willard over for us."

Tortilla Joe could only shrug.

Buck stretched his right leg. "Gettin' ol'. Muscle ties up now an' then in my ham. Hell, pard, there's a heap here I don't understan', an' I know you don't understan', too."

"Like what, mebbe?"

"Why didn't ol' Pothook ship these bulls directly to the Powder country? They's railroads up there, now."

"I've mulled thet over, Buck. I've come to the conclusion thet if he shipped to Wyomin' the bulls would have had to go to New Orleans, then up to Chicago, then out west to Wyomin'—an' by that time—those many weeks—some of the bulls might have kicked the bucket, you know."

"That's logical."

Tortilla Joe scowled. "Then I got another idear, Buckshot. Ol' Pothook might wanna see us in person an' jus' used this bull deal as a way to get us up to his Wyomin' spread."

"What fer?"

"He might be in trouble. 'Member last year when we headed north chousin' them Bar Lazy V dogies into the region aroun' Billings, Montana?"

"Naturally."

"Well, we had a hard time crossin' the middle of Wyomin', remember? Lots of new borbwire fences. Farmers movin' in."

"You're sellin' ol' Pothook's brain cheap, *compadre*. He knows better'n tangle pistols an' rifles with incomin' grangers. They're in the right an' he's in the wrong. 'Mind that's why he left Texas? Was he in a mood to fight the hoemen, I kinda figger he'd have fought up on the Panhandle with 'em instead of headin' stock north."

"That's right. Never thought of that. Odd, how when each spring we head north to punch an' rodeo for the summer we never swung far enough east to visit ol' Pothook an' Ma."

Buck shrugged. "Call it fate er sumpin'."

"We owe him an' Ma a lot."

"Mebbeso our lives," Buck said.

The morning of the fourth day found the bulls in Oklahoma Territory. The Brahmans were getting their legs back and travelled faster now. They'd been well gaunted-down by the little hay in the corral in Dumas.

Noon of the fifth day found Buckshot McKee riding into a little Oklahoma town while Tortilla Joe nursed the bulls around a western waterhole. There Buck bought the *Amarillo Anvil* although the newspaper was three days old. The *Anvil* had a page devoted to Dumas news.

"My God, look at this," the lanky Texan suddenly cried.

"What is it?"

"Here, in the Dumas news." Buck handed his partner the newspaper. Tortilla Joe read slowly, then handed back the newspaper. "Somebody beat the livin' hell out of Tank Willard, it said. Tank's in the hospital an' he might live an' he might not."

"An' nobody knows who hammered Tank down. An' Tank ain't talkin', it says. He was asked if any stock was stolen from his corral. An' he said not a head. That tall guy must've really overhauled Tank's clock."

"An fer why, Buckshot?"

"You got me. Here's another little Dumas item. Says a local citizen was sure he identified a stranger in town as a member of a well-known longrider gang. Said he thought the man was sizing up the local bank to break it open but the man left and the bank wasn't robbed—not at this printin', anyway."

"You mean that tall gink what apparently hammered down Willard—I cain't remember seein' him before—not with the Cassidy bunch, anyways."

Buck looked around at the mention of Butch Cassidy's name.

"Nobody aroun' to hear us," Tortilla Joe said.

"I'd like to forget that day," Buck said.

Ten years or so back the partners—then mere kids—had held the horses for the Cassidy gang while the gang had robbed a Colorado bank. They had aided the gang without knowing it.

They'd been riding out of the Colorado town headed north when a man had ridden out of the brush and asked them to watch a few saddle-horses for a few minutes while his cowboys were in a local house of ill-fame. He'd pay them each two bucks and pay ahead of time.

"We'll report back in less than an hour," the man had promised.

Tortilla Joe and Buck had been delighted. Think of that! Two bucks each—now in hand—and only a hour!

The man and his cowpunchers arrived in less than twenty minutes. They came in crouched over flaming guns, two carrying canvas bags with a bank's name stamped on them. But Buck and Tortilla were not there to see them. They had heard the guns yammering and had fled. They'd unwittingly held getaway broncs for Cassidy's Wild Bunch. The newspaper of a nearby town said a couple of the local youths—out hunting cottontail rabbits—had seen two strangers—not much more than boys—guarding the Wild Bunch's broncs. It also gave a good description of Buck and Tortilla Joe, and their horses were clearly identified as to colour and brands. That night the young partners had *borrowed* two local horses and had turned their original mounts loose on the prairie. And whipped their new horses down the legs heading across the Utah—Colorado line, eight miles west. Once safe in Utah, they'd turned their stolen horses loose. They'd made themselves hidden by working as roustabouts with a local small circus, thankful for their escape. Even now they didn't like to think about it.

They reckoned to cross the Strip on a route a trifle to the north of west. Thus in about fifty miles they'd be in the state of Colorado.

Buck was dubious about crossing the Oklahoma Strip. A few years before more Indian land had been opened for white settlement with the original redskin residents of that land being booted out into the wilderness.

He could remember no redskin uprising in the Strip within the last few years, though—but a man never knew. Plainly there'd be redskins roaming around looking for a place to light, he figured.

They'd forded the Canadian river at nine that evening and let their Brahmans graze on the river's north bank. Here grass was thick and the bulls fell eagerly to foraging.

Buck had ridden drag that afternoon. Tortilla Joe had taken the point. Buck had just got the bulls across the river when Tortilla Joe rode over a northern hill.

"Caught sight of some riders off to the northeast,

Buck."

"How far away?"

"Two miles when I sighted them."

Buck nodded. "Let's have a look. These bulls will be okay here. Anybody try to run them off, tired as they are, an' he'd not get far. Hell, they'd not even move. They'd give 'em the horns."

Buck and Tortilla Joe rode to a hill where they could command a view of the surrounding area. This was a wilderness country of rolling hills and sharp cul-coulees heavy with high grey sagebrush and an occasional cholla cactus. The cactus, though, was thinning out, leaving only greasewood and sagebrush, for at this point the Great American desert was disappearing as you rode further north.

The group Tortilla Joe had sighted was coming in from the east. Buck's glasses showed them to be redskins. He counted six riders well mounted.

"What're we goin' do?"

"Nothin'."

"Them redskins has jumped their reservation. They might decide to butcher one of the bulls."

"Hope they take Flapears and Blacktail if they have to chew on Brahmans, but I sure t'hell ain't gonna challenge six bucks—from here it looks like every one's totin' a rifle."

Buck lowered his field glasses. "They lift a rifle an' we'll both salivant a bullet their direction. Not to kill but to scare."

The Indians came into view. They saw the bulls and stopped.

The bulls then did a strange thing. They swung into a straight line facing the mounted Indians, Flapears and Blacktail holding down the middle.

The bulls then pawed the earth. Forehoofs threw back hunks of Oklahoma sod. They began bawling as they dug.

Two bucks half-raised their rifles. Buck McKee raised his Winchester 1873, the danger in this wilderness-encounter chilling his lanky frame.

Six rifles against two . . . He and his partner could be

shot dead out here a thousand miles from nowhere. And the only persons knowing where their carcasses were would be a handful of reservation-jumping Choctaws.

These Indians would be more than happy to kill a couple of white bastards. Especially since the law would never hear about it . . .

Buck heard the Indians shout. Rifle raised, he waited, cold in saddle, horse solid underneath—but he never shot.

The mounted redskins fled. They wheeled horses, hammered with quirts, and loped madly west. Horns drawn, bawling rage, the long line of bulls seemed about to burst after them, and then suddenly it was over. Flapears and Blacktail broke up the rank and looked around for grazing.

Buck breathed again and slowly, thoughtfully put back the Winchester.

"See how these holy India cows went into a line, not a circle?" he said.

"No cows or calves for them to pertect."

"Thet's right. You hear them Indians holler when the bulls rushed?"

"Them redskins was Choctaw. I know a few words of that *idioma*. You know what they was sayin'?"

"Greek to me."

"They were hollerin' that the Manitou had put these bulls onto this section. Their God had given these bulls eternal life. If an Injun kilt one, he'd fall dead off'n his horse right *pronto*."

Buck hurriedly glanced at the Mexican. Tortilla Joe crossed his ample bosom.

Buck's gut had a chilly feeling. He looked from the brooding Tortilla Joe to the bulls. Flapears and Blacktail each stood with his head close to the other's rump. That way when one slung his long tail around he'd brush mosquitos and blowflies from the other's face. Buck had seen horses stand that way but had never before seen bovines in such a position.

"You don't believe thet, do you?"

"I don't know," Tortilla Joe slowly replied. "Do you?"

31

Buck decided hurriedly to change the subject. "Let's trail-drive these unholy bastards out of this bottom."

"Good idea."

FOUR

Five days later Buckshot McKee stood in the saloon in what was left of Bent's Fort in Colorado on the Arkansas River smoking a long Pacific Grove Havana cigar, the fragrant smoke curling around his battered Stetson, a mug of Walsenberg beer cradled in his rope-scarred right hand.

"This," he said to himself, "is livin' . . ."

Owner Smoky Jones was tending bar. "Long time no see, Buck. Goin' north with another herd?"

Buck shook his head. He wouldn't mention the Brahman bulls cached out in the brush four miles west of town with Tortilla Joe. He figured some of these Colorado punchers might not be too honest. Quite a few thousand bucks were tied up in those bulls. Also, for some reason the bulls were unbranded. And that meant that anybody who threw one and ran his iron on him would be the bull's owner. That was the written—and unwritten—law of the rangelands.

"No other herd," Buck replied. "Barbwire, Smoky—fenced lanes. I got a hunch the days of the north drives are pretty well over."

"Looks thet way, Buck. End of a era an' I don't cotton to it."

Buck shook his head. "Me, neither. But they ain't a damn' thing we can do about it. Headin' north to punch this summer for Dad Sturdivant. He's good to me an' Tortilla. Let's us off to hit the stampedes. We'll take in the shindig up in the Canuck Cypress Hills first an' tie it up at Wolf Point, Montana."

"Seen Charlie lately?"

"Still got the girls an' bar at ol' Mesilla."

"How's the ol' boy look?"

Buck remembered throwing Charlie over his head. "With the same set of eyes." He then put the bee on Smoky for twenty bucks. He got fifteen and had expected only ten. "Pay you when Tortilla Joe an' me go south this fall."

"Your credit's good, Buck. Where's Tortilla?"

"He's ridin' in from Nevada. Meet me up in Billings. How's business?"

Business was slack, Smoky Jones informed. "Trail drives, what is left of 'em, swing way west. Go north along the slope of the mountains. Not so many fences an' gates there. I thought things would be better when McKinley got into office. He's worse than Cleveland."

"Politicians," Buck said. "Legal thieves." His voice lowered. "Who's thet hairpin standin' kinda alone at the far end? Jus' come in, Smoky."

Smoky Jones didn't look directly at the man. He glanced covertly at the man's reflection in the back-bar mirror.

"Never seen him afore in my life."

The saloon-keeper's voice was somewhat guarded. Buck got the idea that Smoky Jones knew the man but refused to acknowledge the fact—but for why?

Buck killed his beer. He bought four bottles of beer—three for Tortilla and one for himself back at camp. He'd liked to have bought Durham at Smoky's but Smoky's price for a sack was double that of a local grocery he knew. And fifteen bucks wasn't much with this Republican inflation period on after the Spanish—American war.

The tall stranger was the man who'd taken over down in Dumas after the Tank Willard brawl. Buck stopped and said, "Buy you a drink, mister."

The man didn't answer. He merely shook his head.

"I'd like to have a talk with you."

"We got nothin' to talk about. I've never seen you before in my life, Buckshot McKee."

"Never seen me? Then how'd you know my name?"

The man's voice was very low. "Get t'hell out, Texas man."

Buck's lips tightened. He looked at the man for a long moment aware that Smoky Jones was watching.

Then he left.

The store-owner was an old retired cowpuncher. When Buck had finished his buying he had a little over four dollars left. He figured that sum would last him and Tortilla at least to Cheyenne, Wyoming. The grocer put Buck's purchases in a woven white sack.

"Never seen a sack like that afore," Buck said.

"Wheat sack. Farmers use 'em. Bemis makes them. Stamps his name on the side, whoever Bemis is."

The oldster's voice held disdain.

"Farmers comin' in?" Buck asked.

"Like lice on a Mexican bull. Most of the sonsofbitches can't even speak English an' most don't care. But I can't holler. They pay cash or get nothin'. Between here an' Kansas is one fenced lane an' borbwire."

"The cow country's done with."

"You don't need to repeat thet, cowboy."

Just then the tall stranger walked past. He glanced at Buck through the big front window, face showing no recognition, and disappeared beyond the window's limit.

"You know thet gink?" Buck asked.

"The one what jus' passed? Never seed him afore thet I can recollect. Stranger in town."

Buck and his sack went out. He tied the sack behind his saddle with Rusty fidgeting slightly, for, like his master, the big sorrel never seemed to be at peace in a town.

When entering the store he'd noticed a big bay gelding tied alone to the hitchrack in front of the town's other saloon. That bay was now gone. Buck got the impression the tall stranger had ridden off on him.

The northwest wind was chilly. Buck wondered if spring would ever come. He had a feeling of loneliness. His talk with Smoky Jones and the old cowpuncher-storeman had been anything but heartening.

The West was rapidly changing. Hell, it had already

changed! What had but a few years before been unfenced open range was now being fenced. Where buffalo grass had grown now grew head crops. Trouble was ahead.

Here on the high plains the only time the wind ceased was at sunset and sunrise. Between those hours the wind continuously blew. And the only reason the land didn't blow, too, was because of the buffalo grass. For buffalo grass was native grass, the grass God had put on purpose on the Great Plains. It hung close to the soil. It covered every inch of the ground. Wind could not penetrate its thick covering. And the roots of buffalo grass also were interwoven into a tight ball. This also kept the soil intact and protected from the ever present strong wind.

When cattle in great herds moved north their sharp hoofs naturally had cut through this buffalo grass protection. The plains had little rain and about the only real moisture they had was when winter came and snow covered the world. Their world, at least . . .

Thus huge dust clouds rose to mark a trailherd's plodding passing. Buck had seen this dust go high into the cloudless sky. He'd sat his horse miles away and had seen a number of dust clouds moving slowly north to the luscious pastures of Wyoming and Montana and lower western Canada.

With open range forever gone, what would he do? He was a drifter—a man of the saddle, of endless open spaces.

He and Tortilla Joe had talked this over. Tortilla Joe had mentioned the upper reaches of Mexico—Chihuahua, Sonora and Coahuila states. Buck had slowly shaken his head.

"They're starvin' to death down there. A cowpuncher's a peon there. A damned slave to the rich. Not for me."

"The Wild Bunch—I've heard they aim to pull out for the Argentine."

"I've heard that, too. They call them big plains down there the Pampas. Still, that isn't like home was, Tortilla."

"Sure isn't, I'd judge. But the Wild Bunch—Cassidy,

Curry, Longabaugh—I don't know, *compadre*. An' wish I did—"

Now, with Rusty setting a long, mile-eating running-walk pace, Buck found himself thinking of the outlaw gang called the Wild Bunch, his thoughts again returning to the point where he and Tortilla Joe, mere striplings, had without knowing it held the Wild Bunch's getaway broncs while the Wild Bunch had robbed a bank.

He and Tortilla Joe had met many of the Wild Bunch hands after that day. First time had been in Chinook, Montana, four years after the first incident.

Kid Curry had been the one to recognize them. He'd poked stocky Butch Cassidy in the ribs. "Remember these two buttons, Butch?"

Cassidy's hard blue eyes had studied the Texas pair. "Hell, yes. They's the ones who held our broncs one time—and was tricked into it!" He laughed as only Butch Cassidy could laugh.

Kid Curry had slapped Tortilla Joe so hard on the back he'd almost caved in the young Mexican, for Tortilla Joe weighed about forty pounds less then.

"Wanna steady job?" Kid Curry had asked.

"Like doin' what?" Tortilla Joe asked.

Curry again laughed. "Holdin' horses again?"

Tortilla Joe shook his head. Buck McKee grinned. He liked these two toughs. They had a good sense of humour, something many people lacked, he had learned.

They had next run into the Wild Bunch south of Lordsburg, New Mexico Territory, where the gang was lying low for a while punching cows in the Las Animas Valley, just inside the U.S. border.

They'd met all the Wild Bunch but Ben Kilpatrick who for some reasons happened not to be with Cassidy and Curry and Longabaugh whenever that trio ran into Buck and Tortilla Joe.

"You two han's is gettin' quite a rep aroun' the West," Kid Curry once told Buck in a Worland, Wyoming, saloon. "Heard you done topped off Lightnin' down in the Cheyenne Frontier Days. First time the hoss has been rid, they tell me."

"He piled me," Buck said.

"You stayed in leather until the whistle blew."

"He threw me a few seconds later."

"But you still rid him by the rules."

Buck made circle with his beer glass on the bar. "Way this son of Texas figgers a man doesn't ride a bronc until the bronc gets so fagged he quits buckin'."

"You got a point there, McKee. You and Tortilla Joe ever get lonesome for different company you know where to find it."

Buck had nodded.

He'd known full well what the outlaw meant. He and Tortilla Joe could join the Wild Bunch whenever they wanted.

"Seen ol' Pothook Malone lately?" Buck had asked Kid Curry.

Rumour said that whenever the Wild Bunch were in Pothook's vicinity the outlaws holed up at Pothook's ranch. Rumour also held that perhaps Pothook in his younger days had ridden with an outlaw gang. Not the Wild Bunch, of course, for at that time the Wild Bunch had not been in existence.

"Saw him about a month ago on the Powder down in Wyomin', Buck. Asked about you an' Tortilla."

Buck smiled. "He saved our necks, onct. Down on the Texas Panhandle. Tortilla an' me was just buttons then. That was about two years before you boys tricked us into holdin' them getaway broncs."

"You two oughta swing by an' visit Pothook. Him an' his missus are gettin' on."

"How is Ma?"

"Ailin', Buck. Ol' age an' hard work."

"We'll try to stop in at Powder River City this fall when me an' Tortilla Joe head south."

But the partners never went south through Wyoming. They had ended up at the stampede in Elko, Nevada. They rode south into Arizona and then east to Charlie's Place. And here they were, on the way to Powder River City and Pothook, if only they could get track of him.

Buck made Rusty quicken his pace. He didn't want

Tortilla Joe's beer to get too hot. He had left the Mexican and the bulls in a draw some five miles west of Bent's Fort.

He rode out of the brush and then hurriedly drew rein, for the clearing held not cow nor horse nor man. The area lay clean of life.

Sudden fear pierced him. Had some unknown guns ridden in, stolen the bulls, gunned Tortilla Joe down? These bulls were valuable animals. And the further north they travelled the more value each and every hide took on.

He cupped his hands to his mouth preparatory to hollering. Then, he changed his mind. He brought down his hands. Were he to holler he might alert some hidden enemy of his presence.

Hurriedly, he pulled Rusty back hidden by the high buckbrush. He wanted no hidden rifle to knock him from saddle. Within a few minutes he was on a high hill sweeping the country with his field-glasses.

This wasn't logical. He'd only been gone about an hour and half. Two hours at the limit. Even if somebody—outlaws, Indians, what-have-you—had stolen the herd, the bulls in that time could not have been driven completely out of sight . . . There should be some trace of them.

He returned to the clearing. Dusk was coming in. But days were getting longer now; there'd be light until eight in the evening, at least. He left saddle. He circled the area keeping hidden by brush. Nothing had gone east. Nor north or south. West was a different matter, though.

Here cloudbursts had washed down tons of loose gravel that would bear no hoofmarks. Buck then saw a pile of smoking cow-manure which told him that the herd had passed this way.

He looked for bloodstains on the rocks. To his relief, he found none. He rode up the canyon. The further he penetrated the wider the canyon became.

He came upon the bulls within a mile. They were peacefully bedded-down, but where was Tortilla Joe?

Then a voice behind said, "Buckshot McKee."

Buck turned rapidly, going into a gunfighter-crouch,

right hand flashing down to his holster. Tortilla Joe stepped out of the brush, grinning widely.

Buck said angrily, "You tryin' to get me to kill you?"

"Testin' your gun-speed, Buckshot. You've still got it."

"Childish play an' dangerous," Buck said shortly. "Why'd you move the critters?"

"Saw somethin' I didn't cotton to in the distance."

"Like what, fer instance?"

"Somebody was on that ridge over there—Thet one to the northwest—"

"Yeah?"

"An' thet somebody was a-watchin' me an' these bulls."

"You sure of that?"

"He had field-glasses. Sun reflected on them. That's what got him my attention. So I moved the bulls to here."

"You use field-glasses?"

"I told you. I ain't got 'em, but I saw him good an' clear."

"Describe him."

Tortilla Joe did. Buck stroked his bottom lip thoughtfully. "Thet sure sounds like the gent who handled Tank Willard for us."

"It was him, Buckshot."

FIVE

On cattle-drives Buck and Tortilla Joe knew that the further north the Texas herd got the slower the progress, for the long gruelling miles wore down the longhorns. Strangely this did not hold true for the holy cows of India, the Brahmans.

With each passing day, the Brahmans seemed to grow stronger despite the fact that spring grass was very green and still held much water. This prairie grass—blue joint and bluestem and buffalo grass—had its full strength in the fall of the year after a blistering summer sun had cooked out its water and replaced the water with dry nourishment.

"These sonsofbitches are tough," Tortilla Joe said.

"Mebbe we oughta ride a bull an' give our cayuses a rest," Buck said.

Tortilla Joe laughed. "Ride a bull! We've tried that at stampedes. An' we failed—and how!"

"I'm goin' try it," Buck said.

That night Buck climbed on board of Flapears. The bull paid him no attention. He gingerly kicked the bull gently with his heels. He wore no spurs. Flapears obediently moved ahead and, to the Texan's surprise, he began herding the other bulls around.

Tortilla Joe stared in wonder.

"This guy's done this afore," Buck said. "Wish I knew where he come from an' who had him afore we got him. Somebody's made a pet outa him. Even used him to bring home the milk-cows, I'd say."

"Like we did when we was children, eh?"

Had Flapears suffered such a fate, also? Buck was sure he'd been ridden before. He gave no hint of wanting to buck. Buck even guided him with the pressure of his knees.

"I'm goin' try thet on Blacktail," Tortilla Joe said.

Blacktail fidgeted while Tortilla Joe climbed aboard. He then bucked the Mexican off in three vicious jumps. Tortilla Joe landed rolling in the sage. He got up and brushed himself off, lips tight as he glared at Blacktail who, chores done, had gone back to grazing.

"I'm goin' put a surcingle on that black sonofabitch one of these days and get on my saw-rowelled spurs and jus' take the hide off'n him!"

"I'll tie your flankin' strap," Buck said drily.

When a Brahman came out of the bucking-shute he usually had a rope tied around him just in front of his hind quarters with a cowbell attached to the rope's bottom. The rope goosed him and the booming cowbell infuriated him. He then kicked at both, which made him much harder to ride.

Summer came on as they slowly moved across Colorado. They drove through fenced lanes. Milk cows stampeded at the sight of the Brahmans. The only cows that didn't run were those in heat. And they welcomed the bulls who boldly waded through barbwire to service them.

The bulls bred three of a farmer's Holstein milk cows. Buck and Tortilla Joe tried to keep the bulls in the lane but the task was hopeless. The farmer came running out with a double-barrelled shotgun.

Buck had to give the irate granger his last three silver dollars. Thus somewhat appeased, the farmer forgot his anger and returned to his sod shanty.

"An' now we're really broke."

"What'll we do?"

"We got to work to the west. Get closer to the mountains an' rough country where they ain't no farmers 'cause the land is too rough to farm."

"Ol' Pothook seems to have deserted us."

"I'll try to get word to him or from him from Denver."

"There's somethin' sure as hell haywire here, Buckshot. We tried to get word from him in Walsenburg. Three days ago, weren't it?"

Buck thought. "Four."

"Okay, four. What the hell's an extra day or two? An' no dice. Spent almost our last buck, too—'cept for those three silvers we gave thet damn' farmer. This started out wrong. It's been goin' wrong ever since. An' way out there on the horizon is that gink—thet tall bastard—thet man handled Tank Willard."

"That might not be him we've seen."

"Too far off for real identification?"

"That's it. I got him in my glasses. But I'd not swear it was that tall button."

Tortilla Joe scowled. "I might be dreamin' up things, Buck. These bulls—this damn' trip—Somethin's wrong, somewhere. You know anybody in Denver who'd lend us a few bucks?"

"I'm thinkin' of one man."

"Who's that?"

"Juan Sanchez."

"*Cantina del Oro*. Juan might an' he might not, but I'll try. These farmers sure look at these bulls. Noticed a few cowpunchers ride by lookin' them over careful like, too."

"They're not branded, remember?"

"An' a cow or horse without a brand is anybody's animal. First one that lays a hot iron on him owns him."

"Unless the calf or colt is still suckin'," Buck explained. "We don't know a danged thing about these cattle except that telegram sayin' they was waitin' for us in Dumas."

Tortilla Joe's face tightened. "I catch the drift. We might be movin' stolen cows. Do they hang cowthieves in Colorado?"

"Jus' horse thieves."

"We could put our own iron on these bulls. Then they'd be ours."

Buck nodded. "Been thinkin' of thet. Anyway, we oughta trail-brand them, if nothin' else."

A trail-brand was a brand put on stock before starting

43

the long trail north. Usually the cattle-owner studied state brand-books listing all brands in the particular state his herd would cross.

He then picked a brand no other state had. He hair-burned this on his stock. Within a few months the hair would grow out. Then the brand would be eliminated but by that time the cattle would be grazing on their northern grass and their owner's brand registered in the state brand-book at the state capital.

"One thing wrong, though," Tortilla Joe said. "You an' me ain't got no registered brand."

"You don't have to register a trail-brand. We're partners, ain't we?"

"Sometimes we ain't but most of the time we are."

They decided to run a wire-brand that evening on each bull just back of his left ear. Their trail-brand would be an MJ. M for McKee. J for Joe. "Now all we need is a piece of wire," Buck said.

A farmer's barbwire fence held an extra few feet of wire. Buck cut it free with his fence-pliers. Two miles further on they met a rider toting a law-badge. His star said he was a deputy sheriff.

He stared at the Brahmans. "What kind of cattle is them?"

Buck told him.

"You got a bill of sale for 'em?"

Buck showed him Pothook Malone's telegram. The deputy went to put the folded telegram in his vest pocket.

"Wait a minute," Buck hurriedly said. "That's mine, not yours." He fairly jerked the telegram from the grimy hand.

"That ain't no bill of sale," the deputy said.

"Is to us," Buck said.

The deputy stood on one stirrup. He gave the bulls another long and probing study. "I oughta take you two in," he finally said. "Impound your stock an' pen you in an' make some inquiries from this Pothook Malone up in Wyomin'."

Neither partner spoke.

"I better talk to my boss." The deputy loped west.

Tortilla Joe looked at Buckshot McKee. "He wants these bulls. An' he wants them free, too."

"Typical county worker," Buck said. "Legal thief. We'd better run thet trail-brand on as soon as possible."

"He looked at them bulls from the left side," Tortilla Joe said. "He saw no bran' there so we'd best hair-bran' from the right side."

"Good thinkin'."

They decided on branding a single M instead of MJ. They'd told the deputy these bulls belonged to Pothook Malone and the M would stand for Pothook's last name.

They left the barbwire lane. They came to the foothills. Here there were no farms. The land was too hilly and rocky to farm.

They drove the bulls into a coulee. Tortilla Joe and Buck roped in a team as they had done in so many rodeos and stampedes. Buck took the head; Tortilla Joe the hind legs.

The bulls were big and heavy. Therefore they were harder to throw to the ground than the cattle roped in a rodeo but Midnight and Rusty knew their jobs. Never did they allow slack in a rope so a bull could kick and struggle. Always they moved ahead just enough with empty saddles to keep the catchropes tense.

Tortilla Joe built a small fire of sagebrush trunks. These coals were as hot as a wood fire if not hotter. Buck's fence pliers built the wire into an M about four inches high. Soon it was red hot and the first bull lying prone.

"I'm not one to escape hard work," Buck said, "but I appoint you a committee of one to hair-brand, Tortilla Joe."

"Now I've heard all things."

Tortilla Joe had a fine touch. Even though the Brahmans had shorter hair than a Hereford or shorthorn he burned only down to the skin, no further.

The stink of burning hair was strong. There was, for once, no wind. The two cowpunchers worked in the coulee—roping, getting down, running back, branding. Dusk was thick when the last bull bore the M.

It would be a nice night with a high moon. They cooked bacon and spuds over the dying sagebrush-branch fire. They were terribly low on grub. Their bank account wasn't. Still, they were free. Suddenly Buck jerked upright from his prone position on the ground.

"Riders're comin'," he said.

SIX

Tortilla Joe also stood. His right hand settled on the butt of his holstered pistol. "That damn' deputy."

Buck said quietly, "No gunplay, pal."

"They ain't robbin' us of these Brahmans."

"Play it calm."

Five men rode into camp. A heavy man on a blue road gelding led them. He had a shiny star on his vest.

The deputy rode at his boss's right. Behind him were the other riders. The three looked like saloon-bums the sheriff had taken along just to fill out his posse.

Nevertheless the partners did not sell the other three short. Each man packed a pistol and the partners got the impression that they knew how to handle those six-shooters.

"Heard you two drifters were hazin' stolen stock," the sheriff said without giving him and his riders an introduction.

"Who are you?" Buck asked.

"Me? Sheriff Breckinridge Monte, sheriff of this county. My deputy Jim Bridges." He didn't introduce the other three.

"Stolen stock?" Buck asked.

Sheriff Monte looked at the bulls. The bulls were grazing along the side hills. "Can't see no brands on them critters."

"They're trail-branded," Buck informed. "Trail-brand registered in Dumas, Texas. Here's the paper."

He handed up Pothook Malone's telegram. The dusk was thickening and the deputy lit a wood match so his boss could read.

The sheriff looked up. The deputy threw away his burned match. "This ain't no bill of sale," the sheriff said.

"Look on the back," Buck said.

Another lighted match. This time the lawman read aloud. "To whom it may concern: The bearer of this— Mr Buckshot McKee—has filed in this county of Texas, county seat, Dumas, that he is owner of thirty two Brahman bulls, unbranded but of good health."

The sheriff paused, then continued: "Signed by Mr Malcolm MacGregor, brand register, Dumas, Moore County, Texas."

Tortilla Joe listened to the last in concealed surprise. Buck had written this latter here in this cut-coulee. He'd seen his partner off to one side sitting cross-legged and writing something but he'd not known what.

It read good. Tortilla Joe's memory soared across mountains and deserts to three years ago when he and Buckshot McKee had been sentenced to six months for inciting a saloon riot in Elko, Nevada.

A local lawyer had brought Buck law books. Buck had learned enough in a short time to apply for a writ of habeas corpus which had liberated him and Tortilla Joe. Buck had used his legal knowledge when writing on the back of the Pothook Malone telegram.

"Looks legal enough to me," Sheriff Monte said.

"How come you don't know he jus' writ that?" the deputy said. "That wasn't on the back of thet telegram when I read it this afternoon."

"You're wrong," Buck coldly said. "It was there then. You jus' didn't turn the telegram over an' read it."

"You callin' Jim Bridges a liar, cowpoke?"

Bridges' hand was on his holster's lip. Anger flooded Buck. He almost matched draws with the arrogant deputy. He caught himself in time. Two guns against five was not a gunfight. It was suicide.

Up coulee a meadowlark's song broke the stillness. The bulls kept on grazing. The meadowlark's song died. The voice of one of the posse took its place.

"I come with you an' the sheriff to collect stolen cows, Bridges. I never come along to sling a gun."

"Me, neither," another posse member said.

Bridges' hand moved back. It settled, palm down, on the top of his wide saddlehorn.

"Much better," Buck breathed.

Bridges said tightly, "Mebbe them words was there when I looked."

Sheriff Monte studied the bulls. Buck could see a cash register working in the lawman's mind. This far north each bull was worth at least two hundred bucks. The further north they got, the more their value increased. But Buck settled at two hundred a bull at this point.

Two hundred bucks time thirty two bulls made six thousand four hundred good old Uncle Sam dollars. Which was probably at least three years' salary as sheriff of this county . . . if not more.

No wonder the sheriff licked his sun-cracked lips.

"Lemme see the trail brands," the sheriff said.

"Hard to see 'em in this dim light," Buck pointed out. "Brand is hair an' not very big. Boss didn't want the bulls marked up by brands."

"Rope one an' bring him over," Sheriff Monte said.

The sheriff's voice had lost most of its original hardness. Evidently he'd assumed a tough voice thinking that he was dealing with two ignorant cowhands. Buck's knowledge of law apparently had taken some of the wind out of the lawman's sails.

"Lay the twine on ol' Flapears," Buck told Tortilla Joe.

Flapears was angry. He'd not been treated too humanely by these things on two legs. Midnight had to drag him by the neck to the sheriff who dismounted and looked at the M hair-brand.

The sheriff looked up at the deputy. "You tol' me these critters never packed no brand."

"They didn't. Not when I was here, anyway."

Buck said, "You didn't ride aroun' them an' look at the other side—the side they was branded on."

"That's right," Tortilla Joe told Sheriff Monte.

The deputy said feebly, "Reckon you're right. I'm

all right down mortified, Sher'ff." Sudden hope rimmed his next words. "But mebbeso they've hair-branded them just afore we rode up."

Buck's heart fell. The hair would still stink. That would tell the lawman the branding had just recently occurred.

Sheriff Monte leaned over to smell the brand. Luckily Flapears at that moment he'd not only had enough—he'd had too much.

He swung his horned head at the sheriff. The flat of his horn hit the sheriff on the side of the head. The sheriff lost his hat. The blow sent him hurriedly back. The sheriff's face turned ashen grey with rage. He pulled his gun. "I'll kill that—"

Tortilla Joe caught the sheriff's gun-arm. "Take it easy." Hardness lay beneath his calmly spoke words.

The sheriff caught his temper. He reholstered his .45. "Brand don't smell of hair," he said. "How long you boys goin' be in my county?"

"We're headin' north," Buck said. "How far to your north boundary? Twelve miles about, eh? Tomorrow night we'll be out of your area."

"Make it out by sundown or I'll throw you into jail and the bulls into the town tax-lot. You boys has caused my bailiwick a lot of trouble."

Buck's brows rose. "Trouble?"

"Coupla complaints has already reached my ears. Your bulls bred a Holstein milk cow. Farmer filed that. One bull kicked down a wire fence. Another damn'—pardon me, gentlemen. Another farmer filed that complaint, too."

"Right sorry about that," Buck said.

The sheriff turned his horse. He rode away with posse—such as it were—following. Buck breathed a sigh of relief when the last horse and rider fell from sight.

"Mebbe we should bunch an' drive north?" Tortilla Joe asked. "Get outa that gink's borders as soon as possible?"

"Good idea."

"We can rest the bulls longer tomorrow."

Soon they had the bulls moving. The bulls didn't want to be driven. They were accustomed to grazing this hour. Here along the foothills were far less farmers. That meant less barbwire and lanes. Moonlight dappled the hills.

At one they met a cowpuncher heading west. He was more than half-drunk. "Had a dance at Rock Crick school," he said.

Buck then remembered it was Saturday night.

"Yeah, you're outa Sheriff Monte's county. Cross the line about half a mile back, cowboy. Sheriff Hans Hagen here in this county. Another no-good parasite sonofabitch."

"Aren't they all?" Tortilla Joe asked.

The drunk spurred on, singing a ribald song. Buck and Tortilla Joe let the bulls spread out along a small valley. The tired animals drank at a creek and tied into the long spring grass.

The partners drew straws to see who'd stand first guard. The unhappy choice fell to Buckshot McKee. Tortilla untied his bedroll from behind his saddle, stripped Midnight, put the horse on picket.

Buck rode Rusty up the north hill. Here he dismounted and looked about. He saw lights to the northeast. He realized they had to be the lights of Denver. They'd driven closer to Denver than he'd figured.

He hoped Juan Sanchez in Denver would lend Tortilla Joe some money. This being dirt poor and without tobacco was getting tiresome.

Much depended on Juan Sanchez's generosity. He didn't know the *senor* Sanchez too well. Sanchez was somewhere somehow a blood relation of Tortilla Joe, but that was nothing new—every border town and some not on the border held a cousin or aunt or nephew and such of the Mexican.

He'd met Sanchez once or twice, no more. He wondered if he'd recognize the *senor* if he saw him again.

The question was decided at eight that morning. A man rode out from the direction of Denver.

The prairie morning was brand new, glistening in

glory. Crocuses showed scarlet faces upward from the spring-growing earth. Meadowlarks flew here, then there, serenading the grazing bulls.

Buck stood against the day and watched the man ride in. Sunlight glistened on a flashing hat-buckle, from conchas on chaps, from the silver-mounted hand-carved saddle.

The man was a dandy. Lithe and short, he rode a saddle as though born there. He drew in a big roan stud and said, "*El senor* Buckshot McKee?"

"*Senor* Juan Sanchez," Buck said.

SEVEN

Juan Sanchez's dark eyes studied the grazing bulls. "They are very, very ugly," he said.

Buck knew the bulls were no beauty-prize winners but he gave no reply, wondering just what had brought the Mexican this distance from his home base, the *Cantina del Oro*, his saloon in Denver's Mexican section.

Surely the man hadn't come that distance just to look at the bulls? Something was amiss here. What was it?

"Light an' rest your saddle," Buck said.

Juan Sanchez dismounted. Buck noticed the *don* was unsteady on his pins. He then knew what was haywire. The Mexican was half-drunk.

"My cousin? Tortilla Joe? Where is he?"

"Over here, cousin Juan."

Tortilla Joe came out of a nearby bullberry bush. He wore only long-handled underward and a .45. The .45 caught Juan's attention. "Ah, you expected trouble, no? You did not recognize me right away. So you went to the brush with your *pistola?*"

"Things haven't been runnin' too smooth," Tortilla Joe said.

"That is what I came to tell you about. The sheriff—he wants your bulls—"

"What sheriff is that?" Buck asked.

"Sheriff Monte. Not of this county but the other south—the one you have gone through—"

Buck felt relief. He thought there'd be another unpleasant session with the local sheriff, He told Juan Sanchez about the meeting with Sheriff Monte and the sheriff's scraggly posse.

"How come you know all this?" Tortilla Joe asked.

Juan Sanchez had heard customers talking in this saloon. "Most of them has never seen a Brahman," the saloonman said. "You'll fin' people standin' along their fences watchin' your cattle."

"We're gonna travel where there are damn' few fences," Buck growled. "We've had too much audience already."

"Be hard to avoid," Sanchez said. "You know, I'm sleepy. Had a fiesta at my house. An' I sneaked away from it."

Tortilla Joe spoke softly. Sanchez did not overhear. "Shall I hit him up for money now?"

"You know the gink. I don't."

"I'd better take him back to town. I'll meet you north of town tomorrow."

They left Buck alone with the bulls. Tortilla Joe would telegram Pothook also. His orders were for Pothook to have some money and word awaiting the partners in Sig Nelson's saloon in Cheyenne, Wyoming.

Buck threw bull-camp that evening on a small creek angling down-hill toward the southeast to eventually join the Arkansas River. Grass was not too high for snow runoff had been too fast on these slopes to allow the water to penetrate to the grass' roots.

Nevertheless it was grass and the bulls fell to. Buck noticed that Rusty kept looking southeast, ears pricked. Rusty looked for Midnight. The two horses had been together since colthood.

Tortilla Joe didn't ride in that night. Next morning Buck again headed the bulls north. Two hours later he came to another settlement of farmers. Grangers stood inside fences. All except one toted a shotgun. This one carried a deadly .45-70 rifle.

Buck later learned these farmers were a fanatic religious sect that thought Brahmans were the cattle of the devil. Were a Brahman bull to breed one of the local cows the settler would shoot and kill the bull. That is, unless Buck got the fanatic first . . .

Within a mile three riders loped in from the east. They turned out to be the local sheriff and two of his deputies.

The trio moved their horses close to the east fence to allow the bulls to pass. Sheriff Jake Russell then introduced himself and deputies. "Matt Hogan an' Bill Mullins. Your name, sir?"

Buck introduced himself.

"Heard about these sacred bulls passin' through our county," the sheriff said. "Your boy came into town an' tol' us you were about to drive through this mess of religious nuts."

Buck smiled. "You don't seem overladen with joy for these farmers, sheriff."

Sheriff Russell spat hugely. "So goddamned stupid they don't even vote. We'll see you run into no trouble, McKee."

Buck said, "You're different than Sheriff Monte. He tol' me to get my ass an' these bulls outa his county as soon as possible."

"He sent a deputy to report to me," Sheriff Russell said. "So these bulls are goin' into the Powder River country in Wyomin' . . . What would one of these bulls be worth on the market this far north?"

"I sure don't know, Sheriff."

"Make a rough guess, eh?"

"Mebbeso fifty bucks a head."

"That ain't enough," a deputy said.

"Thirty two bulls," the sheriff said. "At fifty bucks a head. That makes sixteen hundred dollars. Quite a bit of money. You all alone?"

This last question bothered Buckshot McKee. Sheriff Russell had said that Sheriff Monte had sent over a deputy to tell about these bulls. The deputy naturally would have mentioned two men drove the bulls.

"Had a partner yesterday. Mexican. Pulled out on me this mornin'." Buck shrugged. "Got mad, I reckon. Said he was leavin' for good."

"Can't trust a Mex ever," the sheriff said.

The sheriff studied Flapears. "Ugly sonofabitch. How could even a cow in heat take on one of these terrible-lookin' bulls?"

"They take them on," Buck said.

They came to the last fanatic's farmstead. The sheriff and his men said goodbye and rode east. Within a mile Buck met three cowpunchers. They said they were out looking for strays. They worked for the Bar N Bar. The Bar N Bar ran cattle here.

"Not for long, though," a lanky man said. "Nesters'll come in, run us outa land . . . an' business."

Buck looked about. This was a sort of badland area. Farming land had suddenly ceased. This area consisted of cut-coulees and raw red hills eroded and ugly. There was not even a road into this wilderness north ahead.

"How many miles across this mess of hell?" Buck asked.

Lanky Man said, "Oh, about ten miles, cowboy. Mebbeso eleven. Jus' fin' a coulee an' foller it north. Worse than it looks."

Buck debated. He'd already put almost a day's travel behind. His bulls were getting tired. He studied the badlands. Would there be any feed for them in this hellish area? Or water?

He put the question to Lanky. Lanky informed him that in about the centre of this hell was a spring that would furnish water for his bulls. "Grass aroun' there, too. We lose strays in there." He spoke to his two fellow cowpokes. "What say we drive in with this stranger? Might find some strays aroun' the waterhole."

"We've found 'em there afore," another cowpuncher said.

Two punchers rode point. Buck and Lanky took up the drags. The bulls went unwillingly into the badlands. Buck and Lanky had to pound them with doubled lariats to get them headed the right direction. "Damnedest ugliest critters God ever laid eyes on," Lanky said.

Buck was tired of hearing that. "Don't reckon God pays much attention to 'em," he said. "With all this trouble aroun' the world—wars an' people starvin' to death—I'd say the Old Boy's concerned with more important things."

Once in the badlands the bulls moved easier. The two cowpunchers riding point knew this area. They led the bulls—and McKee and Lanky—through a myriad of coulees. Finally they came upon the spring and the grazing area.

The Bar N Bar men found nine head of strays there, all belonging to their iron. They bunched them and started them south over the trail Buck and his bulls had just traversed.

"How'll I get these critters outa here?" Buck asked.

Lanky answered. "Simple, Cowboy. Just put them north into thet coulee there. Only coulee leavin' here so you can't miss. Then take every draw on your left. Never turn up a draw to the right. First thing you'll know is you're out on level prairie again."

The Bar N Bar cowboys left hazing their strays ahead. Buck dropped from leather, unsaddled, put Rusty on picket-rope after watering him.

The bulls were grazing. Soon they'd bed down for the night. They'd made around twenty miles that day, Buck figured.

Buck's thoughts ran to Tortilla Joe.

He had a hunch the Mexican would ride into camp some time tonight. He wondered if his partner could find his way through these badlands. Then he remembered last night's brilliant moon. Tortilla Joe could make out the tracks entering the badlands. Moonlight would be that bright. And common sense would tell him that Buck had not swung either east or west to circumnavigate this rough area. The partners had agreed to forge north regardless of the terrain. To skirt this badland area would have added somewhere around fifty extra miles to the trek north.

No, Tortilla Joe would follow the bulls' trail in, Buck felt sure. Tortilla Joe might have attended the tail end of Juan Sanchez's fiesta but more than likely he'd laid the day over in Denver for one purpose: to see if he could get a telegram—and money—from old Pothook Malone.

Buck had some cigarette papers. He found some dried sagebrush leaves. He ground them into dust and rolled a cigarette. Didn't taste like much but was better than nothing . . .

He'd shot a cottontail rabbit. The badlands were full of cottontails. He broiled the young flesh over sagebrush coals. They were even getting low on salt, he noticed. His inner man fed, he lay with his head on his saddle, smoking another sagebrush cigarette.

Flapears came close, sniffed at him, then grazed away. Buck wondered if he should stay in this badland area until Tortilla Joe showed up. He hoped nothing serious had happened to his partner. A man never knew in this day and age, he told himself.

He and Tortilla Joe had not lived a clean, trouble-free life. Two years ago they'd made the jail in Denver for beating up on a policeman who'd tried to arrest them for saloon-fighting.

They'd spent a night in jail. Next morning each had paid a twenty dollar fine. That night they'd happened to meet the same policeman. Buck had taken him on alone and when the battle was over the policeman was doubled up knocked-cold in a big alley garbage can.

Memory ran over the back-trail he and Tortilla Joe and the Brahman bulls had travelled since leaving Dumas, Texas. Two days ago Tortilla Joe had declared he'd seen the tall stranger off to the north moving north on horse-back. Buck had searched that area with field-glasses but had seen not a single rider.

Then there was Sheriff Monte and his posse. Well, he was in another county now. Out of Monte's jurisdiction. Still, a man could hit a herd in another county, even though sheriff of the adjoining bailiwick.

And this local sheriff . . .

He wished Tortilla Joe were with him. One man can't watch both back and front. And these valuable bulls . . .

For the dozenth time he wished he and Tortilla Joe had not taken on this bull-nursing job. Were the bulls mere Herefords or shorthorns or Angus—well, those breeds were ordinary breeds, the selling price of each a fraction of the selling price of a Brahman.

He should have recognized these Brahmans

immediately as spelling one word: *trouble*. And to haze them north so many miles . . .

But when you're not much more than a boy—and in jail for horsestealing—and when somebody saves your neck from the rope—No, you weren't guilty. You stole nobody's horse. But you rode a good horse—and the local sheriff wanted that horse—and he wanted to steal it legally—

So he threw you in jail. On a trumped up charge—They hanged horsethieves in north Texas.

No, they'd had to repay . . .

Sheriff . . . Horsethief charge . . . One thing the long dim trails had taught him—and taught Tortilla Joe, too—sheriffs were many times only outlaws—thieves, crooks—parading as citizens behind a law badge—

He'd met two such these last few hours, he felt sure. Therefore caution rode heavily on his shoulders. He was a man alone—one gun only—And he guarded a small fortune . . .

And those three cowpunchers . . . He looked about. He realized he was in a trap.

He saddled Rusty, swung up. He bunched the protesting bulls. He drove them into the coulee the cowpunchers said was the badland's exit.

The bulls were dog-tired. He hammered them savagely with his doubled-up lariat. They lumbered into the coulee.

Lanky had said to keep turning left. He decided to turn right. He met no box coulees. He didn't have to once turn the bulls back. Lanky had lied. To prove it he rode down one coulee to the left.

Within half-a-mile he ran into its blunt end. He spurred back to his bulls. Night was advancing. He hammered them even harder, making them trot. It took him one hour to get on level ground.

Here ran a bubbling creek evidently fed by Rocky Mountain snow. Cottonwood trees and willows lined its banks. Ahead was a flat area on the creek's north bank. He drove his bulls into this section. Grass was high and the bulls began foraging. He looked about. Soon the bulls would bed down. Grass was so high it would almost hide them as they lay down.

Anger touched him. Cold and deliberate anger. The three cowpunchers had lied to him. And for a purpose. They wanted him holed up in that badland trap.

He dismounted. He pulled his rifle from saddle-scabbard. He jacked a cartridge into the barrel. He took a box of .44/40 shells from a saddle-bag. He put a cartridge into the rifle's magazine, thus filling it.

He checked his Colt .44. He always kept the hammer on an empty chamber. He broke the pistol, filled this chamber with a cartridge. He holstered the heavy pistol.

He lifted his lean height into saddle. He looked at his bulls. They were already bedding-down. They were very tired. Rusty was leg-weary, too. His owner was also dog-tired. But not too tired for the chore he figured lay ahead.

He rode back into the badlands.

EIGHT

They hit an hour before dawn. They had it timed so they would have chased his bulls out of the badlands in the growing light of a new prairie day.

His Ingersoll showed four twelve when he first heard them. They moved cautiously and kept themselves well hidden but he still heard them coming.

They left their horses a quarter-mile below the clearing where the bulls had been . . . and now were not . . .

He was hunkered and hidden in the brush half-way up the hill where the coulee led north . . . the coulee through which but a short time before he'd driven his bulls.

He heard a man say, "Christ almighty, the sonofabitch has moved his bulls. They ain't a bull in that clearin'!"

He didn't recognize the voice.

"By god, they ain't a critter in sight," a second voice said.

That sounded like Sheriff Monte's voice. If it were, Monte was completely out of his legal domain. He was in a county where he'd not been elected.

Buck knew many times county sheriffs worked together as a unit in solving a crime and bringing criminals to justice. By the same token couldn't they cooperate in illegal points as a thieving team?

"He's pushed them north, men."

"They had to go north. We never saw tracks leadin' back south. He's put them into thet coulee over there."

"An' we'll fin' him an' them in a box canyon, ready to be took," another voice said. "I tol' him to always turn left in a coulee. That'd put him—an' them critters—in a

61

trap."

So the cowpunchers were in on this, too? Buck saw the men walk openly into the clearing. He counted seven men. Then he heard a man coming through the brush toward him. They sent out a scout or two, eh? The man passed within thirty feet of Buck, who hid behind a big granite boulder. Soon nine men were in the clearing. Buck figured that was all. Two crooked sheriffs, four deputies, three lying cowpokes . . .

"Back to our broncs," Sheriff Monte ordered. "We'll circle through Strawberry Gulch. Run the bastard an' the bulls down!"

Buck waited, rifle raised. They were at the entrance of the coulee when he started shooting.

He wanted to shoot to kill. These gunmen were out to kill him, were they not? Then he had the right to kill them first, didn't he?

He shoved this desire rudely aside. He sent two bullets ploughing dirt behind the last man. The man jumped like a turpentined bull.

"Somebody's shootin!!"

"Get out, men!"

"An' fast!"

Buck had carefully scouted his hiding area. Rabbits and other wildings had made a dim path along the side of this hill. A path that wound through high buckbrush.

He ran ten feet to his right. He screamed, "Shoot the hell outa the bastards."

He shot two more times. Below him bullets spouted in dust. These shots were hard on the spurs of Sheriff Russell, who dived head first into the protective high brush.

Buck quickly shifted positions, then fired once more— but by now his prey was out of sight in the thick undergrowth. Again he hollered, "Follow an' kill 'em, boys! They meant to kill you! Wipe the ambushers off'n the face of the earth!"

"He's got help!"

"He ain't alone, men!"

Buck stopped shooting. He had seen the flashes of a

few guns below him but hadn't heard the whine of bullets. He hunkered, heart hammering; he bent his head, listening to the night.

Seconds moved into eternity. Then, he heard them—hoofs, fast hoofs. Hoofs beathing the earth, hoofs in flight. Grinning, Buck straightened, rifle in hand. Suddenly, he ducked.

The bullet smashed into a scrub oak at his right. He saw the flash of the gun down in the brush straight ahead.

One of the cattle-thieves had stayed behind. He had not counted them as they'd torn into the brush. He hadn't had time.

His rifle flashed to his shoulder. He had only a few shots left, but he emptied the rifle.

A man ran from the brush. He headed for the coulee mouth. He carried a rifle. Buck pulled out his six-shooter. He shot three times, knowing each bullet was a wasted hunk of lead.

The runner was beyond six-gun range. Buck did not even see where his bullets landed but they did not hit the man. Suddenly the man fell violently forward.

Buck thought, I hit him. The bullet's jus' takin' effect. Then he realized the man had merely stumbled over something for he was immediately on his boots. He disappeared.

Buck figured there'd be no other gunman. Had there been one he'd have already joined the pastime. Nevertheless, he took precautions. Crouched, he ran through the brush, heading north to the coulee's mouth where he had Rusty tied to a scrub tree. He hurriedly untied the sorrel, flung himself and Winchester into saddle—then reined in tightly, listening carefully. And heard nothing dangerous.

Somewhere a night-owl hooted softly. Moonlight shimmered in golden beauty. There was no wind. The night was calm.

His mind played on problem points. Strawberry Gulch? Where was Strawberry Gulch? Sheriff Monte—Screaming they'd ride through Strawberry Gulch . . .

And Tortilla Joe? Where was his Mexican partner?

Was Tortilla Joe heading out from Denver this direction? Would he ride into the fleeing bunch of would-be cow-thieves?

One point stood out. The bulls were still in danger. They had to be moved. And moved fast and now. But where?

Common sense came in. He remembered driving Texas longhorns north through this particular area. Not that herds had gone through this badlands; herds had gone east of here on the rolling hill country. But ahead of his bulls there should be a small cowtown not too far.

He'd drive the bulls to this town. Each of these cowtowns had a town corral. Almost all families in these small towns had a milk cow or two, held overnight in a town corral. Once his bulls were corralled in the middle of a settlement they'd be safe. The two sheriffs and their riders would not dare to steal cattle directly in front of the public eye. They might try to get the bulls through some sneaky legal device but Buck figured that was an outside change.

He still had old Pothook Malone's telegram. And the message he himself had scrawled.

There was but one thing to do—get the bulls moving. He knew the bulls were very tired. So was he. Still, they had to be on the move.

He spurred Rusty north through the winding canyons. His bulls were all bedded down. Roughly, lariat doubled, he got them to their hoofs and on their way.

He judged the town to be down-stream. He did not remember its name. Probably he'd never heard its name. Names didn't count. Main thing was to reach the town and get out of the reach of two lawless sheriffs.

He met fences of farmers without a few miles. For once the sight of barbwire buoyed him instead of depressing him. Farmers were moving out to their fields for a day's work.

One farmer had four horses hooked to a gang harrow. He stopped the other side of his fence and stared at the Brahmans. "What's them?"

Buck was sick and tired of this question. "Alligators

with horns. How far to town?"

"Two miles. Straight ahead."

Buck and the Brahmans went on. Buck hoped and prayed no milk-cows in heat would spy the bulls.

He'd had too much trouble the last twenty-four hours. And, for that matter, ever since he'd met these bulls. A bull rushes a barbwire fence and takes it down to get astraddle a cow and—

He caught his thoughts. Actually, these bulls had been good bulls. They'd driven well. They'd pounded out long, dusty, hot—and cold—treks. That they climbed cows in heat was only natural.

He didn't hate the bulls. That was odd. He usually, on a trail drive, got to loathe every critter. Halfway through a trail drive he'd find himself sick to the ears of seeing a cow.

He then realized these bulls were smarter than those stupid, lumbering Texas longhorns. Something along that line, anyway. These were intelligent cattle in comparison to the mangy longhorn. That is, if any bovine could be classed as having intelligence.

Word got ahead of the coming of the bulls. Farmers, their wives, their children and relatives lined up behind barbwire. A collie dog rushed out, teeth clicking. Flapears hoofed him speedily and without conscience.

Buck's nerves were unsteady. He was afraid a boy or girl would run out and challenge one of his bulls. And, frankly, he didn't know what the bull might do. He might charge. And, if he hit, he could kill. Or he might pay no attention.

A small boy on a pony said, "Want me to ride ahead, mister? So no dogs or things get in your way?"

"Suit me fine, Sonny. I got a dime."

"Dime's enough."

Buck didn't mention that was about all the capital he had. Soon the town's outskirts came into view. The boy rode back. "Anythin' else I can do, mister?"

"This town got a town corral?"

"Sure has. You want to corral there?"

"That's right."

The pony's short legs churned dust. Luckily, the corral was on Buck's side of town—a Mexican inhabited village. Within a few minutes the bulls were behind corral bars.

Buck breathed a sigh of relief. He heard hoofs coming in behind him. He turned on stirrups.

Tortilla Joe.

NINE

The bulls' stay in the corral lasted only twenty minutes. This time the town priest headed them north.

"My people are like children," the young priest said. "They think these holy cows of India are devils. They are in my church now and they are plotting, and what they talk is not good."

Buck said, "We'll move them on, Father."

Another dime hired the boy and pony to lead the way north. With the boy at point, Buck and Tortilla Joe rode drag.

Tortilla Joe's trip to Denver with Juan Sanchez had netted two things—Tortilla Joe had a blistering headache from Juan's home-made wine and Juan had finally loaned him ten dollars.

"Well, we've got Bull Durham and papers now, anyway," Buck said.

Tortilla Joe shook his head. "So two sheriffs—And cowpunchers an' others—They tried to highjack the herd—Impossible to believe."

"No word from Pothook, huh?" Buck asked.

"Like I told you—No word. I waited as long as I could, Buckshot. Juan will send word on to us if word comes. To Sig Nelson's saloon. In Cheyenne."

"If he remembers."

Tortilla Joe shifted weight on oxbow stirrups. "That shootin' you did—this mornin'—Two miles from the badlands I met riders—"

Buck's ears pricked up.

"Ridin' fast in the dawn. I saw them in the dim light.

67

But too far away to count—"

"Bunch I ran off, prob'ly."

"They went by me. Oh, maybe a quarter-mile away, to the west. Then later I heard shootin' behin' me, in the direction they went."

Buck looked at his partner. "What caused that, do you figger?"

"I will tell more. Oh, about ten minutes later—maybe a bit more—this rider—he sweeps east of me—"

"He come from the direction of the gunshots?"

"He did. I think he was shootin' at the men who tried to rob the bulls from you."

"You're not sure, though?"

"Of course, I cannot say for sure. I pulled hell-quick back in some brush. He rode fast past me, headin' north. An', Buck, you know who he was?"

"I'll bite."

"He was the tall man. The one in Dumas who said he would handle Tank Williard."

"Couldn't have been," Buck said.

"Why say that?"

"Look, amigo, look. No man's follerin' us an' these damn' bulls north. Why for would he do that?"

Tortilla Joe shrugged. "Still, it was him, Buckshot."

They hazed bulls for some distance in silence, Buck hunkered in saddle, deep in thought. They were leaving the farm-section. Open prairie heavy with grey sage lay ahead.

Buck pulled tobacco smoke in deep. Good to have smokes again. Finally he said, "Let's say you're right. You saw this tall gink. We've thought we've seen him in the distance before. Always travellin' north, our direction."

"Yeah?"

"Why doesn't he come in? Ride with us?"

"I've thought of that. Mebbeso he wants these bulls. Maybe when we get them to the area he wants to have them, then he'll hit us." Tortilla Joe reached to his nigh saddle-bag. He took out a tortilla—the Mexican flat pancake. He rolled it and began eating. "Mrs Sanchez—

la senora of Juan—she made these for me."

"Don't be a pig."

"You want one, too, eh?"

Buck twisted the tortilla into a cylinder. He bit off a chew. "Almost as good as my ol' dead mother used to make. Sometimes I think we did wrong in settin' out as bums, Tortilla. We should have stayed in our hometown of Laredo."

"Not me. Too hot in summer. Sometimes snow in winter. Charlie's Place is better."

"What plans you got?" Buck asked.

Tortilla Joe chewed thoughtfully. "First, we gotta get out of Colorado as pronto as we can. Them sheriffs might not have given up."

"We'll watch a close backtrail."

The boy rode back. "No more farmers for many miles." He got his dime. He loped south, singing.

When they reached Cheyenne Buck rode into town while Tortilla Joe watched the bulls to the west. Buck and Sig Nelson shook hands to the elbows but Sig had heard nothing from Juan Sanchez.

"You ever hear a word about ol' Pothook Malone, up on the Powder?"

"Yeah, about four months back—maybe five, even six—a cowpuncher rode through the Powder. Said Pothook an' Ma were doin' fine."

"Somethin's wrong," Buck said.

The big Norwegian's blue eyes studied Buck. They'd known each other for many years. Usually trailherds stopped a few days around Cheyenne to let cowboys celebrate a few days before hitting the dusty trail north into Montana or even across the Canuck Line into Canada.

"Care to tell me, Buck?"

Buck gave all details about the bulls. "Me an' Tortilla need a few bucks."

Buck felt the big man instantly stiffen. "Buck, if I gave ten bucks or so to every drifter who put the bee on me—Times are tough, Buck. Not a loose dollar in sight."

Buck glanced down the bar. He and Sig stood at one

end. Men jostled for places in the long bar.

"How about five bucks, Sig?"

Sig Nelson considered that. "All right, Buck," he grudgingly said. "For ol' time's sake."

"For ol' time's sake," Buck repeated.

Buck had a little luck. He ran into Mack Smith who ran cattle south of Miles City, Montana, on the Tongue River. Five years ago he and Tortilla Joe had helped drive a trailherd out of Amarillo, Texas, to Smith's Circle Y R outfit.

Smith was travelling by horseback into north Texas. There he planned to buy some good-blooded bulls to breed up his longhorn cows.

"Trail drive 'em back Mack?"

Mack Smith shook his head. "Too much work. Too damn' much borbwire atween here and there and north of here. I doubt if ever a trailherd goes up north again, Buck. I'm shippin' 'em in cattle-cars to Kansas City, then back. Faster an' surer an' a lot cheaper."

"Wish to God ol' Pothook had did that with these Brahman bulls."

"I ain't never seen thet brand of critter."

"Tortilla Joe's holdin' 'em a few miles west of town. This not hearin' from ol' Pothook has run our billfolds damn' short."

"I kin spare you twenty bucks apiece, Buck."

Buck protested. He hadn't meant to bum. Mack Smith waved him aside. He and Buck and Tortilla Joe were long-time friends, remember?

"Well," Buck said, "it sure means a hell of a lot to us. I feel sure Pothook will send you the forty the minute we mention it."

"When God made Pothook Malone He then broke the mould. Mind a drink, Buckshot?"

"Beer, no more."

Mack Smith didn't want to ride out to look at the Brahmans. "I've read about them holy Indian cows, though. They're ridin' 'em in stampedes now, ain't they?"

"They're *tryin*' to ride 'em," Buck corrected.

"The Wild Bunch held up the Northern Pacific fast mail out of Billings a few days ago. Got off with quite a bit of money. Almost all in unsigned paper money, I've read."

"They're tough boys."

"Longabaugh boarded in Billings. A few miles out he came down off the coal with a .45. Old Tommy Adams was engineer. He said that .45 looked as big as a cannon. He lost no time on hittin' the air brakes."

Buck listened.

"Kid Curry handled the dynamite. Butch Cassidy did his share, I reckon. Newspaper said all the gang was in on it but Ben Kilpatrick. I've seen 'em all but Ben, whoever he is."

"I've never seen him either," Buck said. "He seems to be a new hand, isn't he?"

"I reckon so, Buck. Newspaper said nobody seemed to know where this Kilpatrick man was. One reporter said maybe he'd been shot in some holdup and was dead already."

Buck wasn't interested. He had enough troubles of his own. He didn't need to share anybody else's.

"Thet Utah bank holdup the Wild Bunch pulled off a few weeks ago sure had lots of bullets flyin', according to the newspaper. That reminds me. I'm goin' pick up a few newspapers here—today's an' yesterday's an' a few older, if I can get them. Give us somethin' to read in camp."

Sig had today's *Cheyenne Call* and some a few days back. When Buck was leaving through the batwinged door a very tall man also entered. Buck stood politely aside to let him enter.

He immediately recognized the tall stranger from Dumas.

"Well, I'll be hanged," Buck said. "So we meet again, huh? Glad to see you again, stranger."

The man gave him a short glance, nothing more. He entered the saloon without a word. Over the batwings Buck watched the man walk to the bar.

Buck almost re-entered the saloon. The man had been rude to the point of being insulting. Then he caught himself. If the man didn't want to speak to him that was the man's right. This was a free country. If you didn't want to speak to somebody you didn't.

One thing was for sure, though. He'd looked in good health. No bandages . . .

Days were longer now. And warmer, too. Buck figured by the time the bulls hit Powder River City the sun would be really warm. Only two climates in this area, he thought. Freezing or boiling, no other.

He packed two gunny-sacks of grub behind his saddle. Tortilla Joe would be happy to see the Bull Durham and papers—not to mention canned beans and such-like.

Yes, and six Havana cigars, each. Buck knew he'd ration his to one every evening. He didn't care what Tortilla Joe did with his.

But a man couldn't have everything . . . Meadowlarks sang evening songs from high sagebrush. A jackrabbit crouched under a sagebrush fifty feet away. You could see his big brown eyes watching. His long ears were laid back. He wouldn't jump out of his nest until a horse almost walked on him, he was that sure of his natural colour protection against the dark ground.

The bulls grazed in a wide coulee. Grass was high and was beginning to cure a little. Far in the distance he saw a small herd of antelope. He scared up a big muletail buck deer from a draw.

The deer bounded ahead. A doe came in from another draw. She was heavy with unborn fawn. Buck watched the two disappear. He took down his cigar and admired its grey thick ash. He restored the Havana to his lips.

Nothing wrong with God's world . . . Not at this moment, anyway. Tortilla Joe was all ears, but his features sank as he heard there'd been no word from Juan Sanchez. Or from Pothook Malone . . . Or anybody concerned with Pothook Malone and the Pothook iron.

"I got papers to read. Not much light left, either. I'll do double duty tomorrow an' next day."

"Jus' remember that."

Tortilla Joe started building a sagebrush fire. Buck glanced at the bulls. He decided to lay over a day. The bulls needed a rest. Then he silently accused himself of getting soft hearted. And over a damn' ungrateful thing like Flapears, at that.

He read today's *Call* first. Then he went back to the oldest newspaper. He and Tortilla had been in Colorado when that issue had been on sale. He was reading the next to the oldest when suddenly surprise ran across his weather-tanned face.

"Tortilla! For lord's sake, man! Look at this item! Second page, too—important."

Tortilla Joe looked up from his skillet. "You seen a ghost?"

"Come 'ere, manboy."

Tortilla Joe laid down his skillet. He read the head on the story, then stared, eyes widening. Buck watched him. Finally the Mexican handed the newspaper back.

His lips moved and said, "Sheriff Monte—Colorado—Killed by a stray rider—Dead on the prairie—" His dark eyes grew solemn. "Let me think back . . . By hell, that was the day you put the run on them would-be bull-thieves, Buckshot!"

"I didn't shoot nobody. I jus' shot to scare."

"You sure of that?"

"I'm positive. An' if I'd hit him he'd gone down in that clearin'. He wouldn't have been found dead out on the prairie."

"Maybe he didn't get killed outright. Rode a ways an' then kicked the bucket."

"I hit nobody, Tortilla."

"Then who—"

"You said you saw them riders—Did you do any shootin' ag'in 'em?"

"Hell, no. I hid in the brush. Hey, wait a minute—Afterwards I heard shots, remember? An' I saw that tall gink in the distance—"

"He must've shot down Monte," Buck said.

"Had to be him. Unless them thieves got fightin' among themselves. An' Monte got kilt—"

"I doubt that," Buck said. "Thieves hang together, they say. That tall guy must've knocked Monte good out

73

of leather. I saw him today in Cheyenne."

"You—what?"

Buck told him. Tortilla Joe's brown eyes grew thoughtful. Finally he said, "That gink's up to somethin', Buck."

"He's trailin' north with us," Buck said.

TEN

They cut across country. Thirty two holy bulls—tired bulls—and two tough cowpunchers. A Texan and a Mexican . . . Saddlemen . . .

The North Platte was roaring high. Snow-water was still running wildly out of western mountains. The bulls didn't want to go into the spume and mud and skirling water.

They just wouldn't start. They turned, ran, butted, looked at the river, whirled, hooked each other, charged Rusty and Midnight.

Buck said, "I'll start them out."

He took down his catch-rope. He built a small loop. He rammed Rusty in close to Flapears. Flapears knew something was brewing. He knew he was going to be the goat.

He whirled, too late. The noose settled at the base of his horns. Buck pulled the loop tight. He took fast dallies. He allowed Flapears six feet of rope. No more. No less.

"Ride 'em cowboy!" he chortled.

Tortilla Joe whooped, "Hook 'em, cow!"

"Powder River! A mile wide an' an inch deep—"

"An' God knows how long!"

"An' He don't care!" Buck McKee whooped. "Hit that rope, Rusty hoss!"

Rusty rammed into the river. Flapears had all legs braced. He sat on his rump. He bawled in pain and hatred. Rusty had him, though. Rusty pulled the bull into the river.

Once Flapears was in the water, Buck McKee

loosened his dallies. He played out about fifteen feet of rope. Rusty began swimming toward the far bank. He was a water-horse, was Rusty. He swam high and powerfully. Seldom did water lap over the centre of his saddle. Buck hunkered on the saddle.

Flapears wasn't the swimmer Rusty was. He tended to drift downstream. Buck looked back at the swimming big black bull. Flapears was swimming for all he was worth.

At that moment, Buck loved the bull.

"You black ol' sonofabitch," he told Flapears. "You're a fighter, pal. Straighten out an' swim, you bastard!"

Flapears did just that.

Buck looked back across the roiling, muddy waters. The other bulls were swimming in a line behind Flapears.

The bulls made a black line across the river. Tortilla Joe took up the rear. He had his catch-rope coiled and a loop built. Were a bull to begin to tire and float downstream he'd lay the twine on him, and tow him as Buck had towed Flapears.

For now Rusty didn't have to pull Flapears. Flapears swam with slack in the catch-rope. Buck looked to the far shore to the north. They were heading for a gravel-bar to land on.

Rusty's shod front hoofs scraped gravel. Soon he was emerging from the water, wet as the proverbial rat, with Flapears trailing behind, the other bulls following. Buck took the loop from Flapears' horns.

"You did all right, ol' Brahman."

Flapears rushed Buck. Buck jumped aside. Flapears thundered past. Buck kicked him hard in the guts. Flapears kicked back and again Buck McKee did a dodging act.

"He ain't very grateful," Tortilla Joe said.

"He's got a lot in common then with lots of humans I've met. This will be our last big river, won't it?"

Tortilla Joe nodded. "Unless they's a cloudburst somewhere back in the high country. Then a little crick can turn into a big river."

Buck figured twenty odd miles north would find them

at the headwaters of Salt Creek. Then about thirty miles straight north down the Salt would bring them to Powder River City. The long trek had but a few days left.

They bedded down that night in a small prairie valley directly south of Salt Creek's headwaters. Buck took first guard. Coyotes sang and the night was calm. Buck rode past Flapears who stood and watched.

Buck reined in Rusty. "We ain't got much longer to look at each other," he told the bull.

Flapears flapped his left ear.

"I hate to admit it," Buck said, "but I'll miss you."

Flapears flapped his right ear.

"You ain't even listenin'," Buck said.

Flapears pawed sod with his left front foot. He was getting ready to charge. Buck reined Rusty to one side. "T'hell with you and your brothers and all your relatives."

He rode on.

"I must be gettin' plumb loose in the belfry," Buck told Buckshot McKee. "Sayin' goodby to a no-good Brahman bull."

Next night they made camp at the head of Salt Creek. Salt Creek originated on the north side of a ridge in the form of a spring. The bulls and horses watered and Buck and Tortilla Joe took a swim in the pool below the spring. Despite the day's warm sun the water was very cold.

"Wonder what verdict the coroner turned in over Sheriff Monte's carcase?" Buck said.

"Pro'bly death from unknown causes at the hand or hands of unknown people, Buck. Look, there's a big minnow."

"We ever go through that section of Colorado again I'm goin' dig back in old newspapers an' fin' out what happened."

Next day threatened heat. Tortilla Joe rode point. When he turned in at noon he reported seeing not a cow on this range. "Antelope an' deer but no cows."

"Maybe ol' Pothook don't run cattle this far south."

"This is good range. No fences aroun' means no farmers. An' somebody should run somethin' on it."

"Maybe tomorrow," Buck said.

Next day Buck rode point. Summer had really arrived. The sun was blistering hot at three. Buck swung back.

"Ran into some Pothook M cows a few miles ahead, Tortilla. So I guess we got these critters pointed the right direction."

"I'm suspicious, Buck."

"I ain't feelin' so settle-minded either, if you was to ask me. We've gone lots of miles through Wyomin' an' couldn't dig out a word about Pothook an' him one of Wyomin's biggest cowmen."

They began pushing the bulls to their hoofs at dawn. "Last time we do this," Tortilla Joe said. "By this afternoon these critters should be in ol' Pothook's home corral."

They travelled the high country. Thus they'd swing west of the farmer settlement. Tortilla Joe stood on stirrups, hands flat against saddle-fork, and looked far west.

"The Red Wall, Buck."

"Been west of us for miles," Buck said.

"Hole in the Wall is right west of Powder River City, they tell me."

Buck nodded. "You ride in there, you don't never ride out. The Wild Bunch Camp. Cassidy, Curry, Sundance. Or mebbe they're down in the Four Corners country. Or even further south along the Mex border in New Mexico Territory."

"Somethin' up ahead," Tortilla Joe said.

Buck looked and frowned. "Looks like four or five wigwams. This ain't no Injun reservation, is it?"

"I don't think so."

"Where the heck are the houses of those farmers?"

"Can't see no shacks. This couldn't be their settlement, could it?"

Buck shrugged. "Has to be. No other houses atween here an' Hell's Half Acre thet I kin see."

"Them ain't houses. They's wigwams."

There were five of the pointed shelters. New canvas shone in the sun.

The partners passed two hundred yards west of the teepees. "New shiny borbwire aroun' their horse pasture," Buck quietly said. "Look like right good saddle-stock, too. Not a wagon or plough on the spread."

"Men comin' our way on foot," Tortilla Joe said.

"Five of 'em."

Buck and Tortilla Joe drew rein. The bulls loafed on, grabbing bunchgrass. "This has got me stumped," Buck breathed. "What t'hell is this comin', anyway?"

"Got me, too."

The two had cause for curiosity. All five advancing men were exceedingly tall, but their height was not what interested the partners. It was the men's clothing that surprised them. For these men did not wear range garb—high-heeled boots, trousers and shirts. They wore long gowns that completely hid their figures and extended almost to the ground.

These garments looked like they were made of sack-cloth. Occasionally you could glimpse a man's feet. He wore sandals. Tortilla Joe looked at the ground.

This area was studded with prickly-pear cactus, that cacti which grows close to the ground and has long sharp spines. Tortilla Joe caught a good glimpse of one man's footwear. The sandals had thick leather soles.

"Each nightgown's got a pocket on it," Buck murmured. "An' each's got a book in it—a thick book. Looks from here like the Bible."

"It is the Bible, Buck."

Flat black hats covered their heads. The nightgown, as Buck had called it, was coal black. The men neared. Now the partners could see their faces were covered with black cloth from just below the eyes. "Damn if they don't look like train robbers," Buck said. "Think it best we mosey on, Tortilla?"

"They ain't packin' long guns."

"They might pack short guns. Under those night-dresses."

The men were near. Buck and Tortilla Joe, apparently loafing in leather, lifted right hands, palms out, in the Sioux greeting. The five men lifted not a hand. They stopped twenty feet away, just beyond the barbwire fence.

They halted with military precision. They stood in a straight line with the tallest in the middle. They looked at Buck and Tortilla Joe. They looked at Rusty and Midnight.

These scrutinies finished, they looked at the retreating Brahman bulls. They then all turned their eyes back on Buckshot McKee and Tortilla Joe.

The tallest one spoke in a deep voice. "I greet you two wayfarers in the name of the Holy Ghost."

"We accept your greeting," Buck said, "an' in return give ours."

"My fellow sinners here—these four sons of God—have selected me as their spokesman. Those bulls you drive—All thirty two of them—Yes, we counted them from afar."

The partners had no words.

"They are holy bulls, aren't they? Holy animals from the holy people of faraway India?"

"They're from India," Buck said, "but I don't know how holy they are."

"Each is worth a large sum of money, is he not?"

Buck shrugged. Tortilla Joe shrugged. The five began talking to each other in a guttural tongue. Buck and Tortilla Joe exchanged glances.

What was going on here, anyway?

Buck looked across space west to the Red Wall, barely discernible in the dancing distance. Suddenly he got a feeling that these five long-gowns were not speaking a definite language. They were making up a fake tongue to spring on him and Tortilla Joe. He gave the five closer scrutiny. Four were about his height but the fifth was a few inches taller. Religious nuts, Bibles and nightgowns. He said to Tortilla Joe, "Time we ride."

"God go with you," the tallest man said.

"An' with you, too," Buck grunted.

They caught up with the bulls and hazed them again. "What language do you figger them nuts talked?" Tortilla Joe asked.

"Got me, pard. A few times there it looked to me like

they was makin' up their language."

Tortilla Joe frowned. "Never got that idea. Whereabouts on the globe are we, anyway?"

"That must be Powder River City over there a couple of miles to the northeast."

"Look west along the fork," Tortilla Joe said. "If thet ain't a bunch of ranch buildin's an' corrals take off your socks and I'll make a stew outa them an' eat 'em."

Buck used his field-glasses. "Only spread in this area," he said. "That's gotta be Pothook's outfit." He swept the field-glasses around the entire country. "What're you lookin' for?" Tortilla Joe asked.

"I got a danged queer feelin' we're bein' watched. I'm gettin' buggy, Tortilla."

"Them there dresses an' masks back there, Buck. I'm still with the willies over 'em."

Buck lowered his glasses. "Reckon that's what causes it . . . I'm in favour of not drivin' these bulls right into that ranch. I'm thinkin' of sendin' out telegrams an' gettin' no answers."

"I been thinkin' similar."

"Let's drive the bulls down on the crick between the town an' them ranch buildin's. Then one of us can ride into town. Scout aroun'. Other can ride herd on these critters."

"You go, Buckshot."

Buck rubbed his whiskers. "Three of them tall men back yonder I figger would be a little shorter than me but thet tall one—he was as tall as thet gink in Dumas."

"I reckon about the same height."

Buck looked across space. "We ain't seen thet gink since I met him goin' into thet saloon. Maybeso he wasn't trailin' us? Just happened to be headed the same direction we was."

"There's only one fly in that ointment."

"Yeah. What's it?"

"If like you say he was just accidentally headin' north like we was, then why in the hell did he take Willard over?"

Buck could only nod.

ELEVEN

Powder River City was two blocks long with a scatteration of log shacks slung out in the cottonwood trees. Riding in from the west you met the town graveyard first.

Buck drew in Rusty and gave the cemetery a slow perusal. He saw no new graves. He then remembered that every big ranch had its own graveyard. He rode on.

The town slept in heat. Not even a town cur came out with snarling fangs to challenge Rusty. Buck counted four saloons. Three were boarded shut. No more trail-drives. No more thirsty buck-laden cowboys.

The main building was a two-storey frame construction sporting the weather-beaten dim sign: MER-CANTILE. Buck went down, looped Rusty's reins around the tooth-gnawed hitching-rail, and clomped inside, spur rowels chiming.

A few local lads of all ages lounged on the store's front porch. Buck nodded at them, some nodded back, some didn't. He looked at two of the oldest. He had almost forgotten what Pothook Malone looked like, but he was sure neither was Pothook.

The interior was hot and stifling. It smelled of leather, prunes and such. Only one customer was inside.

He was shorter than Buck, but most men were that. He was muscular and tough looking. His chambray shirt covered good shoulders. Buck figured the man was about his age, give or take a few years.

Buck immediately noticed the man packed a six-shooter tied low on his thigh around the barrel of his shotgun chaps. The fact that the weapon was tied-down put him in the gunman class. Few if any cowpunchers ever tied down their short-guns. When riding they merely ran a buckskin thong over the hammer. This thin leather strip then was tied on both ends to the holster. Thus the holster could flap around but the gun could not fall out.

Buck cordially said, "Afternoon, sir."

The man grunted something indistinguishable. His brown eyes studied Buck openly and carefully. Buck got the impression the man didn't like what he saw. Or was he just suspicious of all in this community?

A bald, middle-aged fat man stood behind the counter. He was the type you'd associate as the owner of the store.

Buck again cordially said, "A good afternoon to you, also, sir."

"Thank you, stranger," the bald man said. "An' the same to you. Somethin' I can do for you?"

"A few supplies," Buck said.

"Name 'em, stranger."

Buck glanced at the younger man. He looked out the fly-specked front window at Rusty, the only horse at the hitchrack.

Buck knew the hard-looker was looking for Rusty's brand. Buck had a pleasant thought. The man would not find the brand from this distance. Were he up close and were he to move Rusty's mane to the side right below Rusty's right ear he'd see a small wire-brand—a BM iron.

The man's dark eyes moved back to Buck. He again gave Buck a momentary but searching examination. He then picked up a small woven sack that apparently contained a few supplies.

He left by the rear door.

Buck said, "Bull Durham first, sir," and his attention was drawn to the back end of the store. Here was a small glass-enclosed room. He judged it to be the store's office.

But the office did not interest him. Almost every store had a glass-encased office in that position. What interested him was the young woman who had just come out of that office.

She was a beauty. She stood to just about his shirt pocket, if that high. Her silk blouse displayed hidden feminity and her buckskin split-riding-skirt enhanced her womanhood.

Black high-heeled boots completed her costume, but it was her blue eyes and short stubby nose and red mouth that touched Buck McKee, who'd not seen a pretty girl for a long time.

"Could I help you, Dad?"

"I can handle it, daughter."

Buck said, "I'm lookin' for Pothook Malone."

The girl's luscious frame visibly stiffened. Her father's hands, resting palm down on the counter, became rigid.

"Did I say somethin' wrong?" Buck asked.

He glanced toward the back door. He wondered if the hard-case were not just beyond the door outside, listening. He almost walked back to see, but caught himself in time.

"Pothook Malone?" The storekeeper's voice was catchy.

"Yeah, Pothook Malone."

The girl said, "You'll find Mr Malone at the end of the street."

"Which end?" Buck asked.

"The west end."

Buck looked at the blonde loveliness. His heartbeat picked up. He remembered the graveyard.

"In the—cemetery?" he asked.

The girl laughed shakily. "No, not there. I mislead you, stranger. He's in the house next to the cemetery, this direction."

"Has to be this side," Buck said. "No house west of the graveyard." His heartbeat had calmed.

"You rode in from that direction?" the storekeeper asked.

Buck nodded. "Name's Buck McKee." He watched their faces. Their faces showed nothing. Apparently his name didn't register.

"I'm Cynthia Watson," the girl said. "This is my father, Jack Watson. Dad's been here for many, many years. But there's not much now that the trail-herds swing way west to miss barbwire."

Strangely, although he'd gone north with quite a few Texas cattle, Buck's foreman had never moved his stock through this region.

Buck mentioned the ranch buildings west. That was the Pothook M's headquarters, Cynthia assured. He brought the short conversation around to Pothook Malone. They clearly did not want to talk of the oldtimer. Indeed, Jack Watson said, "We'd rather not discuss Pothook, Mr McKee."

"Okay, folks."

What was wrong here, anyway? One thing stood out: Pothook apparently wasn't dead. If dead he'd not be in the house next to the graveyard. A sudden thought hit Buck.

"That house next to the graves—? Where Pothook is? They don't use it to lay out bodies, do they?"

"No," Cynthia said.

"Pothook's alive," her father said and added, "if you could call his existence living . . ."

He turned and walked into the office. Buck saw him sink into a chair. He returned his attention to Cynthia. "Only the Bull Durham," he said.

"Only that, Mr McKee?"

Buck didn't tell her that purchase just about broke him. "That's all, an' thanks."

He went outside. This thing had started out wrong down in Texas and was still wrong here in Wyoming. He was tying his small purchases to the back of his saddle when a bucking bronc bucked into the street.

The bucking bronc smashed out of the space between the Mercantile and the adjoining building. Shod hoofs hammered viciously on the plank sidewalk. The man in the saddle spurred viciously.

"Ride 'em, Cowboy," he hollered.

Buck immediately recognized him. He was the hard-case with the tied-down holster. Evidently he'd had his bronc at the store's rear.

He bucked straight toward Buckshot McKee. His

horse smashed into Rusty. Rusty shied, jerked bridle-reins from Buck, and jumped to one side.

The bucking bronc's sweaty off-shoulder crashed into Buck. The blow sent the lanky Texan reeling. He landed against the hitchrack rail. This held him up.

Anger roared through Buck. He had ridden more than his share of bucking broncs in rodeos and in cow-camps. This horse was a trained bucking-horse. Being trained, he could be directed by reins.

Buck lunged forward. The horse had no bridle. He had only a hackamore. Buck grabbed the hackamore rope. He jerked it from the man in the saddle. He braced the rope over his right hip.

He planted his boots in the dust. A cowboy uses high heeled boots for two reasons. One is that the heel will not allow his foot to slip forward through the stirrup. Thus the high heel keeps the cowpuncher from getting hung-up in the oxbow or visalia stirrup.

The other reason is that when a cowboy ropes on foot the high heels will dig in and give him a strong anchor. Buck used his high heels for this purpose this moment.

The bucking horse hit the rope's end. Buck's heels dug sod. The bronc went end over end. He landed on his right side with a crash. His rider was thrown from saddle.

The rider landed on his belly. He skidded forward in the dust. Buck released the rope. The horse ran down-street, head to one side so he'd not step on the trailing hackamore rope and throw himself.

The rider scrambled to his feet. His front was grey with dust. He went into a gunfighter's crouch, right hand splayed over holster. Curses spewed from his lips.

"Pull your gun, stranger!"

Strangely, Buck McKee was not down low, crouched. Nor was his hand poised over his holstered Colt .44.

"You ain't got no gun," Buck said.

Nevertheless, the man's hand dipped, hit holster. No gun-butt met his palm. He jerked his hand back, surprise on his ashen face.

"Your pistol fell out when your bronc went down," Buck explained.

Up on the porch, a man laughed sardonically. Buck shot a glance toward the Merc's wide front door.

Cynthia Watson and her father stood there, watching.

Buck directed his attention back to the hard-case. "Next time don't tie down your holster, mister. Jus' tie your pistol into holster. Better yet, never pull your gun against another human."

"Why not?"

Buck said, quietly, simply, "He might kill you . . ."

The man's shoulder muscles bunched. He spoke in a low hard voice. "You got a side-arm. I ain't. I don't cotton to you, savvy? Why don't you hand your gun to somebody an' meet me fist to fists like a man?"

"I got nothin' against you," Buck said. "I don't even know your name."

"Dan Malone's my name."

"Relation to Pothook Malone?"

"His son."

Buck had never heard of a son of Pothook's. He then realized there was a lot about Pothook Malone he did not know. He almost told this arrogant gunfighter his name but then changed his mind.

"You deliberately bucked that bronc over me," he accused.

"That I did."

"You admit that?"

"I do."

"Why?"

Malone hesitated a clock-tick. Then, "I don't like you. That's reason enough, ain't it?"

"It isn't."

"Yellow?"

"Not yellow, Malone. Jus' sensible."

"Then by God I'll make you fight!"

Buck saw then he couldn't avoid trouble. Past experiences had taught him that about all the combatants got out of a fight was trouble. If a gunfight, one or both usually ended up seriously wounded, or dead.

If a fistfight, you got black eyes and bruises. Yes, and if you hit a man hard enough in certain parts, he might possibly drop dead.

But there was one thing for sure, damn sure—you couldn't evade a fistfight when the other burrowed down on you, crouched, fists up, lips twisted with hate and rage, fire burning like hell's fires in his slitted eyes.

Buck thought wryly, "Well, here goes . . ." He crouched, slid under a wicked right hook. Thank you, Charlie, for your lessons, down in ol' Mesilla . . . Good ol' Charlie . . .

The chunky man had some science. He bobbed, weaved, struck. Buck at first hit for the head.

He then remembered Charlie's advice. You're too slow to be a head-hunter, McKee. You hit hard but not fast.

Concentrate on the ribs. The belly . . . Buck tasted blood. A smashing right uppercut brought that.

A punch knocked him backwards. He had not seen it coming. It was a brother to the blow Charlie had knocked him out with back in Mesilla. This man could not hit as hard as Charlie but Buck feared he'd go down to him. And the man would then put the boots to him. He wasn't doing so good, he realized.

Then he felt something behind catch him. It kept him from falling. He'd hit the hitchrack rail again.

For the second time, the rail held him up.

He moved ahead, fists up. He shook his head and cleared it somewhat. And then he used all the fight-logic Charlie had taught him and Tortilla Joe.

He landed a hard right to the man's lips. He wondered if the man's teeth had cut the back of his knuckles. That was of small consequence, though. This man was out to knock him cold.

Buck circled, making his opponent miss. The man breathed sharply. He was running out of wind, young and solid as he was.

Buck liked the wheezing he heard. He conserved his own breath, breathing as Charlie had taught him. Then, he saw his opening.

He sent in a left, followed by a right. The right did it. It caught Dan Malone flat on the tip of his jaw.

Malone toppled. He fell on his belly in the dust. Buck knew he'd knocked Malone out. He'd become aware of a third man circling with him. Now, he turned quickly to confront this stranger.

Buck glimpsed a squat, middle-aged man. The man had a billy club. Sunlight glistened from metal on his vest.

Buck knew that reflection came from a law-badge.

The club came down. Buck tried to duck. The hardwood billy hit him on the right side of his head.

All went black.

TWELVE

When Buck came to he lay on the plank sidewalk. He judged at least half the population of Powder River City surrounded him. He was in front of the Mercantile.

He sat up. Memory returned. He looked about. He looked for Dan Malone. He couldn't find him. "Where's Malone?"

Cynthia Watson answered. "Down at Doc Miller's getting sewed up. You could stand a few stitches."

"Where?"

"On your head."

Buck felt. "It'll heal natural." He got to his feet. He had to lean against the Merc. "Who slugged me?"

"The sheriff," Jack Watson said.

The sheriff wasn't around, either. Buck said, "What's his name?"

"Whose name?" Cynthia asked.

"The sheriff's."

"Ed Fillmore. He hasn't been here but a couple of months. County commissioners appointed him to fill out John Powers' term."

"Where's he at?"

"He had to leave a minute ago. One of those nutty farmers came in after him. Nobody seems to know what the farmer wanted of him. They rode out of town heading west together."

"He had no call to slug me," Buck said.

A townsman said, "He's too big for his pants, that idiot. Here comes his deputy, Jay Beeman."

"Another horse's rear end," an oldtimer murmured.

"Fillmore needs a deputy like I need another arm. Darn near nobody in this county now. All moved west with the cattle."

"Don't say that to Beeman," another oldster said softly.

Beeman was a short man with a gut that hung over his broad gunbelt. He had a scar down the middle of his wide nose.

"Come to, eh, stranger?"

"Hell, no," Buck said cynically. "I'm still knocked out."

Beeman warned, "Don't get flip, stranger. You cain't cause trouble in this town. You deliberately picked on Dan Malone. I saw it from the office down the street."

Buck wisely kept his tongue. He knew these small burgs. Dan Malone said he was old Pothook Malone's son. Naturally Dan drew a lot of water on this range.

Buck didn't know how many head of cattle the Pothook M ran but he did know that when old Pothook had trailed out of Texas a few years back his trailherd had numbered somewhere in the vicinity of four thousand head.

Pothook M would undoubtedly have more head than that, now. A cowman paid nothing for his range—Uncle Sam owned that land—but he did have to pay county taxes.

Logic told Buck that undoubtedly Pothook M was the biggest taxpayer in this desolate county. Therefore old Pothook—and his son—ruled the roost here. County officials held their jobs by favour of Pothook M.

"You able to navigate okay now?" the deputy asked.

Buck nodded. "Why ask?"

"Come with me."

"Where?"

"You're goin' to jail. You're under arrest. The charge is inciting a fight, public nuisance, things like that."

Buck studied the big-gutted man. "You serious?"

"Never moreso afore in my life. Sheriff Fillmore's orders jus' afore he was called outa own."

"Who filed the complaint?" Buck asked.

"We don't need such. An' if we do, Dan Malone will

file one later, right after Doc gets done workin' on him."

"This man didn't start the trouble," the storekeeper said. "Dan Malone deliberately rode that trained bucking horse into Mr McKee."

"Keep out of this, Watson."

Anger rimmed Watson's reply. "Don't try orderin' me, Beeman! I was a citizen an' taxpayer here before you could walk, an' don't ferget it!"

Cynthia said, "Daddy, watch yourself!"

Beeman spoke to Buck. "You comin' peaceful like? Or do I need my 'cuffs?"

"I'll go with you."

Cynthia spoke. "We'll see you later, McKee." She added, "With our attorney."

"No need for that," Buck said. "I don't want to put you an' your father out. Jus' get word to Pothook Malone."

Silence grabbed the group. Buck wondered why. He'd mentioned Pothook's name twice in this cowtown and each time silence had followed. He saw tears in the watery eyes of one oldtimer.

Why was the old boy on the verge of openly weeping?

"I'll notify him," Cynthia said.

"Here's this man's gun," a woman said. "Fell from his holster while he was fightin' that no-good Malone thing."

Buck remembered his gun falling from leather. He'd untied the trigger thong before tying into Dan Malone, he recalled.

The woman handed the Colt .44 to Deputy Beeman. Beeman's big hand touched Buck's elbow.

"Don't rush me," Buck warned.

They went down mainstreet east. Buck looked down at Beeman's huge gut. "You haven't seen your privates for years, I'd reckon. Unless you took down your pants an' looked in a lookin' glass."

"Don't get too lippy, McKee!"

Children and grown-ups trailed Buck and the obese deputy. Buck guessed this would be remembered as one of Powder River City's most illustrious days.

He thought of Tortilla Joe out with the bulls. Tortilla Joe would wonder why he, Buck McKee, hadn't ridden back. Maybe he should ask the deputy to send somebody out to alert the Mexican?

He decided to think this over. His heart warmed toward Cynthia and her father. He apparently had discovered two new friends. He remembered Cynthia's prairie-blue eyes and wonderful feminine figure.

Maybe there was something to this settling down and getting married and raising some kids?

He smiled to himself, seeing himself walking in a furrow behind a team of mules, hanging onto the lurching handles of a walking plough.

The county courthouse was the last building on the main street's east end. It was a single-storey stone building. The jail was a wing of the courthouse. It also was made of heavy native stone.

Buck noticed the bars were set in thick concrete. This would be a hard building to break out of . . . He didn't entertain that thought long. Cynthia would see Pothook. Pothook would come immediately. For the second time in their acquaintance Pothook Malone would get Buckshot McKee out of jail again.

Only the first time it had been accomplished by roaring guns and skirling powdersmoke. A jail delivery, no less . . . Buck once again heard a cell door click shut behind him.

"Rest peacefully," Deputy Beeman said.

Buck looked at him. "I wish I had your delightful sense of humour."

"You might . . . in time."

Beeman locked the steel door shut behind him. His bootheels died. Buck walked to the small barred window. He looked out at a side-hill. He saw sego lilies and grass and boulders. He took his eyes from these. He'd seen them before . . .

He sat down on the bunk. It was hard as iron. It was a concrete ledge hung onto the rock wall. Only a blanket covered it. He knotted the cotton blanket into a ball and threw it into a far corner.

He'd been in one-horse jails like this before. And once he'd got a good case of 'rithmetic bugs off such a blanket.

'rithmetic bugs?

They added to your misery. They multiplied like hell. They divided your attention. And they subtracted from your pleasure.

He momentarily entertained himself thinking how suddenly a man's position in this life can be changed. A few minutes before he'd ridden into this crummy cowburg a free man, riding high in the saddle, complimenting himself and Tortilla Joe about successfully piloting thirty two high-priced Brahman bulls the many miles lying between here and Dumas, Texas.

And now, a few moments later, he was in a two-celled jail, laden with no formal charge—yet a prisoner, none the less.

A strange feeling entered him. It was one he'd encountered while in other jails. When a man was in jail he was utterly dependent upon the people outside. He was completely defenceless.

If they wanted to, they could starve him to death. They could kill him through thirst. It was that simple.

But soon Pothook Malone would come—

Pothook would get him out. Sudden doubts struck him, filling his soul with dread. Maybe Pothook wouldn't get him out?

He'd not seen Pothook for years. He still wondered howcome Pothook hired him and Tortilla Joe to drive those bulls north. He remembered once, years back telling Pothook that if he, Pothook, ever needed him and Tortilla Joe, they could be located by contacting Charlie's Place, down in New Mexico Territory's old Mesilla town.

He tried to think clearly back to that day. He could be wrong but it seemed to him that he remembered Pothook writing down Charlie's address.

Of course some drifting cowpuncher might have told Pothook where he could contact him and Tortilla Joe. He and Tortilla Joe had been partners for many years on the cowtrails. Naturally they were well-known to many trail drive cowpokes.

But why this silence, this hanging stillness, when he said Pothook's name?

The key in the outer door turned. Deputy Beeman entered with Cynthia Watson and her father. Another man accompanied them. He was somewhere around sixty, Buck guessed.

He was bald and small and his grey suit was not the world's cleanest and most perfectly pressed. He had a shuffling gait. He swayed and Jack Watson touched the man's elbow, restoring his equilibrium.

"Thank you, sir," the man told Watson.

"Lawyer Herb Powers," Cynthia said. "Our legal representative."

"And, as usual, rather inebriated," her father said.

"Not more than normal," the lawyer said shortly. His wavering watery eyes settled on Buck. "So this is the victim—pardon me—I meant to say *client* not *victim*."

"Can they jug me without a warrant?" Buck asked.

"I think so," the lawyer said.

"You think so! You're supposed to be a lawyer, remember."

"Have to look up the Territorial Code to make sure."

Buck looked at the Watsons. "My God, the man thinks Wyomin' is still a territory. Send me Pothook Malone."

"There's one sure way to get out," the lawyer said.

"What an' how's that?" Buck asked.

"Break out. Or else stage a jailbreak."

"An' get gut-shot," Buck said. He spoke to the Watsons. "Jus' what's goin' on aroun' here? All them religious nuts on them homesteads. I thought they'd mob us when we went by their shacks this mornin'."

"What'd you mean by *us*?" Cynthia asked.

Buck caught his tongue. It was best nobody knew about the bulls. Or about Tortilla Joe, either.

"Me an' my hoss Rusty," he said. "That's what I meant by *us*."

"We'll stage a jail delivery," the lawyer said. He tried to bow and almost fell down but Jack Watson caught him in time. "Now to my office and studyin' the Territorial Code."

"Still believes this isn't a state," Buck said.

"He'll sober up," Cynthia said with tight lips. Buck

guessed that when little Cynthia swung into action she was a terror—and not a holy terror, either. "I'll see to that, Buck."

Buck liked her calling him Buck and not Mr McKee. "I asked you to tell me what eats this town, remember?"

Jack Watson said, "It's a long story that's taken place in only a few weeks, but this is no place to relate it, McKee."

"You're our last and only hope," Cynthia said.

"What're you talkin' about?" Buck demanded.

Before Cynthia could answer there was a commotion outside the outer steel door. The door opened. Sheriff Fillmore entered. Two men behind him dragged a third man. The third man was putting up a fight.

Buck stared, disbelieving his eyes.

Dan Malone was one of the men. The sheriff unlocked the cell next to Buck's. The door swung open. Malone got behind the struggling man. He kicked him hard in the seat of his pants.

"Get in there, you thievin' sonofabitch," Pothook Malone's son gritted.

The man sailed into the cell. Sheriff Ed Fillmore clanged shut the cell door. He glared at Buck but was silent.

Buck jerked his gaze from his next-door neighbour and looked at Malone. Malone's left eye was swollen shut and black. Buck remembered his haymaker that had done that. Malone's bottom lip was cut. The doc had taken two stitches in it.

The sheriff, Malone and the other tough left. Only upright bars separated the two cells. Buck's eyes returned to his new neighbour.

"Tortilla Joe," he said.

THIRTEEN

Tortilla Joe had a bloody nose. "Where are the bulls?" Buck asked.

"Them religious nuts, Buck . . . Some of them trailed us. Saw where we grazed out the bulls . . ."

Buck nodded.

Cynthia and her father exchanged curious glances. Finally Cynthia asked, "What bulls, Buck?"

"Who's these people?" Tortilla Joe asked.

Buck told him. Tortilla Joe and Jack Watson shook hands through the bars. "Reckon we might jus' as well tell the whole story," Buck said. "Sooner or later it's bound to be known."

"What is the mystery?" Cynthia asked.

Jack Watson said, "Maybe it's none of our business, daughter."

Cynthia's face stiffened. "Sooner or later, father, we got to stand and fight, and what we learn here might help us in that fight!"

Buck was now the curious one. "What fight is that, Miss Watson?"

"The fight to re-establish decency and honour and peace here in Powder River City. But tell us your side first, huh?"

"That won't take long," Buck assured. After he'd finished, Jack Watson said, "An' Pothook sent you word to deliver these critters all this distance—? From Texas to northern Wyomin'—? An' then forsaked you?"

"Sure looks like he did," Tortilla Joe said.

Buck said, "Now bring us in on your story—This law

97

and order thing Cynthia just mentioned—"

"I'll make it brief," Jack Watson said.

The Watsons had been Powder River City's first residents. Jack Watson had read the signs right many years before and had built his store where he figured the cattle-drives would pass through Wyoming going north.

"We had Sheriff John Powers then," the grocer said. "Honest Texan from the spurs up and down. Now he's gone."

"How long's he been gone?" Buck asked.

"Sheriff Powers an' Pothook Malone had to go up north to Buffalo on county business. Comin' back somebody jumped 'em in the night. Murdered the sheriff an' Pothook—Didn't kill Pothook but—"

"How long ago was this?" Buck asked.

Jack Watson looked at his daughter. "How long would you say, honey? You're better at keepin' track of time than me?"

"Well, it was right after that bastard son of Pothook's come into this area an' said he was Pothook's legal heir."

Buck's frown grew. "Bastard?"

"Yes, bastard! And in more than one sense." Cynthia replied. " 'Nough said about him for now . . ."

"What happened to Pothook?" Tortilla Joe asked.

Jack Watson answered. "I think it better you two see Pothook in person than for me to answer your question."

"You're right, Father," Cynthia assured.

Buck spoke to Tortilla. "Where are the bulls now?"

"Give me time, Buckshot. These religious nuts rode up first. Accused me of stealin' them bulls. Said the Scriptures had a passage sayin' them bulls was theirs."

"Now I've heard everythin'," Buck said.

"They threw guns down on me. Jus' then this sheriff an' those other two sonsofbitches rode up. The fanatics left in a hurry. Sheriff also called me a cow-thief. Then him an' this Malone bastard beat me up."

"Buck beat up on Malone," Cynthia said.

Buck momentarily fingered a sore cheekbone. "Feels to me like it was more of a draw."

"Wondered how this Malone bastard got so many

swellin's an' thet black eye," Tortilla Joe said.

"Now you know," Buck said. "Where are our bulls?"

"Druv 'em into town," Tortilla Joe informed. "Put them in a corral on the east end of this burg."

"Town corral," Jack Watson said. "Keep the town milk cows there to milk 'em afore turnin' them out on the night pasture behin' the corral."

"We'll keep an eye on your livestock," Jack Watson said. "Now me an' my daughter better get after thet lawyer an' sober him up."

The Watsons left. Tortilla Joe and Buck were alone in the cell area. "Thet Malone punk rode thet bronc deliberately into me to pick a fight," Buck said. "He wanted guns, not fists—but his gun fell from leather when I threw his horse."

"This whole damn' thing don't make good sense, Buckshot."

"You can repeat thet ag'in."

"Them religious nuts sure scattered out when the sheriff an' his two come ridin' in."

"Why'd they want the bulls?"

"They claimed their holy book—whatever it is—says them Brahmans was sired by the devil an' should be killed. They didn't use the word *killed*, though—they used *slain*."

"Real biblical langwidge," Buck said. "They want 'em so they kin sell 'em. Them boys are thinkin' of money an' not of their god, whatever or wherever he is."

"Like all them high-shoutin' preachers, naturally." Tortilla Joe sat on the bunk. "Hard as a whore's heart . . . The Watsons mentioned a lawyer?"

Buck gave him the unwholesome details. "Here comes somebody," he said.

Sheriff Ed Fillmore bowlegged to a halt in front of their bars.

"Somebody oughta shoot you," Buck said.

"It won't be you," the lawman said. "We hang cow-thieves in this neck of the woods. An' in the eyes of the local law you two's cow-rustlers."

"Them bulls belong to Pothook Malone," Tortilla Joe

informed. "Me an' Buck was hired to drive them up from Texas."

"Not a likely story," the sheriff said. "Tomorrow Judge Seals comes down from Buffaler to hol' his weekly court. He's got a reputation for hangin' each an' every cow-rustler what comes afore his court."

"He won't hang us," Tortilla Joe assured.

Buck said quietly to his partner. "Don't waste words on this tinstar, friend."

"*Tinstar*!" the sheriff said. "Well, by God, I'll—"

"You'll do nothin' but get the crap kicked out of you by me when I get out," Buck said shortly. "Now get Pothook Malone here an' pronto. I wanna talk to that ol' transplanted Texan."

"Talk to 'im?"

"Yes, talk to 'im. That kinda su'prise you, tinstar?"

The sheriff laughed shortly. "That'll be somethin' to see," he said and added, "an' to hear, too."

He wheeled and left.

Buck McKee scowled. "I don't get this crap about Pothook."

"Me, neither."

"The Watsons are goin' bring 'im in," Buck said. "When I mentioned Pothook they both acted as goofy as a goat who's et loco week."

"An' where's Missus Malone?"

"Maybe she's gone over the ridge, Buckshot. Neither her nor Pothook are spring chickens no more. This son—of Pothook's—Cynthia called him a bastard, in more ways than one . . ."

"Pothook will clear up things."

Ten minutes later Sheriff Ed Fillmore entered with an old lady following him. Time had bent her over. She wore a long housedress and a heavy woollen shawl despite the jail's torpid heat. Buck glanced inquiringly at Tortilla Joe. "Now who the hell is this?"

Tortilla Joe shrugged. "Dunno, Buckshot."

The sheriff said, "You got company, cow-thieves. This is Missus Pothook Malone."

Buck's mind whipped back to Texas. He and Tortilla

Joe—in jail—Long time ago . . . He was sure Missus Pothook Malone had visited them in that jail—

But this woman—She was old—

"You boys remember me?" she asked.

Buck nodded. Tortilla Joe nodded. Missus Malone spoke to Sheriff Fillmore. "You can make tracks now, sheriff. I wanna talk to these two in private."

Fillmore didn't move.

"You hear me?" The old woman's voice was knife-sharp.

"I'm stayin', Missus Malone."

"I ordered you to go."

"You ain't my boss. The people of this district is my boss, not you. The days of you an' Pothook Malone an' the PM bein' boss here is went."

"I'm goin' report this to Pothook."

Sheriff Fillmore's thick lips grinned. "Report it an' be damned, Missus Malone."

Shrewd small eyes probed Buck, then Tortilla Joe. "You boys have changed. You were mere striplings then. Now you're mature men."

The partners were silent.

The old woman sighed. "Nothin' I can tell you with this thing's ears both cocked an' listenin'. I hate to bring Pothook outa the house but mebbeso it has to be done."

"Is he sick an' laid up?" Buck asked.

She avoided answering. "I knew them bulls was bein' shipped into Dumas, boys. Then this thing happened to Pothook an' I didn't know 'til today that you two had been notified to move them bulls north."

Buck told about receiving Pothook's telegram and money. "We sent him other telegrams along the way north. Didn't he get any of them?"

"Not that I know of."

Buck sighed. "I wish I *understood* all I *know* about this, Missus Malone. You goin' bring Pothook here, eh?"

"I'll go after him now."

She turned with swishing dress and departed, leaving a puzzled Sheriff Ed Fillmore behind.

"Mebbe there's somethin' here *I* don't understan',"

the lawman murmured.

Buck grinned. "Don't bust a gut tryin' to think, tinstar."

"A human don't think from his belly, McKee."

"People with no brains do," Buck replied.

Anger coloured the lawman's wide face. But he said not a word as he turned and fairly marched out, bootheels savage on the concrete floor. He slammed the outer steel door.

"He ain't happy," Tortilla Joe said.

Buck said, "Neither am I."

"You know, Buck, I done believe I seen Butch Cassidy today. An' beyon' him on thet hill was nobody but Kid Curry."

Buck studied his *compadre*. "You haven't been puffin' on a maryjane cigarette lately, have you?"

Marijuana grew wild along the cow-trails. Most cow-punchers picked it, dried it, and enjoyed it while on a wearisome, dust-thick northern trailherd drive.

"Not that lucky, Buck."

"Tell me?"

"Them religious nuts all rode in to try to steal our bulls. Hell, they was five to one, an' they come out of the brush on all sides. They had me under their guns."

"Vicious sonsofbitches, eh?"

"Well, I'm scared. Dribblin', to be truthful. Then I look by accident west beyon' these locos. An' danged if in the distance I don't see two men on horseback setting on a faraway hill. They was watchin' the proceedin's."

"You see 'em clear?"

"Well, as clear as possible, in that distance. But I'm sure it was Butch an' the Kid."

Buck looked at his scuffed boots. No use wastin' money on a polish job when and if he got out behind these bars. Boots too far gone. Buy new Justins on the money Pothook would pay them for moving them damn' bulls . . .

"Don't seem logical thet the Wild Bunch would be in the Hole in the Wall," Buck deducted. "Newspapers said they held up thet mailtrain south of here around

Casper. Would they hide so close to the holdup scene?"

"I was thinkin' likeways, Buckshot."

"Seems to me they'd a-pulled south after the stickup. Got off with some big money, too—if the newspapers are right."

Tortilla Joe nodded. "Logic says they'd be south in Brown's Park. Or in the Four Corners. Or even down south of Shakespeare in New Mexico Territory."

"Or up north aroun' Kid Curry's home-range, the Little Rockies in Montana."

"I'm sure it was them two," Tortilla Joe said.

"Ain't seen high or low of thet tall gent who we kinda figgered was trailin' us, have you?"

"Not hide or hair, Buck."

"Maybe we was wrong about him. Maybe he was jus' happenin' to go north when we was."

"I'd like to get outa here, Buck."

"Pothook'll get us out."

"When?"

"When he gets here."

Within ten minutes the outer steel door opened again. This time Sheriff Ed Fillmore had his gut-hung deputy with him. Behind the two stalwarts walked bent-over Missus Malone. She led an old man like a mother leads a child.

Buck and Tortilla Joe clutched the door-bars. Tortilla Joe said quietly, "For God's sake, Buckshot—could that be Pothook?"

"Kinda resembles him . . . a little."

"Got to be him," Tortilla Joe said.

The old man was erect but he shuffled his boots, Buck noticed. Grey whiskers covered his jaws and his hat was off and he was almost bald.

The Sheriff and Deputy Beeman stepped aside. Sheriff Fillmore said, "Here's Pothook, prisoners."

Missus Malone and Pothook stood just outside the bars. Buck saw Pothook's sharp grey eyes probe Tortilla Joe for a long second, then turn to him and he wondered what—if anything—those eyes held.

The light was bad but the eyes looked sane and clear,

Buckshot McKee quickly noticed.

Pothook Malone shot out a twisted claw. Buck shook it and then the claw went to Tortilla Joe.

Buck said, "Been a long time, Pothook."

He got no reply.

"We got the bulls up safe," Tortilla Joe said.

Still, not a word from the old cowman.

Buck looked at Missus Malone. "Why don't he say somethin'?"

Missus Malone's eyes filled with tears. She began sobbing broken-heartedly. Buck glanced at the lawman and deputy.

Sheriff Ed Fillmore stood with a sombre, funereal face. Gut-hung Deputy Jay Beeman stared down at his boots. Buck saw the boots were polished and looked new. When he got out he'd ask Big Gut where he'd bought such fine boots.

Suddenly, old Pothook Malone went to his knees. He clasped both hands palms-together in front of him as though in prayer.

Tears sprang from his seamy eyes. They trickled down leathery cheeks to become lost in the grey beard.

Pothook Malone opened his mouth, but no sounds came from the whiskery cavity. Buck stared down into the opening. His blood froze in his veins. He stared down.

Tortilla Joe stared, too. Tortilla Joe's brown eyes were wide with horror and his lips were bone dry. Finally he looked at Buckshot McKee. His words came from a great distance.

"Somebody's cut out his tongue," Tortilla Joe said hollowly.

FOURTEEN

That same afternoon a group of men left saddles and let bridle-reins trail as they squatted hidden in a grove of pines a mile southwest of Powder River City.

The tallest one said, "We didn't do so good, men."

"Thet damned sheriff," one man said. "Right when we're goin' make the kill on thet Mexican—the law has to ride in, big as life and twice as ignorant."

"I figger we didn't time it right," another said.

The tall man said, "Explain yourself."

"Jus' like I said, boss. We shouldn't have tried to steal them bulls in the daylight. We should've waited until night."

"Sounds good," a man said. "But what if the bunch of guns west of here had decided to steal 'em, too? An' come night they'd beat us to 'em?"

"We ain't got no proof them boys got their eyes on them bulls."

"Those black bulls are worth money," a man reminded.

"Thirty two head of 'em," another man said.

The tall man said, "You're right, boys. Chouse them bulls northwest into Montany an' sell 'em to ol' Jake Hoofer in the Bitterroots—He's been lookin' for Brahmans to breed up his string of calf-cows."

"Last time I saw him he tol' me if'n I ran acrost some good he-stuff—bulls like them black ones—he'd pay up to two hundred an' fifty bucks a head, he did."

"He'll pay at least four hundred a head for those bulls," the tall man said. "Or if he don't, on they go up to the Flathead where Bern Gill will spring for around that for 'em, if'n not more."

"When we gonna hit them bulls again?" a man wanted to know.

"I'll figger that out," the tall man said.

"You're figgerin' ain't been so good lately," the other said.

A short pause, freighted with tension. One man shifted position slightly, thus bringing his gun-handle closer to his right hand.

Somewhere in the pines a magpie chattered. The sound was loud in the clearing. Finally a man said, "No gunplay, gentlemen. Don't lose sight of our objective, please."

"Rightly spoke," another said. "We need union, not disunion. We got that bunch of guns west of us. We'll need every bullet—an' gun-hand—we got if we aim to smoke them bastards out."

Another said, "They boys west of here are friends of Pothook Malone, I've heard. Don't know how close a friends but friends jus' the same."

"I've heard the same," another man said. "I don't know if we can bring this thing about, men."

The tall man said sternly, "God damn it, lay off such idle lip! We're here for two purposes. Do I have to state them again, another time?"

"We know, we know," a man hurriedly said. "First, get the Hole in the Wall. Then, from it clean out Pothook Malone's PM iron. We've done good so far for the short time we've been on this range."

"We put Pothook out of the way for all time," the tall man said. "We got rid of that damn' ol' honest Sheriff John Powers. We got an ace man ridin' at Pothook's elbow all because of one of ol' Pothook's so-called sins."

"Sin?"

They all laughed.

"You reckon ol' Missus Malone believes that Pothook years ago put it to a dance-hall slut an' sired a son?" a man asked.

The tall man said, "Makes no never-mind if she does

or don't. By law the so-called son is ridin' high for us."

"For us?" The voice held doubt.

The tall one asked quietly, "You doubtin' him, too?"

"Sometimes I think he's jus' a blowhard hind end. Keepin' that gun of his'n tied down like a bigtime gunslinger. Who's the fool think he is, anyway? Wil' Bill Hickok?"

"Wil' Bill's been dead for years," somebody pointed out.

"I know that. You ain't tellin' me no history. But here he aims to kill this long string of pelican shit—this Texan—who helped bring up them bulls from Texas—"

"Yeah, go on."

"An' the Texican dumps our man off'n his hoss—An' our man's pistol slides out an' he grabs a empty hunk of air aroun' his leather—Hell, the Texican could have kilt him, if he had wanted to."

"You're right."

"I figger he might cave in if there's a showdown, boss."

"I'll keep a close eye on him," the tall man said.

They apparently dismissed Dan Malone from their conversation at this point and a man said, "I circled west. I run across hoofprints comin' from the Hole, but I never seen no riders while the sheriff an' his bunch were puttin' the skeedaddle on you men."

"Then what?"

"Them two horses stopped on a hill west of where them bulls was. The broncs milled aroun' a bit. You could tell by the most hoofmarks on thet spot."

"Go on."

"Well, I put my horse on that spot. An' the flat where them bulls was was open in sight all around, men."

"What's your conclusions?"

"Them horses came from the Hole. They weren't range broncs runnin' loose. They was shod all aroun'."

"Wild Bunch watchin' . . ."

A hot voice said, "We should ride into the Hole. Call the hands on them sonsofbitches. Shoot 'em dead from leather!"

"Good idea," the tall man said and added, "if we had

107

about fifty guns—an' didn't care if we lost half of 'em—"

"I don't like the way things are goin'!"

The tall man said quietly, "You said that afore. We're right back where we started, men."

A few miles further west other men were also holding a conflab, also on a hill in a clump of Douglas firs that threw a rough perfume across the bunch-grass and buckbrush.

"They got McKee an' the Mexican in jail," a chunky man of about thirty said. "An' they're our friends."

"Distant friends," a small man said.

"Why the word *distant*?"

"They wouldn't join an' ride with us, remember?"

"An' we asked 'em to," another said.

Somebody laughed. "Do you blame 'em, men? They got a little bit of grey brains even if they are stupid enough to be cowpokes. When you ride with this bunch you ride to an early grave . . . sometimes, that is."

"Not *sometimes*—you mean *most times*," a man corrected.

Somebody laughed sardonically. "Let's get back on the business at hand," he said.

The tallest man said, "They'll be freed soon. Thet loco lawman can't hol' them in when Pothook Malone hears about it."

"But Pothook cain't say nothin'. He ain't got no tongue. An' he cain't write a word with them there hands of his'n twisted up an' useless with arthuritis. Pothook can't talk an' he cain't write."

"He's learnin' to write, I heard."

"How?"

"By holdin' the pencil between his teeth."

"My God, you don't say!"

"Can't make good readin' yet, I've heard, but his writin's gettin' better an' better each day, they tell me."

"Let's skip over Pothook," the tallest man said. He was taller even than Buckshot McKee.

"Skip over 'im? We can't do that. He's pertected us both up here an' down south. We've et his grub, free. He even years ago rode with us on a raid, ain't thet right?"

"That's right."

"Okay, that's settled. We see Pothook gets a fair shake. That means we kill whoever cut out his tongue. We know who did that. We know who wants to run us out of the Hole. We got a hunch one of them sonsofbitches—or mebbeso more than one—ambushed Smoky."

There followed a short and heavy pause. It was like a silent memorial respite for the ambushed and dead Smoky, the outlaw now sleeping the big sleep in the Hole in the Wall bandit burial ground.

"We gotta wipe out thet other bunch," a man said shortly. "Kill 'em like they killed Smoky . . . From ambush like they kill, if necessary!"

"I doubt if I can sink that low," a man said.

"What's ahead?" a gruff voice demanded, plainly speaking to the leader. "We've taken enough off'n this bunch of bastards . . ."

"I've got a belly-full friend."

The leader said, "It all depends on one point, and that point is them Brahman bulls."

"What're you talkin' about?"

"The bunch wants them bulls. They'll kill to get them. They almost had them when that Mexican was alone with 'em an' would've if the law hadn't accident'ly ridden in."

"Now we're on this tinhorn sheriff. An' that big-gutted deputy of his'n. What's your opinion on them two?"

"I don't think thet sheriff an' deputy have any idea what's goin' on underneath this whul mess."

"How'd them two get their offices? They ain't local men. Shipped-in guns."

"Governor appointed them after Powers got killed an' Pothook got his tongue cut out. I figure them thet jumped Powers an' Pothook meant Pothook to bleed to death out on that Buffalo trail."

"But he didn't. He's a tough ol' sonofabitch."

The leader said, "We're talkin' aroun' the point, men. The bulls is what count. They're the centre of the whul damn' mess."

"You speak truth."

"We watch them Brahmans, cowboys."

FIFTEEN

Attorney Herb Powers that long summer evening hung onto the bars fronting Buckshot McKee's cell. "I kin git you out on a writ of habeas corpus, gentlemen," he said.

Behind the attorney stood lovely Cynthia Watson. A deep frown tormented her forehead as her prairie-blue eyes regarded Buck McKee.

Buck KcKee knew a little bit about law. During other previous jail-stays he'd studied lawbooks, most of them coming from the library of the county attorney designated by the voters to prosecute him and Tortilla Joe.

"Gotta get a judge to sign it," Buck now said. "An' from what the honourable sheriff tells me the judge won't be here until tomorrow."

"I could ride to Buffalo and get in there by midnight," the attorney said. "And get Judge Seals to sign it and hurry back."

Cynthia laughed cynically. All eyes swung on the blonde beauty. "What's so funny about that?" Buck asked.

"Sure, he'd get fast to Buffalo," Cynthia said. "Kill a horse getting there. Saloons and whorehouses there, you know. He'd not even get to the judge's house. Or office."

Attorney Herb Powers turned watery eyes on the girl. He still clung for safety—and equilibrium—to the bars.

"And he'd be there a week at least," Cynthia finished.

Powers returned his liquid gaze to Buck and Tortilla Joe. "Cynthia reminds me of my sixth wife. She didn't trust me, either." He blinked a half dozen times in rapid succession. "A hacksaw blade, perhaps? One of you must today have a birthday?"

"Why a birthday?" Tortilla Joe asked.

"A birthday cake, of course. Ideal hiding place, gentlemen."

"I took Mr Powers here to show you he was and is still drunk but also to show you my father and I are doing all we can, gentlemen," Cynthia Watson informed. She was close to tears.

"This Powers any relation to the former sheriff?" Buck asked.

The attorney said, "Sheriff Powers was my only brother. Two years older than I. We came to this country right after the Watsons."

"Ain't you anxious to fin' out who murdered your brother?" Tortilla Joe asked.

"Not particularly, sir."

"That's an odd attitude," Buck said.

"We all have to die," the attorney said. "Well, no expense paid trip to the glories of Buffalo. And no lucre lining my pockets. Maybe if I saw some gold ahead of time—my palm holding it securely—I could forsake the bottle and become sober and able to think by tomorrow morning?"

Despite the seriousness of the situation Buck McKee had to laugh. "That'd come from Pothook Malone's treasury because me an' my partner ain't got none such, Attorney."

"Unfortunate humans." Attorney Powers released the cell-bars, turned, almost fell, caught his balance and lurched out, the steel door clanging behind.

Buck spoke to Cynthia. "There are some things here I don't understand. Mayhap you can help me?"

"I'll try."

"Sheriff Powers? Why was he killed, and how?"

"Sheriff Powers was an honest man. Honest men are hated and feared because they are honest. He and Pothook were returning at night from Buffalo. About halfway between here and Buffalo they were undoubtedly jumped on in the dark. Assailants had knives. No bullet wounds."

"Powers have any trouble with anybody aroun' here or anywhere else right afore he got killed?" Buck asked.

"I don't know. If he had, I never heard about it. Neither has my father. Nobody knows who killed him. And cut out Pothook's tongue."

"Who'd have it in for Pothook?" Tortilla Joe asked.

Cynthia could only shrug.

Buck asked, "This Dan Malone, now? You all call him a bastard?"

Cynthia told the partners that Dan Malone was an illegal son of old Pothook. "Mother was a saloon girl in Texas, I understand. Pothook didn't try to evade the stigma of being the baby's father. Missus Malone knew about the baby all the time, I understand—but she refused to raise it."

"An' Dan Malone only jus' made contact with his father?" Buck asked.

"Not too many months ago. Maybe six months since Dan showed up, maybe a month or more less. He came just before those crazy religious nuts of farmers moved in."

Buck nodded. Tortilla listened.

"Are the farmers any threat to the land Pothook Malone's cows run on?" Buck asked.

Cynthia shook her head. "PM runs back in the rough country. Farmers can't farm back there. No, farmers are no menace to PM. In fact, they could be a boon, in one sense of the word."

"Howcome that?" Tortilla Joe asked.

"Winters are terrible in this country. Cattle can't live out on the range in winter when snow is feet deep. Cattle need hay. Farmers can raise hay for Pothook's spread."

"Pothook mad at the grangers?" Tortilla Joe asked.

"Not that I know of."

"Dan Malone get along good with them?" Buck asked.

"I've never heard of trouble between him and them."

Buck nodded thoughtfully. "PM losin' any cattle? Long loop men, riders in the dark, things like that?"

"Before they cut the tongue off of old Pothook—Well, he and my father are close friends. Bound to be after being together so many years. And Dad has hinted that Pothook hinted something like that."

"That he was losin' cows?" Tortilla Joe asked.

Cynthia nodded. "But I don't know how true it is, of course. But I have to get back to the store."

Then, she was gone.

Buck sighed. He remembered the girl's hips as she walked away. "She'll make some man a good wife." He looked at Tortilla Joe.

"Don't look at me, Buck. She don't how how to pound out *tortillas*."

"You could teach her," Buck assured.

The cells were getting dark. Mosquitos buzzed in and out the open high-barred windows. To the surprise of Buck and Tortilla Joe Sheriff Ed Fillmore ushered in nobody but Dan Malone some ten minutes after Cynthia Watson left.

"What the hell you doin' here?" Buck demanded.

The stocky man grinned. He needed a shave. He pointed down at his holster. "Took your advice, McKee."

Buck noticed the man's gun was tied into its holster. But the holster was not tied to the man's hip.

Sheriff Ed Fillmore was retreating through the steel door.

Buck said, "Sheriff, come back here."

Fillmore stopped. "What's eatin' you, McKee?"

"Stay in here. This man tried to kill me once. He might try again. Your job is to pertect my life."

Fillmore stopped. "Jeezus," he said. He closed the steel door. He leaned against the steel. "All right, I'm here," he added.

Dan Malone said, "I never tried to kill you, McKee. My horse busted out buckin'. You can't guide a buckin' horse. He jus' hogs down his head. He goes where he aims an' no man on him can change his mind—or his direction."

Buck knew this was not true but said nothing against it. He mentioned that about the time he and Tortilla Joe had taken charge of the bulls in Dumas, Texas, was about the time Sheriff John Powers was assassinated and Pothook Malone had his tongue cut out.

Dan Malone watched through crafty eyes. "That's about right," he finally said. "But what're you drivin' at, McKee?"

"When Pothook got laid up, who took charge at his ranch?"

"I did. Naturally. His only son, only child."

Buck asked, "Did you get the telegram I sent you from Texas?"

"I did. An' I didn't answer because I didn't know you for what might be a bum, a schemer, who'd get the coin an' then jus' disappear. With my father not bein' able to speak, I could learn nothin' about your character, McKee." He looked at Tortilla Joe. "That goes for you, too, Mexican."

The word *Mexican* brought yellow hardness to Tortilla Joe's eyes, for it had been spoken a little too loud. Buck made a hand gesture that Dan Malone didn't see. Tortilla Joe settled back.

"You get the wires I sent you—or Pothook, rather—from Walsenburg, Colorado? An' from Denver an' Cheyenne?"

"I did."

"An' the telegram from Fort Collins, down in Colorado?"

"I got it."

Buck realized the man lied. He'd sent no wire from Fort Collins. He wondered why Dan Malone stood before him. Maybe curiosity had driven the cowman into the jail?

That didn't seem logical.

"Howcome you come to see me an' my pard?" Buck asked.

"I'll drop charges against you."

"Why?"

"All a mistake, McKee. A big mistake."

Buck looked at Sheriff Fillmore. "Did this guy file charges against me? An' against Tortilla Joe?"

The sheriff hesitated, then said. "No complaint was

114

ever signed or filed. I jus' decided to jug you two for your own pertection."

"Pertection from who or what?" Buck demanded.

The heavy jowls reddened. You could see the red even in the dim light. "Jus' thought it best," the lawman said.

Buck returned his attention to Dan Malone. "Where are the bulls now?"

They were as Cynthia had guessed—in the night pasture behind the town cow-corral. "Purty good grass there," Dan Malone said. "An' plenty of water. Crick runs right through it."

Buck said, "I'm not turnin' them critters over to you, Malone. They was bought by your father—manifest in Dumas said that—an' when I get shut of 'em it'll be a signed release by none other than Pothook Malone."

"My father can't write, McKee."

"Nothin' else will get them bulls away from us," Buck said.

Tortilla Joe said, "That goes for me, too, United States Citizen."

Dan Malone clipped his words. "I'm legally my father's guardian. I signed the papers in Lawyer Powers' office right after my father and Powers had their—well, accident."

"Who signed for your father?" Buck asked.

"My mother."

Buck nodded. "An you prob'ly had a hammerlock on the ol' woman almos' tearin' her shoulder outa joint."

Dan Malone doubled his fist. He stepped forward. Buck didn't step back. Sheriff Fillmore started forward. Malone stepped back.

Malone spoke to the sheriff. "This long string of pelican shit is loco—completely loco."

"The whole world's loco," the lawman said.

Malone sent flinty eyes over Tortilla Joe, then over Buckshot McKee. "Nothin' good I kin do here," he said. "I come in peace. They drove me up a wall. Goodnight, you two sonsofbitches."

Malone stalked out. Fillmore dug out a big dirty blue bandana. He mopped his brow. "Sure got hot in here all of a sudden. You two hairpins want out?"

"We could sue you an' this county for false arrest," Buck reminded.

"You get nothin' from me. I got a wife and nine kids down in Cheyenne. Won't live outa that town. Hate the prairie. But you might get a buck or two out of the community. I asked a question: you two hellions want freedom?"

"Lemme think about it," Buck said.

"Me, too." Tortilla Joe looked at Buckshot McKee. "Let's have a conference, partner?"

"Good idea."

The partners went to the rear of their cells. They mumbled something and Fillmore even cupped an ear to hear. The partners returned.

"We want to know a few things first," Buck said. "Then we'll give you our decision."

"Fire away, men."

Buck asked, "You guarantee we'll live through the night if we went outside?"

The sheriff studied him. "I guarantee nothin'. Who t'hell would want to kill you two drifters?"

"Dan Malone tried it onct, remember?"

"Dan jus' stood here an' said he didn't ride you down on purpose an' thet his hoss jus' bucked in your direction."

"Dan Malone's a liar," Buck said.

Tortilla Joe listened.

"An' besides," the lawman continued, "who'd wanta kill you two—an' for what reason?"

"I don't know the *who* would be," Buck replied, "but the *why* would be simple—somebody wants them expensive Brahman bulls."

The sheriff said seriously, "They're worth plenty of money, that's right . . . Read other day in the Montana Stockman's Journal where them Brahmans live good and get fat in the snow an' bad grass where a Hereford or Angus would starve to death." He looked at Tortilla Joe. "Well, what you two goin' do? Stay or git out?"

Before the Mexican could answer loud boots were

heard in the corridor beyond the big steel door. The door hurriedly opened and three men entered, gun-harness gear creaking.

Buck McKee stared. "Well, I'll be hanged."

"Double hangin'," Tortilla Joe said, beaming.

They shook hands through the bars. "Butch Cassidy," Buck said. "An' Kid Curry. An' Harry Longabaugh, hisself."

The Wild Bunch shook hands with a happy Tortilla Joe who demanded each move close to the bars for a short Mexican *abrazo*. Buck McKee hurriedly noted that with the arrival of the Wild Bunch Sheriff Ed Fillmore had quickly stepped back and now stood by the steel door.

The Wild Bunch had paid the lawman not a bit of attention.

"Heard about the mess you two is in," Butch Cassidy said, "an' we decided to bend a few cell-bars an' get you out."

"I feel awful strong tonight." Kid Curry grinned.

Harry Longabaugh said, "I'm as strong as the Kid."

Buck said jokingly, "Ain't you three gonna say *hello* to our sheriff?"

"Why?" Kid Curry asked.

"Those black holy bulls now," Butch Cassidy said. "We can get you three hundred bucks apiece an' don't ask who'll buy them."

Three hundred times thirty two equalled over nine thousand bucks, Buck McKee figured hurriedly. More money than he and Tortilla Joe had had combined in their lives. And more than they ever hoped to have singly or in combination.

"They ain't ours," Buck said.

Tortilla Joe said, "They belong to Pothook."

"I got a hunch Pothook's goin' out of the cow business," Butch Cassidy said. "Talkin' to his missus here in town t'other day. She said her husban' ain't in no condition to rod a cow spread, an' southern California's sun an' warm winters was beginnin' to look good to them both."

"How about the son?" Tortilla Joe asked. "That

bastard of a Dan?"

"Son?" Butch Cassidy's brows rose. "Oh, yes, that hind end of a mule. He don't count, men."

"You look over the bulls?" Buck asked.

The three outlaws had done just that. "They're safe where they are," Kid Curry assured. "You two want out?"

The trio acted as though Sheriff Ed Fillmore didn't exist. Buck and Tortilla Joe exchanged glances. With the Wild Bunch watching the bulls the bulls were safe. Just then heels tapped beyond the steel door. Ed Fillmore opened it. Blonde Cynthia Watson entered.

She carried blankets and two pillows. "No hotel in town," she said. "Mrs Rothwell boarded it up when cattle drives moved west." Then to Cassidy, Curry and Longabaugh. "How are you men?"

Hats flew off. "Jus' fine," was the chorus.

"Brought these blankets and pillows for Buck and Tortilla Joe. Dad said those cot beds are concrete. He should know. A couple of years ago John Powers jailed Dad for being drunk even though he and John were close friends."

Cassidy looked at Buck. "You're stayin' behin' bars for the night, eh?"

"Looks that way," Buck said, smiling.

"Purtiest girl in town brings us beddin' so we stay," Tortilla Joe said.

Cynthia smiled. "I guess I am the prettiest girl in town, seeing I'm the only young girl in Powder River City."

Buck looked at Tortilla Joe. "First time we've slept under a roof for a long time, *compadre*."

"Since Charlie's Place."

SIXTEEN

Next morning early Sheriff Ed Fillmore moved too close to the bars of Buck McKee's cell, plainly to unlock it.

Buck's long arms shot out. He clamped both tough hands around the sheriff's leathery throat stifling immediately the lawman's surprised yelp.

The lawman struggled, face fuming. Tortilla reached through the bars. He snagged the lawman's pistol from holster. He jerked the jail keys from the wide belt.

Tortilla Joe spun the .45, centring it on the sheriff. He said, "You can let him loose now, Buck. If he starts to run I'm puttin' a lead slug through his back right opposite his heart!"

Buck released the sheriff. Fillmore sagged back against the iron door, fumbling at his throat which held Buck's stern blue fingermarks. The sheriff coughed phlegm.

"Why t'hell did you do that, McKee?" he snarled. "I was jus' goin' unlock your cell an' let you two free!"

"Practice," Buck said.

The dull eyes widened. "Practice? What the hell does that mean?"

"Practicin' for a jailbreak that might be necessary," the lanky Texan said.

"An' teachin', too," Tortilla Joe said.

The sheriff still rubbed his neck. "Where does the damn' *teachin'* come in?" he demanded.

"*Teachin'* you not to move too close to a prisoner's cell," Tortilla Joe pointed out as he unlocked his cell door and handed the keys through the bars to Buckshot McKee.

Buck unlocked his door and stepped into the corridor. "Thanks, Sheriff."

"Never in my life have I ever met two bastards like you two," the sheriff said.

"An' no doubt you never again will," Tortilla Joe said.

"I got breakfast cooked for us three," the sheriff said.

Buck studied him. "You're jokin'?"

"Nope, cooked it myself, I did."

Tortilla Joe spoke to Buckshot McKee. "Mebbeso we shouldn't have treated him so rough?"

"How were we to know?"

The breakfast lacked much. Eggs were boiled rock hard. Pancakes were as tough as a Navajo saddleblanket. You could dent the coffee with a hammer and chisel. Despite these failings the partners fell to. They hadn't eaten since last noon out on the prairie.

Buck leaned back, belched. "Inner man fed."

"Darn nice cookin'," Tortilla Joe told the sheriff.

"You boys is liars," Sheriff Ed Fillmore said good-naturedly. "An' what is more I think you both were born liars."

"You got a good point there," Buck assured. "You goin' stay aroun' when bullets start singin' or are you goin' take it whippin' your bronc down the hind legs for more speed?"

"What bullets?"

"I don't know whose just yet," Buck said slowly. "But them Brahman bulls are worth a small fortune. I don't know who'll come out on top an' ownin' them but me an' my pard want to go on record right now as them bein' our sole property, Sheriff."

"On what grounds?" the lawman asked.

"We druv them up from Texas. That's quite a distance, you know."

"I bin on a few north trail-drives."

"An' we ain't been paid yet," Tortilla Joe said.

Buck McKee said, "So Sheriff Powers was knifed to death. An' then a knife cut out ol' Pothook's tongue . . ."

The sheriff and Tortilla Joe watched Buck.

"Knife work . . . up here in north central Wyomin'," Buck said, as though musing. "Knives belong down on the Mex-Texas border . . . an' in ol' Mexico. They're silent. Not noisy, like a fire-arm."

"I looked the death scene over careful," the sheriff said. "Me an' Deputy Jay Beeman . . . Lots of boot tracks an' hoss prints but nothin' pointin' to who the murderers could be."

"Maybe Pothook will get so he can write with his pencil in his teeth," Tortilla Joe said.

"Let's hope so," the sheriff said. He shifted in his chair. "You boys seem to know Curry an' Longabaugh an' Cassidy an' them other long riders. Jus' tell them boys I don't want no how-to-do with 'em 'cept as peaceful humans. Tell 'em that if they get rough aroun' here I'll be long gone."

They thanked the sheriff, went out into the cool of morning and sauntered over to the town corral. The bulls were on the milk-cow lot. One townsman was rather angered. Flapears and some of his black friends had been playing husband and wife with the townsman's pet milk cow.

"She must've been in heat," Buck said.

"She wasn't when she was put in the pasture. But I guess she saw your bulls an' got in the motherly disposition right soon. Not that she got bred—but man alive, I wanted a heifer calf that we could use as a milk cow."

Buck spoke to Tortilla Joe. "Do Brahman cows give good milk?"

"How would I know? All I've ever seen in that breed is a bunch of bulls an' I know you can't milk a bull."

The townsman looked from one to the other and then rapidly walked away. "He doubts our sanity," Buck said.

"Sometimes I do, too."

"Here comes some cowboys," Buck said. "From the southwest."

The *cowboys* turned out to be the religious nut farmers. They drew rein and looked at the bulls on the other side of the fence.

Buck quickly noticed each farmer packed a rifle in his saddle-boot and each had a six-shooter holstered on his thigh. Evidently their religion made no stipulations about the carrying of deadly weapons.

Not a one looked at Buck or Tortilla Joe. Not a one said a word of greeting or lifted a hand in recognition. They just sat saddles and looked at the bulls.

"All well armed," Buck quietly said.

"Don't look like preachers to me," Tortilla Joe also spoke softly. "Never afore have I seen such tall men all in one bunch. You figger one or some of them was thet tall gent who trailed us north?"

"They got the bottoms of their faces covered," Buck said. "Look more like highway holdup men with them masks then they do like God's Chosen."

"How about them packin' toad stickers?"

"I'll do my best to look, Buckshot."

Their scrutiny evidently finished, the tall men turned horses and rode west to go down Powder River City's main drag there to rein-in and dismount in front of the Mercantile.

"How about the knives?" Buck asked.

"Hard to tell, Buck. All them loose clothes—Hard to see if any holstered knife was under them. One had a knife hung from his gunbelt, though. You notice that?"

"I saw it."

Cynthia Watson rode over on a pinto gelding. "The bulls seem to be doing okay," she said. "When you going to deliver them to the PM ranch?"

Buck scowled. "I don't know . . ."

Cynthia looked at him. "I understand. You don't know who really owns the bulls? Might be Pothook; might be Dan. Dad and I are like you two: we just don't know what is what, either."

"We ain't been paid yet," Tortilla Joe explained.

"Didn't Missus Malone yesterday mention anything about pay?" the girl asked.

Buck said, "Not a thing. She looked in bad shape to me. Almost as bad as poor ol' Pothook hisself."

Cynthia shook her head slowly. "Dad says he don't

think either of the Malones have many days ahead, but he said that about ol' Plenty Horses twenty years ago when that ol' Crow was supposed to be in his eighties."

"An' the ol' buck's still alive?" Buck asked.

"Looks to me like he'll outlive my father." She studied Flapears' flapping appendages. Flapears studied her, the picture of contentment. The other bulls were bedded-down under the wide cottonwood trees, also apparently at peace with the world. "They're ugly brutes," the girl said. "You two want me to ride with you to PM ranch? Show you the way?"

Buck liked the girl's company but he didn't want to put himself and partner deeper into debt to her and her father. The Watsons had done much for two drifting cowpokes now.

Buck hated debts, monetary or personal. He knew Tortilla Joe felt the same. Neither of them owed a soul in the world a cent if memory were correct—and in this case Buckshot McKee knew it was.

"Seen the ranch from the ridge when we rode in yesterday," Buck said, "So we oughta fin' it easy. Jus' ride straight west, eh?"

"About six miles."

The girl looked disappointed. Buck realized she undoubtedly was very, very lonesome, stuck in this almost unpopulated wilderness. So he said, "We'd be glad to have you ride along, Miss Cynthia—that is, if your Dad don't need you at the store."

"The store business here is almost done with, Dad says. The few farmers—like those religious things—can go to Buffalo for supplies. We doubt if any other farmers will move in. Dry land farming hasn't paid, the State Agriculture Office says."

"But the would-be homesteader doesn't read such," Buck said. "He reads only the lies and untrue things put out by the railroad companies and thieving companies who settle ignorant people on land that turns out to be worthless."

"That's right," the girl said. "And some of the settlers can't even read English—or even talk it."

Buck looked about at the rolling wilderness. A few years ago buffalo by the million grazed on this land. Buffalo grass then covered most of it but that grass was now almost all gone—along with the buffalo.

They rode along a wagon trail. Evidently PM rigs had worn the trail through the sagebrush as ranch wagons had gone into town for supplies. Powder River City had no railroad.

"Pothook's outfit ships cattle out of Buffalo," Cynthia explained. "Most of them go to the Chicago stockyards, I believe. The farmers will have a long way to haul their wheat and oats and corn—that is, if they can grow any such with the little rainfall this area has."

"Wind an' drouth will drive 'em out," Tortilla Joe said. "But by that time the damage will be done. Their ploughs will cut the buffalo-grass and turn it under and leave bare ground and the wind will move that from here into Nebraska or South Dalota or even further east."

Things at PM ranch looked no more encouraging. Pothook was at his breakfast table trying to eat without a tongue. Ma Malone fed him with a spoon. They were the only two in the rambling log ranch-house set on the side of a Wyoming gentle hill.

"Where's your son?" Buck asked, forgetting Pothook couldn't talk.

Pothook forgot, too. He tried to speak, couldn't. Despair lit his grim face.

Ma Malone answered. "Sonofabitch is aroun' here somewhere. Snoopin' aroun' as usual, I reckon. Wish the bastard would drop dead."

Pothook watched her in eternal silence.

"Now cowpunchers on the ranch?" Buck asked.

"Got only our ol' hostler," Ma said. "Two men out west about thirty miles watchin' the bog potholes along the river there. No need for hands this time of the year. Be months yet afore beef roundup."

The partners understood. Big ranches laid off men after spring calf-branding was done. There were then a few dull months until the outfits again stocked up on cowhands for fall beef gather.

Buck noticed that Ma and Cynthia had moved to one side and were quietly talking. Woman talk, the lanky Texan figured. Ma left the kitchen and soon returned with a small buckskin sack. Buck recognized it immediately as a money-poke.

"Ain't paid you boys yet fer bringin' up them bulls," the woman said. "How much you figger each one has earned, Pothook?"

Pothook could only nod.

"Hundred bucks each?" Ma asked her husband.

Buck's breath caught. Quick mathematics told him one hundred times thirty two was thirty two hundred—sixteen hundred for him and the same for Tortilla Joe.

Pothook Malone nodded.

Buck said, "Missus Malone, that's too much money."

"It sure is," Tortilla Joe said.

Ma Malone's shrewd eyes appraised the partners. "I always figgered you two as fools ever since the day you was young-uns an' Pothook an' our 'punchers peeled them jail bars off'n you down in Texas, but now you're provin' thet all these years I've been correct!"

Cynthia smiled. "Convicts?" she said jokingly.

"They ain't got enough brains to be good crooks," the woman said, a wide smile touching her sun- and wind-cracked lips. Seriousness suddenly gripped her. "Pa an' me might pull out for California. Sell out an' jus' leave. So what will we do with all thet money twenty thousand odd head of cattle will bring?"

"What about Dan?" Buck asked.

"T'hell with him," Ma Malone said.

Something moved across Pothook's dull eyes, Buck noticed. The cowman opened his mouth, then apparently remembered, and closed his mouth again.

"Well, under such circumstances," Buck said, "Tortilla Joe and I take sixteen hundred each, and thanks almighty, Missus Malone."

"You earned it, Buck."

Buck remembered Comanche war parties, big rivers to swim, and long dry marches with the tongues of the bulls lolling. He saw sixteen one hundred dollar U.S. treasury notes put in his hand. The hand of Tortilla Joe received the same.

Buck folded the money and put it in an old poke he toted in his right hand pants pocket.

He knew now why Cynthia had taken Ma Malone aside. He thanked the blonde girl with his eyes. She smiled prettily back.

Ma Malone said, very seriously, "Pa an' me is goin' keep one-third of what we get when we sell out. The whole rest is goin' to the orphan home in Cheyenne—lock, stock an' barrel."

Buck wondered why the woman told them this.

"If anythin' happens to me or Pothook, them bulls are yours, you two drifters."

Buck and Tortilla Joe exchanged glances. Something was transpiring here they didn't clearly comprehend.

"None goes to Dan," the woman said. "Jack Watson has been our closest friend for years. This girl's dead mother—God bless her big soul—was the closest friend I ever had, or ever will have."

Tears filled the old woman's eyes. Buck glanced at Cynthia. She, too, had tears.

"I speak for Pothook, too," Ma Malone said. "We had this plan arranged before those bastards cut out his tongue. If somethin' happens to Pothook an' me, then Jack Watson an' Cynthia take over and sell our cattle and donate all to the orphans, poor little souls."

Buck said, "You two'll live to be a hundred, Missus Malone." He heard horses come into the yard. Tortilla Joe looked out the window.

"The Wild Bunch, Buck."

"What part of 'em?"

"Cassidy. Sundance. Kid Curry. Then a real tall gink with 'em—never have seen him afore."

Buck glanced out the window. "That's the tall gink that straightened up Tank Willard in Dumas, ain't it?"

"Sure looks like him but at this distance—"

Ma glanced at the battered old alarm clock. "Boys right on time. Bring 'em in, please, Cynthia, daughter."

The four Wild Bunch members came in with clomping

126

bootheels, jangling spurs and creaking gun-harnesses.

Buck spoke to the tall man. "How'd things turn out down in Dumas?"

"Jus' fine, McKee. Willard saw the light, at last."

Buck said, "Last time we met was in Sig's saloon down in Cheyenne, an' you didn't know me."

"Wasn't my day to make friends."

Buck looked at Butch Cassidy. The outlaw was smiling. "This is Ben Kilpatrick, Buck. The Tall Texan, the want ads call him. Cripes, he's two inches taller than you, at that."

"How come he get in Dumas?" Tortilla Joe asked.

"Pothook tol' me about these humpbacked bulls comin' in there," Cassidy explained. "That was right afore they cut his tongue out. Us boys thought maybe somethin' might happen to the bulls. So we sent Ben down to kinda ride herd on you an' Buck."

"How'd he get down there so fast?" Tortilla Joe asked.

"He had a good start on you. Went by train."

Buck looked at Ben Kilpatrick. "How come you never tol' us who you were? An' why you was in Dumas?"

"Jus' thought it best you didn't know," the tall man said.

Butch Cassidy said, "Well, that's settled." He spoke to Ma Malone. "How's Pothook gettin' along with his writin' by holdin' a pencil in his mouth?"

"Not much," Missus Malone said. "Can write a few letters, but the're almost impossible to read. I was jus' tellin' Buck an' Tortilla Joe thet if somethin' happens to me an' my husban' them bulls are their's."

Cassidy scowled. "I don't get it," he said. "What could happen?"

"Lots of things," the woman said.

Kid Curry sighed. "Lots of things could happen to each an' every one of us, people." He looked at Butch Cassidy. "You wanna do the talkin' or shall I?"

"You got a gift of gab," Cassidy said, grinning.

Buck said, "There's a whale of a lot here I don't understan', men."

"Same for me," Tortilla Joe said.

Cynthia said, "Something important is coming up. I feel it in my bones. Would you want me to leave the room?"

Butch Cassidy shook his head. "You're Jack Watson's daughter," he said pointedly. "Kid, look into the hall, eh?"

Kid Curry silently went to the kitchen door. He opened it suddenly, then said, "Nobody in the hall."

"I don't trust that Dan person," Cassidy said and to Ma Malone, "He on the ranch?"

"He was a short time ago. I think he's in the office down by the bunkhouse. I didn't hear anybody ride out."

"An' we didn't meet him or anybody else when we rode out," Tortilla Joe said. "Evidently you don't trust him, Cassidy?"

"No further than I could throw one of your Brahman bulls by his tail." The outlaw looked at Buck. "The deal is this, you two Texas drifters. This gang of religious nuts, now—well, they ain't as religious as they put on."

"I didn't read them as such," Buck said.

"They're what's left of the Matt Ketchum gang," the outlaw explained. "We didn't hol' up that train a couple of weeks back, down south of here. Them bastards did that—and when they called to each other during the holdup, they used our names. That put the law on our tail again."

"Not again," Kid Curry corrected, smilingly, "but more *tongh* again."

Butch Cassidy nodded. "They're posin' as farmers so they can be close to us 'cause they want the Hole in the Wall where no law can touch them. So the way we figger they're out to kill the Wild Bunch off—and it wouldn't su'prise me if they hankered for a bunch of expensive bulls, too."

"Brahman bulls," Buck said.

"Right," Ben Kilpatrick said.

Butch Cassidy said, "An' what about them hittin' the Wild Bunch at the same time they try to rustle them bulls?"

Buck asked, quietly, "An' who'd set the trap, Butch?"

There was a moment's pause. Buck glanced at Cynthia. Her mouth was slightly open. Her tongue wet her lips. Ma Malone stood listening. Pothook Malone stared, mouth tightly shut.

Tortilla Joe's brown eyes watched Butch Cassidy. Buck swung his gaze back to the four outlaws. "Who's the bait?" he asked.

Butch Cassidy smiled. "Two drifters I know . . ."

Buck said, "One named Tortilla Joe?"

Cassidy nodded.

"An' the other?" Buck asked.

"You make a guess," Cassidy said.

Buck nodded. "Spring with details, Butch."

SEVENTEEN

The only thing Pothook Malone could do was to listen. Although he disagreed with certain points in the Wild Bunch's plan he knew there was no way to voice this disagreement. He was a man without hope, and he knew it.

Within him boiled hate for the men who had cut off his tongue and killed his good friend, Sheriff John Powers. He knew that hate was wasted energy. There was absolutely nothing he could do.

He raised his hands. They came up with pain surging knife-sharp through his shoulders. They came up very, very slowly. He knew that within a few more days he'd not even be able to raise his hands.

The pain became too great. He had to let his hands drop. They plummeted to his sides like dead metal weights. Tears filled his watery eyes.

His tool-shop was off his bedroom. Here he kept his side-arms and long-guns. He stood stooped and studied his three shotguns. One was a ten-gauge single barrel. Another was a double-barrelled twelve gauge. The third was a short-barrelled twelve gauge pump gun. He had liked it the best for hunting mallards.

All the weapons were loaded, he knew. They'd always hung on the wall with cartridges in their barrels. Had he had children in the house he'd not have allowed the arms to be loaded.

But he and Ma had never had a child. That was one sore point between them, although neither ever mentioned it. He had only this bastardly get from a saloon whore. And there were times when he seriously wondered if Dan Malone really was of his own semen. But the boy had even from birth resembled him. So he'd taken over the doubtful paternity.

And he'd been honest with Ma. He'd told her all details. She had grudgingly accepted. She'd even gone to see the baby. The boy had then been four years old. She'd viewed him from a short distance. She'd not revealed to the mother she was the wife of Pothook Malone.

Next day the child had been playing with other children in the street. She'd got a close look at him. She'd also seen the mother. The mother worked as a charwoman. Her whoring days were over. She'd grown too old. Also a customer had slashed her face a few years ago. The sharp knife had cut the bridge of her nose in two and scarred both cheeks under the eyes.

The mother was an ugly, pitiful character.

Ma Malone returned home. "They're poor as a church-mouse," she said. "You double what you have the banker send them. You hear me."

"You're the boss, Ma."

Now Pothook hobbled to the window. He looked out on the hills back of the house. Ma was outside, puttering around in her flowerbed. Here a concrete stairway went down under the house. The root cellar was there.

Pothook Malone crossed the room to his shotguns. He acted as fast as he could. He built a loop on a stout cord with his teeth. He wished he could work faster. But he couldn't. And that was that.

He rose on tiptoe, the loop in his mouth. He snagged it over the barrel of the short-barrelled shotgun. He pulled the loop tight. The front sight held it firm to the blue barrel.

He moved back, cord between teeth. He hoped to ease the deadly weapon from the wooden pegs. He couldn't. The shotgun came down fast. The butt hit the floor. To him it made a loud noise.

He stood poised, pain lancing, tongueless mouth dry. He listened. He was sure his wife had heard the noise. He breathed in short, gasping sounds. He waited patiently.

But he heard no feet coming toward the door. His breathing became normal.

He backed to the door, the gun pulled behind him. He opened the door and looked out through its crack. The hall was empty. Three doors down was his bedroom.

Where was Ma? Still outside the cellar door?

He fell to his knees. He thus lowered the shotgun silently to the floor. He rose. He hobbled to the window.

Yes, she was still there.

He returned to his shotgun. Cord again in his mouth, he hurried down the hall, the shotgun trailing stock-down behind.

He froze at his door. What was that sound? Was it the back door opening? He heard it again. No, the wind. The wind, the never-ending Wyoming wind. The wind brushing a tree branch on the eaves. He should have recognized that sound. He'd heard it for years.

He bent his aching knees. He put his mouth around the doorknob, somehow also keeping control of the cord. He opened the door with his mouth. He pulled the shotgun inside.

He closed the door. He stood against it a few moments breathing heavily. So far, so good.

He'd lain on his back in the dead dark night after night, hour after hour. Planning this, working out each move, each detail. All was going as planned. He looked across the room at his bed.

The bed was made up. A gaudy homemade bedspread covered the double bed. Ma had made the spread. She'd sewed it piece by piece last winter in front of the fireplace with her arthritic hands working as best they could.

He dragged the shotgun to the bed. He got on his knees beside the bed. His head came down and he rutted like an animal against the spread and blanket and sheet, spreading them back.

He then got on the bed. He got on all fours. He pulled the shotgun between the sheets. He then released the cord. He pushed the bedding back into place with his head. The bed was again complete. He got to his feet and looked down at it.

"Goddamned human billy-goat," he told himself, smiling a little at his accomplishment.

The shotgun was hidden. It made no bump under the bedding. He hobbled back to his gunshop. He looked out the window. Ma still puttered around in her flowerbed.

He walked slowly into the living-room. He sat in his old easy-chair before the fireplace. He looked at the fireplace's sooty back-wall. His thoughts returned to the conversation with the Wild Bunch and Tortilla Joe and Buckshot McKee.

He closed his eyes in utter weariness. It was the terrible weariness of old age and incurable sickness. He knew it would never leave him until death came. When young he could go to bed dog-tired but in the morning he'd wake up new and refreshed and ready for the challenge ahead.

Now when he awakened mornings he was just as tired—if not more so—than when he'd gone to bed the night before.

He realized Ma was spending more time than usual in her flowerbed. He did not know that Ma's sharp eyes had detected bootprints left by one particular pair of high-heeled riding boots in the dust in front of the cellar's door.

Ma Malone nodded slowly, eyes closing in thought. A person in the root cellar would be directly under the kitchen floor. Anybody secreted there could hear each and every word spoken overhead.

She knew from experience. Up to lately she'd always had a Cheyenne squaw as a housekeeper. Only the last few months since government rations to the reservation Indians had been more than doubled had she failed to have a housekeeper but now with so much coming in no squaws would now work.

She'd been in the cellar many times when her housekeeper or others had been talking in the overhead kitchen.

Kid Curry had wasted time and steps when he'd unexpectedly opened the kitchen door.

She checked the ranch's buildings for human occupants. Besides her husband in the house and she herself only one other human was on the spread and that was the old hostler and roustabout, an ex-cowpuncher now physically broken by bucking broncs and other range mishaps. He slept in a manger in the horse barn, half-covered with hay. He snored loudly and drunkenly.

Her stepson kept him drunk most of the time. Before the coming of Dan Malone the oldtimer had been a sober and industrious worker. Oh, yes, he got off on the bottle for a few days a year, but now he was drunk day after day.

Things had more or less gone to pot since Pothook's illegitimate son had arrived. Pothook waylaid, his tongue cut out. Sheriff John Powers—Honest John, as he was called—murdered by the knife.

And maybe PM cattle missing, too? She heard rumours around town lately to that effect. Dan had too much money . . . Far too much, she'd heard—big gambling games in the pool hall's basement, things like that . . .

She went to her husband's bedroom. He lay sleeping on the covers. She looked at him with tears. He was nothing any more—just a shell, bones and skin and gristle, no more.

And once he'd been—

She began to sob. She left hurriedly. She didn't want her sobs to awaken him. He needed sleep. He was a good man. He was the only man she'd ever loved. She'd been a virgin when they married. She had not been able to give him children. And he'd wanted children years ago.

She'd gone to doctor after doctor. Some had told her she could conceive. Had the trouble been in Pothook? She had never asked him to go to a doctor for a physical examination. She'd never mentioned—even when they'd had spats—that the fault could lie in him, not her.

Had she conceived, Pothook would never have lain with that saloon whore, the mother of Dan. She felt sure of that. She felt it in her bones. And she had wanted children. Three girls and three boys, she'd told Pothook the night of their marriage.

Now their wedding night seemed centuries ago. How peaceful, how serene, life had then been, down there on the limitless Texas Panhandle. No pain, no problems, the man she loved, children with him, see those children grow, to school they go, they marry . . . and then other small ones, your grandchildren.

Suddenly she remembered something. A piece of notebook paper on Pothook's dresser. She returned to his room, crept inside, left the door open to allow air to enter, and stopped in the kitchen to look at the paper.

And her heart leaped. Her breathing came in gasps. She stared at the paper. Just a simple piece of notebook paper. Like school children use. The type Pothook used to run his pencil jerkedly over, the pencil clamped between his tobacco-stained teeth.

She read four words, crudely drawn:

CUT TONGUE POWERS SON

What did they mean?

She put the note tremblingly on the table. Then she stood and stared blindly out the window onto the hills and their brown drought. Finally she looked back at the note.

She had made her husband's bed this morning. This note had not then been on his dresser. She realized he must have written it before going to take his nap.

Yes, just recently written.

She sat wearily at the kitchen table, unmindful of the dirty dishes it contained. She'd wash those later, she thought vaguely.

Right now dirty dishes didn't count.

Only the note—and the four hardly-legible words— was what counted. She'd question Pothook when he awakened. She'd put her questions. He'd nod either yes or no. She'd talk to him then . . .

She never spoke to her husband again, though.

The shotgun's blast saw to that.

The roar came from Pothook Malone's bedroom. She did not hurry. She knew what had happened. She had feared this for some time. Now that it had come she felt a sort of odd relaxation.

"You're a brave man, my husband," she told the wall as she went down the hall. She corrected her statement to, "You *were* a brave man," and she glanced into the gun-

135

room and saw which shotgun was missing. "So you took the short-barrelled one, eh?"

The scene was terrible. It was blood and gore and death. Yes, and the stink of black powder, seeping through the room's air. She calmly surveyed the scene from the doorway.

Her face showed no emotion. Later the shock would pass and tears would come, but now she just felt a strange numbness.

Her husband had put the shotgun's barrel in his mouth. He lay naked. He'd triggered the trigger with his big toe on his right foot. He'd been killed instantly.

The number five shot had ripped off the top of his head. It had driven blood and hair into the wall. The pillow was torn and saturated with his blood.

She looked at his hands. They lay eternally idle, now. Warped, twisted, useless then—useless now.

"So this is the way it ends," she said quietly.

Slowly, she closed the door. She returned to the kitchen. She began washing the dishes in the sink. Upon building this house Pothook Malone had run in one-inch galvanized pipes from a spring back of the house on the hillside. Thus the house had something few pioneer ranch-houses had—running water and bath-rooms.

"He thought of lots of good things," she told the dishes. "He always was workin' to do somethin' good for me. He laid with another woman but I guess he truly loved me."

She washed a plate.

"An' I loved him," she told the plate.

She wondered if the shotgun's blast had not awakened the old roustabout. She walked through the living-room and looked out the big window. She could see the entire barn from here. No human was advancing up the path leading to the house.

"He didn't hear it," she said. "Damn' ol' fool, too drunk."

She went to the storage shed. There were six five-gallon cans of kerosene. This was used for lamps and lanterns. She took a can to the house. She opened it with the ice-pick. A small steady stream jetted out.

She first walked around the outside of the house jetting kerosene over its foundation. She then went inside and soaked the base of each room with kerosene. When she saturated her husband's bedroom she also soaked the bed and bedding with the fluid.

"You'll be cremated, my love."

The eternal wind blew outside. Were the house to be on fire the wind would carry the flames to the other buildings. To the barn, the bunk-house, the cook shack. All would go up in flames. The wind blew from the right direction, too. "Thank you, Wind."

She took her husband's pistol from its holster. It hung on his den's wall. Pothook had taught her how to shoot with shotgun, rifle or pistol—but she'd never been a good shot.

She'd always flinched as she pulled the trigger. Closed her eyes against the oncoming explosion and kick against her palm. He used to joke with her about that.

"Don't flinch. Don't close your eyes."

"I can't help it, Pothook."

Pothook shot a Colt .45. She tried to hold it out straight as though shooting. It was too heavy. She didn't have enough muscle. She put the pistol back into holster.

She went to her bedroom. Pothook had bought her a new little automatic pistol four years ago when the ranch had shipped fall beef to South Saint Paul. She didn't know its calibre. She didn't care to know. It was a light little weapon. And it could kill.

Well did she know that. Cottontail rabbits summertime plagued her garden. They ate up the peas and beans and even dug at the carrots. She'd lain in wait and killed quite a few of them at close range with the pistol.

She knew the weapon would kill a man at close range. She awaited the man she intended to kill in the barn. Time ran slowly past. She kept thinking of her dead husband and of blood and hate and human gore.

Hate was the most useless thing in the world. She'd learned that long, long ago. She told herself she didn't hate this man. She told herself she was just ridding the world of an undesirable person—an evil, scheming, brutal person who deserved to die.

Who should never been born, in fact . . .

The man rode into the barn at dusk. He went down and began unsaddling. She watched him from her hiding place among the heap of old saddles and gear at the barn's far end.

The old hostler kept on snoring.

The man's horse dripped sweat. He'd been ridden hard in this heat. The man carried his damp saddle-blanket and saddle to a sorrel horse tied in a manger. He led the sorrel out.

The blanket went down on the sorrel's back. The saddle followed. The *cincha* swung, he snagged it, he threaded the latigo through the cinch-ring, pulled, made his latigo tie.

He then crammed the bit between the green-grass stained teeth. He pulled the split-ear headstall over the bronc's head. His rifle rode in saddle-boot, shiny wood stock upraised. His pistol was tied low on his right thigh.

He was with one boot in the off-stirrup and ready to swing when Ma Malone walked out of the saddles and gear, her automatic ready. She said, "Where are you goin'?"

The boot dropped. A right hand flashed down to land on the holstered pistol. Fingers began loosening the buckskin-thong tied over the gun's hammer.

"What's eatin' you, Ma?"

"Don't call me Ma! Your mother—" Ma Malone caught herself. No use going into old and sordid details. "You killed John Powers. You cut out your own father's tongue!"

The man laughed sardonically. "You're full of shit, ol' lady. What makes you make such crazy statements?"

"Your father—He finally wrote some words—Wrote with his teeth—pencil in mouth—like I've been learnin' him—"

"I doubt that, ol' bitch."

"The note he wrote—Over there on thet manger partition—I laid it there—"

The man looked.

"Read for yoreself."

The man read the note. She noticed his hands were very steady. She was the only one who was nervous.

The man balled up the note, threw it aside. "Maybe Pothook wrote that. Maybe he didn't. Maybe you wrote it. But that cuts no ice either way."

"What counts?"

"That I kill you. The time has come. I should have killed you before. Then goes that snorin' ol' drunk—Then Pothook himself—"

"Powers knew you rustled your father's cattle. So you killed him to silence him forever. Your father knew you stole from him, too. You cut out his tongue so he couldn't talk against you!" She still had her gun half-raised. It was growing mighty heavy in her grip. "I wonder why you jus' didn't kill my husban' an' be done with it." She would not tell him Pothook had taken his own life.

"I intended to. But at the last moment I got soft-hearted. Poor dumb ol' sonofabitch—payin' money to a whore. Even my mother used to laugh when she got his checks. Said I could be the son of any of the thousands of men she laid down under."

She raised the automatic. Her old arm was slow. She'd heard of gunmen who could draw, lift, fire, like chained lightning. She hadn't believed it, though.

No human could be that swift, she'd told herself. Now she realized she'd lied to herself. For this man was that fast.

His gun leaped upward. He was now crouched, down low, gun levelling. She didn't get in but a delayed shot. One shot, no more. And it went low and ploughed into the barn's liquid manure-dust.

It went low because his bullet hit her in the right chest. It spun her and almost dropped her but somehow she held her feet. Never before had something hit her so hard. Never again would she be hit this hard.

She was stunned. But still, she had sense enough to run. The back door was fifteen feet away. She hurled her old body toward this door. She did not remember dropping the automatic.

The creek was lined with high buckbrush. It was about twenty feet away. A trail led to the water—a well-defined trail. Horses had made it when led to the water.

She expected a bullet to hit her back. Strangely, none came—she fell into the buckbrush. She got to her feet. She twisted through deep brush that shielded her.

She wondered why he'd not shot again. She did not know that he'd stumbled as he'd turned in the barn to follow her, pistol raised. He'd caught his heel in the flooring of a stall.

He went down. He got up rapidly. He ran to the back door. Ma Malone was not in sight.

He saw her automatic. She was disarmed. He'd ride her down. He'd kill her from his saddle.

He spent thirty-four minutes searching for the wounded woman. He didn't find her. Dusk was turning into night. Time pressed him. Had she fallen in the creek? And drowned? And floated downstream?

He doubted that. It hadn't rained for weeks. The creek was low. It held water only because of the beaver dams.

Ma was dead somewhere back in the brush. And brush was so thick a man on foot had a hard time piercing it. She had taken his bullet solidly, he remembered. If indeed alive she was somewhere in the buckbrush. Either dead or bleeding to death.

He returned to the barn. He rode into it by the wide tall door. He glanced down at the fallen automatic. Popgun, no more . . . He wondered if the shooting had awakened the drunken hostler.

He rode close to the manger. The man still lay passed out, arms wide as he lay on his back. He still snored. Dan Malone raised his pistol. He took aim at the man's head.

Then, he lowered his gun. He rode out the front door. He rode to the house and dismounted and went inside without knocking. The house had the acrid smell of kerosene.

He sniffed this smell. Ma must have been filling the lamps for the night. And spilled some coal-oil.

"Pothook."

Echoes, but no answer.

"Hey, Pothook."

Again, the echoes. Again, no answer.

He went from room to room. No Pothook Malone. Had the old man heard the shooting and had he run outside to hide?

He came into Pothook's bedroom. And then, he stopped. Tough, gun in hand, all killer, he stood there—and stared. Stared at the blood, the torn head, the wall behind the head.

Had the pioneer cowman killed himself? Or had Ma Malone gone loco? And killed her husband?

Spurs clanging, he crossed the room, stopped beside the bloody bed. He saw the shotgun's barrel under the man's jaw. Dried blood hung around the man's lips. Already blowflies had gathered.

He saw the bare foot. The big toe, close to the trigger-guard. He drew back. Pothook had committed suicide.

"Sleep good, you ol' stupid sonofabitch."

Again, he caught the stink of kerosene. Looked like the bedding had been damped with coal oil. He gave this little thought. Accidents happened. You spilled water and kerosene in your life. And beer and whiskey, too. He found his stirrup. He swung up. He used his spurs. His horse loped east on the road leading to Powder River City.

He did not know that Ma Malone heard him leave. She had hidden under the logs and debris facing the second beaver dam. She'd seen him searching for her, gun in hand.

Water had come to her neck. Her head was hidden by water-soaked logs. When she heard his horsehoofs pound toward town she came out of hiding, dripping water like a drowned beaver, her dress flat against her belly and breasts and thighs, clinging to her aching old flesh.

His bullet had hit her under the right arm. It had torn through the muscle by the armpit. It had grooved a groove on her ribs. Her arm could be raised but with difficulty.

She lurched to the house. She took down an 1873

Winchester 44-40 rifle. The rifle was loaded, she knew—Pothook always kept weapons loaded, dangerous as that habit was.

But she made sure. She saw the rim of bullet in the barrel. Carrying the rifle, she went to the barn. She had a tame old gelding saddle-horse in a manger. She led him out and somehow managed to bridle and saddle him.

She was about ready to mount when she remembered the kerosene. She went out the front door, leading her horse.

She didn't smoke so she carried no matches. She went to the kitchen. She got a box of wood matches. She then went to the bunkhouse, the most westerly building, for the wind blew in strong from the west.

She entered the bunkhouse. Although unoccupied some weeks now it still stunk from humans. Dirty feet, unbathed flesh, unwashed stinking clothes under bunks. She'd sprinkled one bunk heavy with kerosene.

The match flared, broke, went out. The second caught fire. The bedding leaped into flame. She hurried as fast as possible to the open door. Already another two bunks were flaming.

She smiled wickedly, happily.

She fired the house in the kitchen. Soon the room roared with flame. She'd trailed kerosene down the hall and into each side room. The fire ran like a scarlet runner out the door and into space.

"Thank you, prairie wind," she said.

She mounted and turned the horse east toward Powder River City. She remembered the old hostler then. She turned her horse to ride through the barn and warn him. Already the west end of the big barn was on fire.

She drew reins. The hostler ran from the barn.

"Fire, Pothook, fire! Pothook—"

The man stumbled. He went sliding forward on his face. Ma Malone had seen enough. Her shoulder was one throbbing, painful ache.

Despite this, she smiled.

EIGHTEEN

Dan Malone's rendezvous with the Ketchum gang was in a grove of cottonwood trees south of the wagon-road running between PM ranch and Powder River City. Dusk was thickening over Wyoming's desolation when he rode into the clearing.

The cottonwoods topped a high hill. From this altitude a man could see many miles in all directions.

Many thoughts plagued the tough rider. Most were far from pleasant. He wished he'd never hit it with the remnants of the Matt Ketchum gang. He blamed his joining the outlaws on old Pothook Malone.

Dan Malone always laid the blame on anybody but himself.

He'd never known how he stood with old Pothook. Fear had ridden with him his few months on this range— fear that old Pothook would kick him out, boot him out for good.

Dan Malone had lived to this date in almost abject poverty. He'd had many brushes with city-law as a boy and he'd fled to this section to escape arrest in a city holdup.

His god was money. He wanted money. With money, a man could do anything—he could love, murder, hate, kill. Money bought you out of all difficulties. He'd seen money save man after man from jail and hanging.

He'd started rustling old Pothook's cattle. He'd stolen alone until the Ketchum riders had come into this section. He'd sold his stolen PM cattle to army sutlers who bought beef for the neighbouring Indian reservations.

The sutlers were as crooked as he, if not more so. Rumour had it that if a man was an army sutler for only five years he could have stolen enough money from Uncle Sam in that time to retire for life under the palm trees of Florida or southern California. Or some distant far land . . .

Then had come the Ketchum gang. One thief gravitated to another thief and the gang began secretly rounding-up Pothook Malone's far-flung beef. And now the pockets of Dan Malone and the long riders carried more gold than ever before. The rustling was even more profitable to the gang than robbing trains and banks. And much less personal danger was involved.

Dan Malone stood on stirrups and looked about—and then he saw the fire slashing the darkening sky in the direction of PM ranch.

He stared, not believing his eyes.

Were the ranch buildings on fire? Yes, the spread was that direction. Northwest about three miles. Had to be PM buildings. No other buildings were in that area.

Suddenly, he remembered the acrid smell of kerosene. It stung his nostrils, clung to his palate. Somebody had set the spread on fire. But who was that somebody?

Not old Pothook. Hell, Pothook was at the Pearly Gates now, getting checked in. And Ma Malone? Had he killed her? She'd run from the barn and into the brush— and he'd not found her. Or her body . . .

Hell, Ma had to be dead. When he shot, he shot to kill. Never before had he lifted his side-arm against a human and failed to kill that mortal. No, Ma was dead, blowflies around her corpse, in that thick brush.

Damnit, why hadn't he looked longer for her body? No, he'd had this meeting with these bastardly so-called religious nuts at this hour—and they were not even here yet.

Had the drunken roustabout torched the buildings? He should have killed the old bastard, he now realized. He remembered pointing his pistol at the scraggly bead.

But hindsight is always stronger than foresight.

One point stood out. Somebody wanted to get rid of PM buildings. If the buildings went, the ranch went. You can't operate without headquarters.

This was a riddle. When this was over, he'd ride back and look for Ma Malone's body. With this, he put PM aside. He concentrated on what lay ahead. He thought first of the remnants of the Ketchum gang.

With PM a thing of the past, whoever laid a rope and a branding iron on PM cattle became owner of those cattle. With Pothook Malone alive, the Ketchum gang had needed a man at PM ranch as a listening post.

Now, that listening post was not needed.

And Dan Malone felt terror eat at his guts. The tall tribe, with its false black robes and Bibles never read, needed him no longer. In fact, he was now a menace to the gang. He had a mouth, hadn't he? And if things got tough and law—real tough ranger or range law—moved in, that mouth could blab and turn state evidence to protect its owner.

He was about ready to rein his horse around and feed the brute the spurs when a voice behind him said "Been waitin' long, Malone?"

He stood on stirrups. He twisted his muscular body in saddle. One of the tall outlaws had come in behind on foot.

"Why the sneakin' in?" Dan Malone asked. His voice was unsteady.

"Precaution, no more." Then, "Okay here, men."

Dan Malone's fear spread. These men were experienced trail-hands. They'd led him into a trap. They'd apparently left their horses hidden in yonder timber. And had been hiding with rifles and short-guns in this brush while he'd sat saddle, an open target.

Why hadn't they simply shot him from saddle? Well, they'd not done that. Which meant they still had use for him.

"Fire northwest," one man said.

Dan Malone said, "PM ranch buildings. I fired them."

"Why?"

"Get rid of them."

"You're burnin' down your own property. That don't make sense to this man, Malone."

Dan Malone considered his answer carefully. Finally he said, "I'm leaving men. My record ag'in the law—well, it's just too much. Them tinstars catch me it's either guns to death or a life behin' bars."

"You got company in that respect. Where would you go?"

"South America." Dan Malone had heard some outlaws had already left the U.S. for South America, mainly Argentina.

The Ketchum gang considered that. They did not now wear their long black robes. Nor did they now carry Bibles. Now they were dressed in ordinary range gear—old boots, star-rowelled spurs, ordinary pants and shirts. Yes, and their guns—their short-guns, their rifles on saddles.

"What do you know about these Brahman bulls?"

"Quite a bit," Dan Malone said, and told them what he'd heard from his hiding in the root cellar.

One Ketchum rider summed it up, "So this McKee an' the Mex will haze them bulls alone west out of town for the PM. When they come to that flat in the timber between here an' town they'll let the bulls graze. That'll be a sucker play to pull us in with Wild Bunch guns surroundin' us to cut us down, eh?"

"That's the deal," Malone said.

One man said, "Don't sound logical."

"Why?" Malone asked.

"McKee an' the Mexican ain't that stupid. That'd pull them right into a trap, us there with guns. What's to keep us from knockin' them pronto from saddle with us hid?"

"I don't credit either that long string of pelican shit or that fat spick as bein' men of brains," Malone said. "An' they're too dumb even to be thieves. They trailed them black bulls all the way up from Texas, remember? No pay on the way up, an' them almost starvin' to death an' bumming money for bacon an' tobacco. You consider men that ignorant to have brains?"

146

"You got a point," a man said.

Another said, "Can they see thet PM fire from town?"

"Reckon not," another man said. "Too many hills between town an' the fire. Red glow in the sky, yes—but most would think it was the moon risin'."

"Moon don't come up over there."

"Who's at the PM?" somebody asked.

Dan Mason almost blurted out that Pothook Malone had killed himself, and that he had shot Ma Malone and she had fled to die in the brush—or so he ardently hoped.

He caught his tongue in time. Were they to know that Pothook and Ma were dead it would mean his death.

"My father an' Ma and the ol' hostler. All three waitin' for them bulls to show up. Big deal for 'em, this event."

"Which won't happen," a man said. "Them bulls are as good as ours. Six hundred bucks apiece at the Quarter Circle N north in Montana on the Yellowstone River."

"Even if the bulls got through—which they won't—it wouldn't be much of a event for them ol' people, their housin' an' out-buildin's burnin' down. How come you torch them, Malone?"

"Because I hate those two sonsofbitches. Ol' Ma treats me like a dog. Even called me a bastard to my face."

Nobody spoke.

"An' besides, I got enough money. I'll have more after we free these black bulls. Enough for one man. Transportation out an' out forever."

"I see your viewpoint," one man said. "But now where'll we hit these bulls, cowhands?"

"Not where the Wild Bunch figgers we should," one said.

A man said, cynically, "Why not there?"

"Us in an ambush? Cowboy, with the Wild Bunch out in the brush, pickin' us off like kewpie dolls in a cow-town celebration?"

"They don't know we know what Malone has tol' us. We got the jump on 'em, the su'prise element. We circle them without them knowin' it when they figger they're circlin' us."

"You got a strong point there, bronc rider."

"Can't miss. Look at this thing from the outside for a minute, eh? Lemme have my say without interruptions."

"Okay, talk."

"What's the main thing we're after?"

"The Hole in the Wall."

"Okay. But to get the Hole we have to do what?"

"Kill off the Wild Bunch."

"We're man to man in numbers, I'd guess. We got ambush on our side. None of 'em knows what Dan jus' tol' us. So they don't ambush us. We ambush them!"

"Wipe 'em out completely?"

"To the last man, cowboy."

The gang went into details. Evidently it had ambushed many, many times before, it seemed to Dan Malone, who sat a silent saddle and listened, his mind made up—he'd kill these men before they killed him.

He reasoned they'd not gun him down until after the ambush. They'd need his gun until that time. He grinned inwardly in wolfish glee.

"We kill off Pothook an' Ma, an' we operate outa the Hole an' no law in the world would be loco enough to go in after us. We kin rustle PM cows when there ain't no trains or stages or banks to rob."

"That's right, bronc rider."

NINETEEN

Tortilla Joe held out a broad dark palm. "I see my life line. Moon's that bright. Reckon it's time we move these critters."

Buck got afoot. "For the last drive," he said.

They swung into leather. Tortilla Joe on Midnight watched the gate while Buck cut out the Brahmans, who didn't want to leave the high grass and flowing water and handy milk cows.

As usual, Flapears was the orneriest. He put his head down, pawed up a half-ton of dirt with his forehoofs—and then charged Rusty, who long ago had learned all of Flapear's angry mannerisms.

Buck, too, had learned the bull's signs. So when Flapears charged, head down, legs churning corral dust, Buck quickly reined Rusty to one side. Rusty leaped south. Flapears roared by on the north.

The moon was now very brilliant. It washed yellow and mystic across the low grey sage and scraggly greasewood. A jackrabbit leaped up and Flapears and his brothers acted as scared to death.

Buck rode around the bulls, whipping them into shape with the end of his catch-rope. Tortilla Joe from behind beat them over the rump. The jackrabbit disappeared into the distance.

They were about a mile west of Powder River City when Buck said, "Rider comin' in fast from town. I sure hope it ain't who it looks like it'll be."

Tortilla Joe looked. "Cynthia, sure as shootin'."

Cynthia Watson rode a black and grey pinto gelding.

149

She said, "Couldn't sleep. Dad took the screen windows down to clean them today. An' he didn't put them up again, the lazy lout."

"An' the mosquitos—?" Buck said.

"Almost ate me up in bed. Damn' things got tin-snipper's bills, I do declare. So seein' I couldn't sleep I thought I'd ride Patches out to keep you boys company. I knew you'd be happy to see me."

"I am," Tortilla Joe said, and meant it.

"I am, too," Buckshot McKee said and didn't mean it. Or did he? She made a nice picture of femininity on that little high-stepping pinto. Plenty in front sticking out nicely from her buckskin blouse and nicely rounded thighs fitting under the swell-fork of her saddle.

Buck ran over the battle-plan drawn up in Ma Malone's kitchen. According to the Wild Bunch the Ketchum gang would never allow these bulls to reach Pothook Malone's home-corral.

Butch Cassidy claimed the Ketchums needed the bulls right now. They'd trail them into Montana pronto. There a rodeo promoter would pay top prices for the bulls. The bulls would be rebranded and then shipped to various stampedes for bucking stock, for Brahmans were scarce and drew big prices from the show-promoters.

How Cassidy came to know this, Buck could only guess. But Butch was a man of many friends and with an ear close to the ground, two reasons he'd lived as long as he had on the Outlaw Trail.

Tortilla Joe circled to Buck's side of the herd, leaving Cynthia to pull up the drags. "We gotta get shut of this woman," Tortilla Joe said. "We don't wanna be responsible for her death, Buck."

Buck seriously nodded. "I know that. A bullet don't care who it knocks into Kingdom Come. As it is, I'm wonderin' if you or me will see the Wolf Point Stampede . . ."

"We're in a hell of a mess," Tortilla Joe admitted. "But what'll we do? You jus' can't ride up an say, "Lissen, baby. Bullets might fly anytime now. An' you'd best get your purty ass way back where a bullet can't carry!"

"That's what a man should tell her and I elect you to be that man."

"Hell, no. Not this boy. She's your woman, not mine. You don't see her blue eyes get big an' roun' an' soft when she looks at my dark-skinned mug."

Buckshot McKee sighed. "Okay, I'll tell her."

But the lanky Texan never got to tell pretty Cynthia Watson to neckrein her paint horse around and go home, for at that moment Cynthia had ridden to the opposite side of the herd to turn a bull in and suddenly she reined in and stood on stirrups, staring ahead.

"What—What's that, Buck?" she asked.

Buck and Tortilla Joe reined in and stared, too. A rider had come out of the trees to the north about a hundred yards ahead. Dancing moonlight showed it to be a woman.

A woman bent over saddle-fork, barely hanging onto the saddle. Buck stared in wonder. Tortilla Joe said, "That's a woman, Buck?" He made his sentence a question.

Buck said, "If my eyes are right that's Ma Malone."

Cynthia cried, "That's Mrs Malone!"

The three spurred forward, bulls momentarily forgotten.

TWENTY

When moonlight came the Ketchum gang sent out two scouts. Within an hour the first came back and said, "They're movin' the bulls outa the night-pasture. An' headin' 'em this way."

"How many?"

"Two. The Texan an' the greaser."

"Okay. Good work. Now slip out ag'in an' keep both eyes peeled."

The second scout came in thirty minutes later. "The Wil' Bunch are at the Malone ranch—or what used to be that spread. Cripes, boss, that whole outfit went up in smoke. Only foundations left. Thet an' red hot ashes."

"I wonder if anybody got cooked in the fire," Dan Malone said.

"Yeah, they's one body. I think it's thet ol' roustabout you mentioned, Dan. Couldn't make out no features."

The old woman dead; Pothook a corpse. Must have been the old roustabout who'd torched the buildings. Dan Malone frowned. That didn't make sense. Or did it?

The Ketchum boss's voice broke into Dan Malone's thoughts. "With the ol' man an' the ol' lady dead that spread'll be all yours, Malone."

No, he'd milked PM ranch for all he safely could. So he said, apparently joking, "Nope, she's all yours, boys. I'm through here. An' fer good, too."

"Logical thinkin'," a man affirmed.

"Ownin' property jus' ties a man down," Dan Malone said. "I've had enough of this country to last me a life-time."

"Property finally owns the man an' not the other way around."

"Can that crap," the leader growled. "We out first to kill off the Wild Bunch. Get the Hole in the Wall. Second we're out to steal some valuable bulls. How many hands ride with Butch Cassidy?"

"Four."

"Only four?"

"That's all, boss. I kin count, you know."

"I know you know simple sums, man. I'm jes' su'prised there's so damn' few of them."

"Gang must've split up, some pullin' out after we stuck up that mail train an' we called each other Cassidy and Kid Curry an' Ben an' Sundance an' all them other Wild Bunch names."

"Screw such gassy talk, men," the leader ordered. "Head back an' keep a close eye on the Bunch, Ole."

"On my way, boss."

Ole departed with hard hoofs, heading west. Ten minutes later the other scout came in, bronc running hard through the moonlight.

"He tryin' to kill that hoss," the leader mused. "Must be somethin' buggin' him hard to use his hooks that-away."

"They're changing' direction, boss. They've swung them bulls off the trail north. Ma Malone jus' rid in on 'em. Not more'n fifteen minutes ago, if that long."

Dan Malone's heart sank. "Ma—Ma Malone?"

"Ma it was, Dan. Come ridin' on an ol' nag from the direction of PM. Came ridin' slow with the plough-horse plodding along like each step was to be his last."

"You sure?"

"Absolutely sure. Got close enough in the brush to make damned sure. But somethin' must be wrong with Missus Malone."

"Why say that?"

"Thet Watson heifer—She was with McKee an' the spic. Her an' Missus Malone started back toward town. An' Missus Malone—looks like she was sick, or some-thin'. Ridin' bent over that way with the girl helpin' her

153

stay in saddle."

"What the hell has happened?" the leader said.

Dan Malone knew. His heart was pounding heavily. So the old bitch had not died in the buckbrush . . . She'd hid an' then got a horse an' then burned down PM ranch . . . And now she was riding into town to tell everybody in the world that her stepson had shot her and—

Sheriff Ed Fillmore would hear her story. The town loved the old girl. A posse would ride out—And if they caught one Dan Malone they might just stretch his neck with a manila catch-rope tied to a strong high branch of one of these old cottonwood trees—

He shivered despite the cloying night heat. A man noticed this and said, "Feelin' cold, cowman?"

"None of your damn' business."

"No fightin' here," the leader said shortly. "Save thet for McKee and the Mexican an' the Wil' Bunch. So the bulls would be druv through thet grove of cottonwoods where we aimed to circle aroun' the Wil' Bunch an' get them an' the critters at the same time?"

"They sure ain't pointed that way, boss."

"What'll we do?" Dan Malone asked. "Them bulls are still my property, you know. Wil' Bunch touch one of 'em an' they're stealin' private property. Rustlin' cattle."

"You tryin' to be funny, Malone?" the leader asked.

"Damn it, no!" Dan Malone was putting up a front. "Nobody's stealin' my stock with me lookin' on an' doin' nothin'."

One rider said, "Dan's got a good point, boss. We could buy them bulls from him."

"An' we'd not get the Hole in the Wall," a man reminded.

The leader laughed. "Buy the bulls? Think we're fools, Malone? All we'd have to do is shoot you from saddle. We'd get the bulls free."

"You wouldn't do that." Malone's voice trembled.

The leader laughed again. "Not right at this moment," he said. "Come on, cowboys! We head straight north! We intercept those bulls afore the Wil' Bunch gets there."

The Ketchums did not know that Buckshot McKee

had covertly trailed the messenger from the bulls to this rendezvous. Now Buck crouched in the buckbrush some two hundred yards south with Rusty hidden in a coulee behind him. The lanky Texan counted the enemy.

He wondered how many rode with the Wild Bunch. He heard a noise to his left. He twisted on hips, Colt .44 rising, then falling, as recognition came in.

Butch Cassidy said quietly, "The bulls—Over north of the trail—You're not followin' our plan. Why?"

"Ma Malone."

"What about Ma?"

Buck told him. "She claims Dan was hidin' in the root-cellar under the kitchen when we had our conflab. She saw his boot tracks outside of the cellar door."

Cassidy nodded. "So you changed plans to throw the Ketchum gang off the trail. But they got two runners out. We've located one."

"One watches the bulls, too."

"Where's Ma now?"

"Went to town with Cynthia. To Miller, the doctor. Dan shot her."

"How bad?"

"I don't know. She looked poorly and she's lost lot of blood."

"The Malone ranch buildin's—All burned down."

"Ma fired 'em. She cremated Pothook. Pothook committed suicide. Shot himself with a shotgun, Ma said."

"Holy smoke, Buck!"

"Ma said the old roustabout was alive when she left the ranch. See any sign of him?"

"Yeah, saw his corpse. He got caught between two fires—bunkhouse an' blacksmith's shop—Never made it out—Where's Dan Malone now?"

"Not far away. With the Ketchums."

Butch Cassidy made a fist. "Sonofabitch," he said. "This moves the fight out in the open an' we ain't got but four of us—"

"Only five of them, Butch. Anyway, that's all I could count."

"How about you an' Tortilla Joe?"

Buck looked at the longrider. "Meaning?"

"You gonna fight? Or you goin' drift?"

"Pothook hired me an' Tortilla Joe to take them bulls from Dumas Texas to Powder River in Wyoming—to deliver 'em to his ranch. An' we still got a few more miles to go before we end the trail, Butch."

Cassidy said, "You answered my question. I can see the Ketchums hittin' for your bulls about two miles further on where the hills level out."

"I can see the same, Butch."

"They come in. We have them between our rifles."

"It'll be rifles," Buck said. "At a distance, Butch." Buck spoke slowly, deliberately. "But I don't like them bein' between our rifles an' yours, Butch."

"I get the drift, Buckshot. With them atween us bullets might hit one of us—your side or mine—by accident. What's your answer?"

"Me an' Tortilla Joe put them bulls hell-for-leather west down that slant onto that flat region you mentioned. They come down slidin' in gravel and crap but we pull back and swing north while you an' your rifles come in from the west."

"Good thinkin', McKee."

"The Ketchum bunch will have to hit from the south. They ain't got no other direction to come in on."

Butch Cassidy got to his boots. "See you later, Buck."

"I hope so," Buck said, and grinned.

TWENTY-ONE

But the Ketchum gang upset the cart. The gang did not hit the bulls from the south. The gang swung in behind and rode in on the Brahmans from due east.

Buck and Tortilla Joe had just driven the bulls madly down the slant. Below the critters lay a flat area dotted with grey sagebrush and dried buffalo grass.

The bulls went over the cut sliding and skidding and bawling. Buck and Tortilla Joe hammered them with doubled catch-ropes. Flapears went skidding on his rump, tail extended, bawling in anger. His fellows followed him, tumbling and rolling in the bright moonlight.

Dust rose. Rocks were jarred loose. They rolled down hill. Suddenly Buck pulled in Rusty, setting the big sorrel on his rump.

"My God, Tortilla! Look behin' us!"

Tortilla Joe's stern rein drew Midnight to a skidding halt. He stabbed a backward look. A group of horsemen was rapidly approaching, cutting through the sagebrush, moonlight bright on their trappings.

Buck hollered, "That's not Cynthia comin' back with the sheriff! Them's the holy roller sonsofbitches!"

"Hittin' from behin'," Tortilla Joe uselessly yelled.

"Come, on, Tortilla!"

"We gotta get outa here, Buck!"

Both had hurriedly snaked rifles from saddle-boots. Buck was sure he heard a bullet whine overhead but between the rolling and bawling bulls and the dust and moonlight a man couldn't be sure of anything.

157

Dust was so thick Buck couldn't tell one bull from the other. All was a roiling mass of bovine backs and flying pebbles, but the bawling bulls undoubtedly saved the lives of the partners.

The Ketchums wouldn't fire into the herd for fear of killing or maiming a bull. Also dust almost completely hid the partners as they rode plunging through the herd.

The partners headed west. Suddenly, Buck reined Rusty sharply to the north, the big sorrel knocking a bull galley-west.

"Ridin' into Wild Bunch guns ahead, Tortilla!"

Tortilla Joe then pointed his labouring gelding north. He rode high on stirrups, reins looped around saddle-horn, rifle half-raised as he studied the eastern horizon for Ketchum killers.

"Don't see nobody behin' to shoot at, Buckshot!"

Buck McKee also rode high in leather, Winchester rifle half-raised. "Right you are, *compadre*. Dust hides 'em—"

Without warning, they broke through the last of the herd. They were on open prairie, still protected from Ketchum rifles by the hanging thick dust. But that would not last long. The wind was already whipping the dust away and leaving only the brittle blue moonlight.

Bulls thundered directly toward the approaching Wild Bunch. "Split up," Buck screamed, "or they'll ride you down, Butch!"

But already the four Wild Bunch riders had split up. Two swung out to ride up the south side of the herd. The other two swung north to ride that side. These two were Ben Kilpatrick and Butch Cassidy.

Butch Cassidy's reins made his bronc cake-walk, front legs flailing dusty air. "The bastards pulled a windy on us," he hollered. "Come in from behin' instead of from the side."

Ben Kilpatrick brandished his rifle. "Come on, cowboys. Let's wipe out those Bible shoutin' fakes!"

The two Wild Bunch men spurred east, heading for a showdown with the Ketchums. Tortilla Joe started to ride behind them but Buck caught Midnight's reins.

"Stay with the herd, partner. The bulls won't run long. Once they get scattered it'll take from hell to breakfast to bunch them again. An' besides, we can swing in front of 'em."

"Good idea, Buckshot."

Rifles spat whining lead. Somebody brought a six-shooter into action. The sixgun's loud roar smashed over the sounds of hoofs and the singing lead of rifles.

"There goes two of 'em," Tortilla Joe screamed, rifle pointing southeast. "Pullin' out, they are."

"Let's get 'em," Buck said.

"Thet off-side one from here looks like Dan Malone, Buck."

"Could be that bastard. Shootin' down an ol' lady—"

Tortilla Joe raised his rifle. Buck McKee batted the barrel down. Tortilla Joe stared angrily at his partner. "What the hell's the matter with you?"

"Ain't you got eyes, Tortilla? They two's shootin' at each other an' not at the Wild Bunch or us!"

"By golly, you're right, Buckshot." The Mexican peered through the moonlight, eyes narrowed. "I might be wrong, but one has to be Dan Malone."

The tall rider suddenly sagged over his saddle-horn. He'd plainly been shot. His horse galloped on. For some moments the rider was poised over the saddle's fork. Then he toppled to the off-side. He fell to the prairie. He became a black dot in the sagebrush. A dot that didn't move.

"One of the Bible toters gone," Tortilla Joe said.

"An' looks like he went for good," Buck said. "He hit the groun' awful hard. If'n the bullet didn't kill him thet fall sure as hell would have."

" 'Specially if he landed on his head. Thet other one— Dan Malone—Looks like he stopped one, too."

"I thought so, too—at first. But he's ridin' up in leather now an' whuppin' his horse down the hin' legs."

"Should we start after him, Buck?"

"Not me. We got thirty two bulls jus' a few miles from where we was hired to deliver 'em. An' our job is not to shoot down an' kill the owner of the bulls. Our job is to deliver the bulls safe an' get paid an' drag ass out."

"We've already got paid."

"Then we deliver . . . and drag," Buck said.

Tortilla Joe stared southeast. "Looks from here like Kilpatrick just got one. There goes two ridin' fast to the south. They got enough. Hell, another jus' went down, Buck."

"Good long range shootin'," Buck said. "Well, let's round up these bulls for the sure last time and get them movin' west."

The Brahmans had run themselves out. Even Flapears had lost his fight. Soon the bulls were in a bunch with the partners behind them pounding them for more speed.

"Gunfire runnin' out behin' us," Buck said. "Looks to me like the Wild Bunch won ag'in. How many riders you see off to the south, Tortilla?"

Tortilla Joe stood on stirrups and looked. "Five of 'em, Buck. One in the lead, ridin' south as fast as his nag will take him."

"That'll be the last preacher," Buck said. "Them four behin' is ridin' close together which means they're friends—an' they have to be the four of the Wild Bunch."

"That's the Wild Bunch."

Buck hit a bull over the rump with the free end of his lasso. "Cynthia knows that if it should work out that way we want to see the money for these critters go to the Sisters and them orphans up in Terry. You tol' Butch that if he ever wanted to reach us all he had to do was write Dad Sturdivant at Malta. Just thinking ahead *compadre* that's all."

"PM ranch—or what's left of it—in sight. We leave these bulls along the crick," Tortilla Joe said.

The bulls began grabbing at the buckbrush. All was calm and peaceful here close to the ashes of the burned down ranch buildings. Not a living soul in sight save two dog-tired cowboys . . . and thirty-two Brahman bulls.

"We've delivered," Tortilla Joe said. "Our job is done." He coiled his catch-rope. "I see what you mean. We leave no untied points behind. Yep, time we leave you, bulls."

Buck looked at Flapears. Flapears looked at Buck. "Goodbye, you black sonofabitch," Buck told Flapears. "Hope I never see you again."

But Buck's wish was not granted. Three months later he sat on Flapears in a bucking-chute at Roundup, Montana, on the last day of the Mussellshell Basin Stampede.

The stampede had lasted three days. Flapears had piled every man who'd tried to ride him and some of Montana's best bronc kickers had bit Flapears' dust. Now Buck tugged on the loose rope around the bull's rib cage.

"Get a good hand-holt," Tortilla Joe said.

Tortilla Joe stood outside the chute. He had hold of the flanking strap hanging loosely around the bull just in front of his hind quarters. When Flapears—and Buck—left the chute Tortilla Joe would just then pull the flankin' strap tight.

The flanking-strap made the bull buck harder. He'd kick back at the tight strap. This made him harder to sit on, for his rump would come violently upward while his forelegs dug the arena dust.

The arena boss rode up on his mule. "Ready, McKee?"

Buck paid the short man no attention.

Tortilla Joe said, "Man we knew down in Powder River City jus' talked to me from the stands. Ma Malone got well. She sold off all her cattle. Gave the bulls to Butch."

"Well, we already know that. Butch sold the bulls to a rodeo promoter. He sent our money to the Sisters in Terry. Sisters wrote thanks to Dad Sturdivant in Malta. Dad got word to us. Now I'm sittin' on ol' Flapears ag'in."

"This gent said Dan Malone jus' disappeared. Some claim he was shot an' died in the brush an' his carcase was never found. Others say he made good his getaway."

"Doesn't matter to me, Tortilla."

Buck's guts was a mass of wriggling knots. His belly

161

always acted up when he was ready to ride out on a bucking-horse or a bull.

The arena boss snarled, "Hook thet critter outa thet chute, McKee!"

Again, nobody paid him attention.

"Sheriff Fillmore rode out with Cynthia an' the town bunch to watch the fight. Sheriff claims all of the Ketchums were knocked down by Dan Malone. Now why would Malone kill his own side?"

"Man never can tell, Tortilla."

"Ma Malone is down in southern California. Sold off the PM cattle, lock stock and barrel. Wild Bunch helped her make the last gather."

"Good for her," Buck managed to say. "Cynthia?"

"Got married a few weeks ago. Cowboy drifted through an' she put her loop on him."

"Good for her."

Buck felt Flapears' big back muscles tighten. Flapears didn't flap his ears now. Flapears waited for the chute gate to open. No cowboy had ever sat on him the necessary ten seconds. Ten seconds meant a much-needed one hundred bucks.

"Snow'll be hittin' us in the ass soon," Tortilla Joe said. "Then we'll head south? Charlie's Place?"

"Charlie's Place," Buck said.

The arena boss's wide face was red with rage. "God damnit, McKee, five thousan' people are out there—Waitin' to see you kick out this bull—"

Buck looked at Tortilla. "Did I hear this scissorbill here say somethin'?"

"I never heard him say a word!"

Buck raised his spurs high. His hooks would come down hard on old Flapears the minute the chute gate opened.

His belly had settled down a mite now. Always did just before the violence and action started.

"Pull that flankin' strap tight, Tortilla." Then to the gate tender, "Swing her open, Charlie."

The chute gate opened.

THE GRINGO

ONE

This was the weekend of the first full moon of August, and the *pueblo* of Santa Barbara was celebrating *fiesta*. Cliff Blanton left his tired dun at the livery-barn and walked down the crowded main street, the sound of the violins and the clink of the castanets hanging on the warm California night. He was definitely out of place—a tall Texan wearing shot-gun chaps marked with trail-dust—and he saw this in the glances of the men and women.

He put his broad shoulder against the door of the *Cantina de Luna*. The silence inside was in direct contrast to the gaiety on the street. The heavy oak door closed behind him.

Cliff spoke to the man behind the log bar. "I am hungry, *senor,* and I would like some food. I would like a room for tonight, too."

"My wife will serve you," said the bartender. Cliff had spoken to him in liquid Spanish. "You talk good Spanish for a *gringo, senor,* if I may say it."

Cliff said, "Texas."

Two men, the cantina's only other customers, were eating at a far table. The elder looked up suddenly, his aged eyes clear and quick across the room. Cliff felt their swift probing; the man looked again at his companion.

The bartender came back, waddling like a black bear. "You will have a drink, *senor,* before the meal?"

Cliff ordered whiskey.

"You *gringos, senor,* if I may say it—you drink hard drinks."

"We fight hard, too," said Cliff.

This time, both of the men at the far table looked at him. The elder one, plainly a man of some importance, was about sixty, thin with a rawhide strength. The skin had pulled back against his cheekbones. He wore a beaded velvet jacket that showed the red front of a silk shirt and his trousers were of finest cloth, trimmed with black braid. The other was a middle-aged man, plainly an *Americano,* stocky of build and thick of thigh. He had brush-scratched leather chaps, runover boots with silver-inlaid spurs, and he wore a gun on his right thigh.

The middle-aged man asked, "Where you from, stranger?"

Cliff repeated, "Texas."

"What's your chore in this town?"

Cliff was silent for a long moment, measuring the man's arrogance. Finally he said, "If it's any of your business, fellow, I'm looking for a bite to eat, then a place to spend the night."

"There ain't a vacant room in Santa Barbara. This is *fiesta*, Texan, an' all the rooms are taken. You'll prob'ly keep ridin' on, huh?"

"Maybe," said Cliff, "and maybe not."

"This town, and this range, don't like Texans, fella."

"You ought to know," murmured Cliff. "You look like one."

The man's face went hard, narrow. He started up but the old man reached out, brought him down. Now the old man spoke, "Perhaps we should introduce ourselves, *senor*. My companion is my *primero*, Jeff Garland, and I am Don Alfredo de la Mesa, owner of the land-grant called the Santa Isabella Rancho."

"Cliff Blanton."

Don Alfredo, said slowly, "You are the gringo— the Texan—who is to start the cattle-ranch on the Cuyama river, *no es verdad*?"

"My cattle are coming over Ventucopa Pass," said Cliff. "I left them there and rode into Santa Barbara, intending to see the county surveyor."

"You are moving onto my land," stated Don Alfredo.

Cliff smiled "I am sorry, *senor*, but I believe you are wrong. In my pocket, I have a deed to twenty thousand acres of the Cuyama river bottom. I bought it from the United States Land Office in Washington, D.C. You forget, I believe, that governmental decree has broken up all the original land grants in California. California is a part of the United States now; not a province of Mexico."

Jeff Garland said grimly, "You're trailin' into trouble, Blanton. Santa Isabella Horseshoe cattle have been running for almost two centuries on Cuyama river and no Texan is moving in, shoving them back."

Cliff spoke quietly. "I think you're wrong, too, Garland."

Garland crossed the room, a big man with a strong tread. He said quickly, "I don't think so," and he hit suddenly, bringing his fist up swift, hard.

Cliff Blanton went back against the bar, then he hit Garland. His head cleared, and he drove Garland back. Garland fought hard, legs wide, but Cliff knocked him down, spilling him across Don Alfredo's table.

Cliff had his gun out. "Don't pull, Garland," he said.

Garland braced himself and got up, wiping blood from his mouth. "I didn't come here for trouble," Cliff said slowly. "I left Texas to get away from trouble."

Don Alfredo bowed stiffly. "Good night, *senor,*" he said. Then, to Jeff Garland, "You will come with me, *senor?*"

The question was soft, yet Cliff felt the steel that underlined it, gauging this man's character. Garland said to Cliff, "This isn't the end of this!"

"I didn't figure so," replied Cliff.

They went outside then. The bartender was silently picking up the scattered dishes and putting them on the table he had set upright.

"I'm sorry that happened," said Cliff.

The food was good, boiled beef and potatoes, with enough spice but not too much. For the first time in months, Cliff had coffee cooked from freshly-baked beans that had come up the west coast by boat, and unloaded at the Santa Barbara docks. He should have enjoyed the meal, but his mind was not on this food.

Now and then, merry-makers slipped in, got a drink, glanced at Cliff, and left. Cliff knew that word was going around the *pueblo* that he was in town, that he had fought with Jeff Garland.

For *gringoes* were a rarity here in Santa Barbara. Few *Americanos* had wandered south of Salinas. Now a Texan was intending to run Texas cattle on a land-grant awarded centuries before to the de la Mesa family by a king of far-away Spain.

Cliff had known all this before he had left Texas. He could remember standing in the United States land office in Houston, talking to the grey-haired land-commissioner, some months before.

"You will undoubtedly move into trouble, Cliff. Although the government has ordered the Santa Isabella land-grant property, except for the ten thousand acres surrounding the old de la Mesa *hacienda*, undoubtedly Don Alfredo will not let his land go without a struggle."

They had gone to the big wall map. "Where is the Santa Isabella *hacienda*?" asked Cliff.

The land-commissioner had put his thumb on a spot on the Cuyama river. "Right about there, Cliff, judging from the correspondence from Washington. The land sells for fifty cents an acre. That makes it ten thousand dollars for the deed."

"So you think Don Alfredo will fight anybody who drives cattle in?"

"I'm led to believe that, Cliff."

Cliff had said, "I'll take the deed, sir." He had written out a cheque, and the deed had arrived a month or so later, there at the Pecos ranch. He had built a herd of cows, some two thousand head including the bulls, and he had pointed them West, heading across New Mexico and Arizona territories.

Cattle-running on the Pecos, in his estimation, was through. Cotton was moving into Texas since it had lost its identity of the Lone Star State and become a part of the Union. Southerners were coming in from Louisiana and Mississippi—and the other scattered southern states—and Northerners, too, were drifting in. Texas range was poor range and this California grass—

"Good grass out there," his trail boss, Shorty Nolan, had said. "I was out there about ten years ago one summer, if you remember. Fella told me the Santa Barbara country was about like the territory I was in, and that was good cow-country I saw, Cliff."

"Keep 'em pointed west," said Cliff.

According to the land-commissioners, his deed had also been sent to Santa Barbara, there to be filed with the county surveyor, who also acted as tax-collector, assessor and recorder. Cliff had left his tired herd at Ventucopa Pass and ridden west toward Santa Barbara that lay beside the Pacific, its log docks stacked with cow-hides bound by clipper ship around the Horn for the great manufacturing cities of Boston and New York. The land-commissioner and old Shorty had been right. This was good cow-country.

The slow wind rustled the dried autumn grass that covered the mountain meadows there in the Sierra Madre moutains. Mountain slopes were studded with scrub-pine and clumps of *manzanita* and *chamiso*. This would hold the winter rains, making them soak into the earth, conserving the rain so that it would sustain life in the grass during summer and fall.

"Ain't *mucha agua* in that river now," grumbled

170

Shorty Nolan. "But I reckon when it rains, Cliff, there'll be plenty of run-off here. This rain usually comes in January an' February, and when it rains the sky just turns upside down an' lets loose. Far as I reckon, from that map back on the mule-pack, Santa Barbara's over this way." He jabbed a thumb toward the west.

They sat on the high summit of the pass, almost a mile above sea level.

"Wagon road down there along the ocean, Cliff. *Peon* back yonder tol' me it run from Ventura south of here to Santa Barbara, which should be about fifteen miles away, hid by that bend in the mountains."

The cattle were tired and leg-weary. They had been on the move since spring, and their ribs showed. The cows had not been bred the fall before, therefore they were without calves, but breeding time would be soon, and they needed some fat on their ribs.

Cliff had told Shorty to drift the herd down on the head of the river, water the stock in the pot-holes that showed down on the sandy river-bottom. Another day's short drive would bring them to the new Box N ranch, an adobe structure built, according to the land-commissioner, by the Franciscan *padres* years before as a dwelling place for travellers to stay over-night when going through the Cuyama district.

Cliff finished his coffee, looked up at the man. *"Cuanto, senor?"*

The man said, *"Viente centavos,"* and Cliff put an American dollar on the bar.

The woman said, "Please *senor*, do not come back."

Cliff stood, face stony. "Because I am a gringo, *senora?*"

"You are a *gringo, si.* But not so much for that do I ask you to stay away. Don Alfredo is our friend; his

171

daughter, *Senorita* Linda, and his other daughter, *Senorita* Maria, they are our friends, as is his son, *Senor* Miguel." Cliff murmered, *"Gracias, senora,"* and left.

Outside, it was like stepping into another world. There was laughter and song, and a moon that smiled from behind leafy clouds. Cliff stopped an old man "Where can I find the county surveyor, *senor?"*

"Don Pablo Morales? He lives down that street, on the corner." The *viejo* looked up, aged eyes pulled back into deep wrinkles. "You are the *gringo*, Cliff Blanton, *si*?"

"Word travels fast in this pueblo, *senor."*

"There is trouble here for you."The *viejo* shuffled off, ancient head shaking.

Cliff moved through the crowd, conscious of the quick glances. He went a block, and was crossing the street, when the man called to him, voice clear in the night. *"Gringo!"*

The words stopped him, holding him slim and hard against the night. He turned slowly, resentment rising inside of him. *Gringo* was a cruel word, denoting disrespect for these *Americano* adventurers who had torn California from Mexico.

"You called to me, *senor?"*

The man was moving toward him, stepping into the dust. The moon showed him as a California dandy, huge sombrero set back on his head, a blouse of yellow oriental silk, a red *sarape* encircling his thin waist, the end of the *sarape* almost dragging in the dust against his blue woollen pants.

Cliff saw his face, thin and young, and judged him to be about twenty.

"Yes, I called to you. You are the only *gringo* on the street, are you not?"

172

"I'm a Texan," corrected Cliff. The dandy had a pistol stuck under his *sarape,* the butt of it black and cold. "What do you want?"

"I am Don Miguel de la Mesa," said the Mexican.

Cliff decided to evade this trouble. He said, "That's nice," and turned. Don Miguel crossed the strip quickly; he grasped Cliff's left arm.

Cliff stopped again. "Take your hands off," he said.

"You tried for trouble in the cantina," stated Don Miguel. "My father is old, *senor.*"

"I did not hit your father."

"No, but you insulted him. You knocked down Jeff Garland."

Cliff stood, smiling faintly. This dandy was drunk. Muscatel and sauternes, drunk in the heat of the festivities, had gone to his head. "Garland is old enough to take care of himself."

"*Gringos* aren't welcome here!"

Cliff deliberately placed his right hand flatly on Don Miguel's chest. He pushed hard, straightening his elbow; the blow sent the don back, loosening his grip on Cliff's shirt. Don Miguel went back two paces, steadied himself, and let his hand fall to the pistol in his *sarape.*

Cliff stood wide-legged, eyes missing nothing. People were moving back, pulling away from them. He said clearly in Spanish, "I don't want trouble with you, Don Miguel. With these people as my witnesses. I state that again."

Now a girl came running across the street, and Cliff turned sharply as she moved into his vision, his hand falling to his gun. She held Don Miguel by the arm and cried, *"Hermano,* brother, don't, please don't!" She looked at Cliff, "Please, *senor,* do not use your gun! He is drunk with too much wine—Please!"

Two young men came up, took Don Miguel back toward the street dance that had gone on undisturbed. The girl looked at Cliff.

"I am sorry, sir." Her English was concise and clear. "I wish to apologize for the actions of my brother and my father."

"You are *Senorita Linda?*"

"No, *senor,* I am *Senorita* Maria de la Mesa." She was dark and small, pretty in black silk. Cliff bowed, a little stiffly.

"*Gracias, senorita,*" he said. "Thank you."

TWO

Don Pablo Morales had celebrated too early in the evening and too well, and when Cliff Blanton reached the assessor's adobe house, the man sat limp in his chair, big and wide and reeking of sauterne. His wife, a heavy, shuffling woman, came to Cliff's knock.

Cliff told her he wanted to see her husband on business. She let him in then and they went into the living-room where the whale-oil lamp showed the official slack in his chair.

His eyes opened, and he saw Cliff. "You are the *Americano,* no? The one who bought the ranch, from Texas?"

Cliff assured him he was correct. Don Pablo Morales sat up straight, brushing imaginary dust from his silken front. "I was catching a little nap, *Senor* Blanton. *Si,* your papers have arrived; they are in my office. The title of the land is recorded here in your name."

Cliff asked him to ride out the next day or so and definitely establish boundaries for the land. Yes, there were cattle on this graze, now.

"Whose cattle?" asked Cliff.

The cattle of Don Alfredo de la Mesa, bearing the Horsehoe brand. Yes, and the stock of Jeff Garland, who ran the Big Circle iron, with headquarters high in the Sierra Madres, the home-ranch on the south fork of La Brea Creek.

Cliff frowned. "I thought Jeff Garland was range boss for Don Alfredo?"

Don Pablo Morales hastened to assure him that Jeff Garland held that position, but he also ran cattle on a thousand head of stock from the Horseshoe brand, turning the iron into his brand, The Big Circle.

"Who else has settled on Santa Isabella land?"

"You and *Senor* Garland are the only ones—now, between all three of you, the Grant is just about sold. You see what you are moving into, do you not, *senor*?"

Cliff thought of his fight with Jeff Garland. He nodded and smiled. He left with the assurance that the surveyor would be out within the next week to show him the boundaries of his newly-acquired property. "You are not going to use barbed-wire, are you, *senor*?" asked the official.

"I have heard of that wire, *senor*. But you have none here in Santa Barbara, have you?"

"Some rolls of it were unloaded on the dock the other day, after a trip around the Horn from Pittsburg."

Cliff considered. "I probably won't use it, *senor*."

176

Then he added, "Unless I have to, of course. Garland and *Senor* de la Mesa will have to move their cattle off my grass."

Morales shrugged thick shoulders. "I am only the surveyor," he said. "The *grin*—the *Americanos*—they enforce the laws now. Once a month one of them rides through here; they call him a *Californio* Ranger. His name is Burnett. A big man, with red hair." He considered, thick face grave with its deep wrinkles. "The *Padres,* they are the ones who kept the law, and they did it through God's race. We were a happy people here, carrying on our cattle and our olive and orange and lemon growth, but then when gold was found at Sutter's Mill . . ."

Cliff nodded "I believe I understand, sir. But if they leave me alone, there'll be no trouble." He went out into the night that was bright with moonlight. From where he stood he could see the beach with its white sand and the blue Pacific, lazy and tired, curling up on the sand, then running back. He felt a vague, uncertain feeling, something akin to loneliness. This town had no place for him or his kind, and it made no overtures in so informing him. He had caught the pathetic, lost tone in Don Pablo Morales' words, and he knew the man was right. With the coming of the *Americano,* these people would have to change, or there would be violent, open conflict. The end of their peaceful, happy era was at hand. Men would move in, aggressive *Americanos,* and their ambition, and greed, would shatter their world.

Standing on this high spot, he could see the dock that ran out to the sea. Fishing boats rode at anchor. Beyond them, riding the ground swells, stood a tall clipper ship, probably loaded with cowhides to take to the New England States. Even as Cliff watched, the clipper moved out into the channel, sleek and slim in the moonlight.

He went to the livery-barn. The brief rest had put new strength into the dun, shoving back some of the weariness. But the bone-tiredness of the long trail had seeped deep into the animal. Only weeks of rest and good grass could take that tiredness away.

Cliff saddled his horse, paid, led the beast outside, twisted his stirrup around, then slowly lowered his boot to the sod again. He turned and looked at the girl who stood beside the palm tree.

"You are the *Americano?*"

Cliff thought, at first, that this was Maria de la Mesa, but this girl was smaller, thinner. Her *mantilla* had been pushed back, showing her dark face with its full lips and dark eyes.

"I'm Cliff Blanton, *senorita.*"

She said, "Allow me to present myself. I am Linda de la Mesa, and I want to apologize for the conduct of my only brother tonight."

Cliff murmured, "*Gracias, senorita,* but your sister, the *Senorita Maria,* has been kind, too."

There was a bench under the palm; she sat on this. "Will you sit by me, *senor,* that we may talk?"

Cliff sat, holding the reins.

"My father, *Senor* de la Mesa, is an old man, *Americano.* Our land has passed from generation of de la Mesas to the next generation; he is the last to hold it. For over two centuries, it has been in the hands of those of our blood. This is a hard blow on him, *senor.*"

"I understand," said Cliff slowly

"He cannot understand," said the girl slowly. "My sister and myself—we can see that it had to come. But my brother again, he is a different person—he is under the influence too much of our *primero*, Jeff Garland. He drinks too much, too."

"When did Jeff Garland come to this region, and where did he come from?"

"He came years ago, I was a small girl. Over ten years, by far. He came one day with a boat from Colombia, and he stayed to work on the Santa Isabella."

Cliff figured that Jeff Garland was a renegade Texan, probably run out of the Lone Star State by the Rangers. He had probably caught a boat out of Galveston or some port, fled to South America, had finally worked up the West coast to California. That meant that Jeff Garland was a hard man, a tough man.

"We do not want trouble, *senor*," said the girl slowly. "Neither my sister nor I want this to turn into trouble. We have talked this over."

Cliff waited, quietly.

"We want to work with you, *Senor* Cliff. At home, in every way we can, we girls will talk with father. We have great influence over him. We ask that you be tolerant with him and with our brother."

"What if one, or both of them, run trouble against me?" asked Cliff flatly.

Her answer was prompt. "Then you would defend yourself, of course. We do not ask you to be clay, but we ask your tolerance and good will."

She got to her feet, said goodnight then, her voice small. Cliff found his stirrup and lifted himself, turning his dun toward the south.

He skirted the edge of Santa Barbara, riding along the hills. When he came to the well-travelled road, he

179

knew he had found San Marcos Trail. As he rode higher, the plain and the hills spread out below him, washed by the silent moonlight. They ran to the edge of the Pacific where their darkness changed to white sand.

The lights below him were pinpoints of flame suspended between mountains and ocean. There was festivity and song down there on that street, here in the pine and buckbrush was a silence century-deep. Cliff was tired. His weariness was deep; not close to the surface. Miles of desert and mountains had put it into him, as they had ground utter weariness into his mount, and only sunshine and laziness and time would take it from his bones.

But through this, depressing as it was, came a sudden lift, a surge of energy. First, there was the sudden, striking longing for this land; with great fertility locked in its dark bosom. There would be rest here and green grass for tired cattle.

Once a Texan, always a Texan, he thought. *Thinking of cattle all the time* . . . But that was a cowman's way: cattle to him were his occupation, they were his lifeblood.

He reached the summit of San Marcos Pass. It would be downhill now to the buildings on Wells Creek, miles to the north-east.

Now and then, on the flat parks of the Sierra Madres, he saw cattle grazing and read some brands. The Horseshoe was a clear iron, burned thick and big on a cow's right ribs; the Big Circle was located on the ribs too, of course. Jeff Garland had run the broad side of a hot running-iron around, completing the bottom of the Horsehoe and turning it into a Circle. Evidently Don Alfredo must have trusted his foreman. All Garland needed to get more cattle was to brand more Horseshoe cattle of the Santa Isabella Grant and, unless Don Alfredo demanded a roundup and count of Big Circle cattle, he could not tell exactly whether Jeff Garland had branded the five thousand he bought, or if he had branded anywhere within a thousand more than that number.

Cliff smiled, reflecting that his brand, the Box N, could not be changed to either the Horseshoe or the Big Circle. He was skirting the head of the badlands south of Santa Ynez.

According to his calculations, and evidence supplied by the surveyor, Santa Ynez was the trading-post closest to his Box N on Wells Creek.

Sunrise would find him miles from the Wells Creek ranch site. He took into the Sierra Madres again, coming to a wide stretch of shallow water settled between two ranges. Here grass grew knee-high and curlews ran ahead. This was the primitive area, the home of the mountain lion, the bobcat: this was, he believed, the Sisquoc River. He had one more ridge to climb, and then he would go down to the plains of the Cuyama River.

To get to Wells Creek, he needed to hit a canyon called Abel's Canyon, marked by its red rock formation. He had swung west too far. He put the dun on a trail to the ridge. With the wilderness below him, he would get his bearings again.

Dawn was colouring the east when the dun, sweaty and dirty, came down a steep incline heading toward adobe buildings scattered along a creek bottom. Here, at this ranch-house, Cliff could get his directions, and maybe a bit to eat.

When he came up to the corrals, a man came out of the brush behind him. Cliff heard him and turned the dun. His nerves were raw and lack of sleep pulled at his muscles.

The man, stocky and bowlegged, carried a rifle, the barrel raised a little. He had a black patch over one eye, and his cheek below it was scarred. A knife had made that scar, Cliff realized, and a knife had blinded him.

"Who are you, stranger?"

Cliff lied suddenly, "Just riding through. Heading for the Cuyama, up towards Wells reek."

"You're too far west." The man studied the dun's brand. "I take it you're with that Texan who's trailin' cattle in? I understand he runs a Box N, like your sorrel carries."

Cliff shrugged, remained silent. This fellow, he saw, was an *Americano*, and unless he were mistaken—and he felt sure he wasn't—he was a renegade, an outlaw. He carried two Colts, both tied low; cartridges glistened from his gun-belts. Finally Cliff spoke. "What outfit is this?"

"Jeff Garland owns this spread. The Big Circle, on South Fork."

Cliff thought, *I've ridden miles too far to the west,* and his weariness grew. Coupled with this was a watchful wariness directed toward this Big Circle guard.

"You ridin' for Cliff Blanton?" demanded the man.

Cliff thought, *Here is trouble staring at me again.* He said clearly, "Look fella, I don't know who you are, nor I don't give a damn. I traded for this horse in Santa Barbara; I want to get to Maricopa. Somebody told me Wells Creek was the water to follow, after I'd got over the ridge."

"He told you wrong. I think you better light here for a while, cowboy, and rest your hooks. Jeff Garland'll be ridin' out from Santa Barbara today an' he might want to talk a little with you. Be good, now, and do as Leo Edwards says."

Cliff considered that briefly. He decided to play along. "All right with me, Edwards. I'd appreciate a hot cop of Java an' a mornin' nap."

Edwards smiled, the effort tipping his face strangely. "Now that's talkin' sense, stranger. If you just turn that dun and—" Cliff's words had dropped his rifle a little. Cliff was over him, leaning from leather, anchored on one stirrup hard. His pistol rose and arced, and Edwards went down on his belly, prone in the brown grass.

Cliff wiped his gun on his chaps, then pouched it again.

He turned the dun east.

THREE

Cliff had breakfast with a goat-herder, there on a high mesa. The man, who could speak no English, talked a broken jargon of Mexican that was difficult to understand. Then he headed north-east, the goat-herd's words clear in him.

Big Circle riders were using the prospective Box N buildings for a line-camp, stationed there to turn cattle back south again, and to keep them from crossing the Cuyama river. The herder had lifted two grimy fingers. *"Dos hombres, senor."*

Cliff had also found out he was only fifteen miles from the ranch. He looked toward the mountains to the east. His Box N herd had already crossed that range and now, unless he were mistaken, his riders would be working them toward the prospective Box N headquarters that were now occupied by Big Circle riders.

The sun rose steadily freighted with a sullen heat. The dun was lathered again around the headstall and the edges of the heavy Chimayo saddle-blanket. A mesa ran out, jutting over the Cuyama valley. Cliff drew in here among the buckbrush and looked down at the range below them with the river in its centre.

He saw the Box N buildings below him. These were old abodes, grouped in a square. The centre of the square was a *patio,* a square strip of sun-baked, hoof-pounded adobe soil. Two saddled horses stood to a hitchrack there.

He studied the buildings for some minutes, knowing that much of his life would be spent down there on that flat covered by greasewood and marked by white alkali. A thin column of spruce smoke rose lazily from a chimney. The Big Circle riders were preparing a late breakfast.

Riding down the slope, Cliff kept covered by the high brush. He came to a great sandstone rock some distance behind the buildings and he left the tired horse there. Rifle under his arm, he went into the patio, coming between two thick adobe walls. One of the saddle-horses saw him and snorted, the sound trumpet-loud in the stillness. Cliff moved into the room almost leisurely, slipping through the open door that hung on hand-made strap hinges.

The two men were eating at a heavy table hewn from live-oak. One saw Cliff then, and the other, catching his companion's surprise, turned and looked at Cliff.

"Who are you?" demanded the smaller man.

"I own this place," said Cliff flatly.

"You're the Texan, huh? Blanton?"

Cliff nodded. "Get your horses and ride."

They exchanged glances. The taller said, "Don't jump too far, Blanton, because we might snap you short suddenly. We've got breakfast on the table, fella. We wanna eat, *sabe*?"

"Jeff Garland might not like this," muttered the shorter.

Cliff said, "We don't give a damn what Jeff Garland likes. I tangled with your boss down in Santa Barbara, fellow, and I'm not giving him an inch from here out. That goes for his hired guns too."

"You talk tough," said the trail man.

Cliff came forward suddenly. He swung the rifle barrel sharply. The steel swept across the table; crockery fell, coffee spilled. The tall man, face flushed again, reached for his iron. Cliff raised the rifle's steel and brought it flatly against the man's forehead, knocking him down. He was groggy but not out and Cliff said abruptly, "Get to your feet, and ride out!"

The man got up, his hand against his forehead. Cliff gestured toward the door with his rifle. The smaller man was through, his fight gone. With Cliff behind, they went through the door. The smaller man got his boot in stirrup. As he went up, Cliff lifted his pistol out of the holster. The man found his seat, looked down and said, "I'll need that gun, fellow."

"You'll get it," assured Cliff. "It will be left for you in Santa Ynez." He felt a sense of weariness and made his voice tough. "Jeff Garland called me in Santa Barbara. He wants war, and he's going to get it. Ride with pistols light from here out and with a rifle in your saddle-holster. And stay off Box N range."

"T'hell with you!" growled the short man. "How about our duds, fellow? We got clothes in that

187

bunkhouse . . .

"You'll get those . . . in Santa Ynez. Now hit steel to them horses. He went to one knee, the lever working on the rifle. He shot three times, placing the bullets over their heads. Horses reared and straightened out in fear. They raced across the *patio*, steel hoofs slamming into the soil, Cliff ran across the packed yard, and by that time the riders were fanning across the flat, riding low on their broncs' necks. He did not shoot again. Powder and bullets were scarce. He watched them run into the hills to the south-west.

They'll have a story to tell Jeff Garland, he thought. He found no warmth, no assurance, in that summation. Trouble rode with short stirrups here, and Trouble had a gun in either hand. Garland was tough and he ramrodded a tough crew.

Cliff had acted this way deliberately. From here out, it was dog eat dog, bullet against bullet. Jeff Garland had so decreed that by his actions in Santa Barbara.

Cliff turned, his rifle barrel rising. He steadied it, then let it slack. The woman was ageless, and her face was wrinkled. She grinned from toothless gums, yet her black eyes, hidden almost by the wrinkles, were sharp with life.

"You are Cliff Blanton?" she asked. She spoke English, too.

Cliff nodded.

"I thought so, *Senor* Cliff. Word had come to me—Magdalena Cortez—that you would be here soon, with your riders. The goatherd, Enrique Verde, he told me last week, and the *Californio*, the ranger—Pete Burnett—he told Enrique."

"And you, *senora*?"

"This was the *hacienda* of my forebears." She was

talking Spanish now. "I was the last girl; I married, but not to the man my father, Don Juan Cortez, desired me to marry. I married the man of my choice, the Sierra Madre Indian, Silver Springs. He lies up there now." She gestured toward the silent Sierra Madres.

Cliff nodded.

"They died, my father, my mother. That was *anos* ago, twenty-five, at the most. Don Alfredo de la Mesa purchased our hacienda and abandoned it; he took it into his great King's land-grant. He let me live here, *senor*. I can cook, *Senor* Cliff."

She turned and waddled into the room where the Big Circle men had been eating. Cliff heard her starting to clear away the debris his rifle barrel had caused. He turned to his horse, led him to the barn and stripped him, noticing that two Big Circle horses ate at the manger. The manger held hay: a coarse, tough slough-grass. Coarse feed, Cliff reasoned, but probably good feed. He carried two buckets of water from the pump and the horse drank eagerly, nose deep in the cold, pure water.

"Food is ready, *senor*."

Cliff ate his second breakfast. But that at the goat-herd's camp did not compare to this. He had wild hog flesh, prepared in salt vats, fried to a lean, brown goodness. A white linen tablecloth covered the table and muscatel wine sparkled in a goblet. The change in the room was miraculous.

"Did you do all this—in such a short time?"

"Si, senor." The dark eyes were sharp.

Cliff smiled. "And you cooked this meal, too?" He looked at the pancakes made of corn flour and the honey syrup.

"Si."

"*Gracias*," murmured Cliff. he saw the sharpness leave the sunken eyes, and a softness came in. He had the impression suddenly that this ancient woman had known great pain, that it had not been of the flesh but of the spirit. He ate slowly, enjoying the good feed, the fine coffee. Maggie had left, evidently going to her room. This was a good range and he had good holdings.

He stirred himself, got to his feet. Outside, Maggie came out and he said "I ride for my herd, *senora*. This evening me and my men will come in. There are five of us and we will be hungry men. The job of cooking for us will be big, and I do not want to ask you to do it, *senora*."

She shook her head. "No, no, no," she kept repeating. "No, I will do that."

Cliff said quietly, "All right, if you care to. When you need supplies, let me know, and we'll send a rig into Santa Ynez."

She was smiling again, the smile bright, quick. Cliff went to the barn where he put his hull on one of the Big Circle broncs. The horse was young and strong, grain-fed and ready for the trail. Cliff rode toward the east and the ridge of the Sierra Madres.

The sun was almost at noon, and autumn heat was across the land. The air was still and he saw cattle—Big Circle cattle. He drew in knowing that he would have to rid his range of this stock.

Ventucopa Pass, he reasoned, was at least twenty miles away, a good day's drive for hoof-sore cattle and leg-tired broncs. He had never seen a range so desolate, so lonely as this, brooding like some maimed, broken giant. Man had scarcely set foot across it, the edges of it only punctured. And over it all, looking down without emotion, were the peaks of the Sierra Madres.

The Big Circle horse was sure-footed as a mountain goat, steady on the thin trails. From here, Cliff saw the range clearly, the limitless panorama unfolding below, undulating and endless. An hour later, he met the goat-herd, Enrique Verde, holding his small flock in the rocks of a mountain pasture.

Cliff said, "You range far, *senor*."

The man smiled, "This is not far from where we had breakfast this morning, *senor*," he said slowly. "You rode around a great circle and I ranged my goats across it. You ride to your herd of cattle, I suppose?"

Cliff nodded.

"You have seen your *hacienda* by now? You have met Magdalena Cortez, the *vieja*, who is as old as the wind, and with a heart of yellow gold?"

Cliff assured him that he had, and that by this time the Big Circle men should be close to their home ranch, ready to pour their troubles into the big ear of big Jeff Garland. Enrique Verde's seamed face broke into a wide smile that slowly died.

"There are cattle on your land, *senor*. Cattle belonging to the Big Circle and to *Senor* de la Mesa, the Horseshoe cattle. What do you do with them?"

"Run them west," growled Cliff. He saw a twinkle come into the brown eyes. "Head them toward the Big Circle and the Santa Isabella Rancho, and run them off my grass. You are smiling widely, *amigo*."

"There is another method, *senor*."

Cliff ran his thumb along his jaw. "I could pen those Big Circle and Horseshoe cattle and demand that both Jeff Garland and Don Alfredo pay me range-dues for the grass they have eaten on my land. That is right, according to law."

191

"Jeff Garland would not like that," said the goat-herder.

Cliff considered that. If he held these cattle, Garland and Don Alfredo would have to pay for them or else fight for them. Maybe it was best to clash with these two right away, and get this problem settled for once and always.

"I could run my cattle this side of the *hacienda*, I guess. See that neck of land that juts out into the river? I could bunch these Big Circle and Horseshoe critters and hold them there."

The goat-herd nodded. "*Senor* Jeff Garland, he made me pay a toll to him, so my goats could eat on this land. I have ten goats—no, twelve, for Nancy had twins—and the cost is ten *pesos* for the year. I suppose you will do the same, *senor*."

The goats were long-haired angoras valuable only for their hides and what little milk the nannies gave. Enrique Verde probably had a *senora* and a bunch of *muchachitos* and *muchachitas*. Garland made life miserable even for this goat-herd.

"There'll be no charge for grazing on my land," he assured the goatherd.

He rode off, the man's thanks in his ears. He saw the head of the Cuyama below him. Box N cattle were moving along the edge of the river, heading toward the ranch buildings. Cliff rode down the slope, one hand high in the air, and Shorty Nolan sheathed his gun, recognizing him.

"We been worried about you, Cliff. Danged near come headin' toward Santa Barbara my ownself to look you up. What's new?"

Cliff told him. "So the land lays tough, huh? Say, this is good range, Cliff! Better'n Texas, I'd say. Here comes Sis Johnson up. Kid's been worried pink about you, Cliff."

Sis Johnson was a lanky, gawky kid of nineteen. Some years before, Cliff and Shorty had taken him out of a Juarez *cantina*, a homeless waif, and taken him into Texas. The 'punchers had started calling him *sister* when a kid, and his anger had been so great they had promptly dubbed him *Sis*.

"Any good-lookin' gals down there on the Ocean?" asked Sis, buckteeth showing. "Or what did keep you so long, Cliff?"

The rest of the crew came loping up, letting the tired longhorns graze along the river bank. Mack Dunn was a young man, not more than twenty-five, yet nights in the saddle had marked him with an oldness. Gene Creston, somewhere in the neighbourhood of fifty, had ridden in the Panhandle Wire Cutter's War with Rawhide Blanton, Cliff's father, and when Rawhide had passed on, the veteran saddleman had transferred his allegiance to Cliff. He told them about Jeff Garland and Don Alfredo de la Mesa.

"We'll reach the *hacienda* by sundown," said Cliff. "We'll corral our stock on the point, then get a good night's rest. You can bet on this, men—I'm here on the Cuyama to stay."

Cliff took the point, because he knew the way to the *hacienda*. Shorty Nolan rode beside him, while Sis Johnson and Mack Dunn pounded the laggards with their free catchropes.

Gene Creston rode the north flank, keeping the hungry stock from turning down toward the green rushes and foliage along the river. These cows and the scattered bulls had stood up well under the all-summer drive, but they were getting tired. This weariness was not on the surface; it was deep, ground into bone and tissue. Cattle men, and horses alike, were its victims.

The pack-mules, laden with grub and bedding, followed behind the herd.

"Maggie will have dinner ready when we come in," said Cliff.

Shorty smiled slowly. "Don't take you long to get a woman, huh, Cliff? So she goes with the deed, huh?"

The cattle were strung out, walking in single-file, threading their way across the face of a bluff that overlooked the Cuyama. Cliff rode ahead, figuring to scare any Horseshoe or Big Circle cattle out of the way of the herd. He did not want them intermingling with his herd. The afternoon had run out and the sun was falling rapidly. He decided that they would reach the *hacienda* about dusk, he figured.

And his assumptions proved correct. With dusk falling across this range, the cattle came over the last ridge; there, below the riders, lay the *hacienda*. They studied it, their eyes keen; Cliff felt a stir of pride; they liked the set-up.

They pushed the cattle past the adobe structure, turning them down on the neck that ran into the Cuyama. Here grew grass that was sheltered by cottonwoods and oaks. Willows concealed mottes of fresh bunchgrass. A trail led down off the hills; they put the cattle along this.

Cliff discovered somebody had built a fence across the neck, and they would be able to pen the cattle in for the night. They shut the gate on the rail fence and rode toward the *hacienda*.

"We'll station guards, huh?" asked Shorty.

Cliff nodded. "After chuck, men."

They left their broncs in the barn, feeding them

from the small haystack. They trooped toward the pump, and Cliff pumped water while they washed, splashing and grunting.

"Plenty nice," said Gene Creston.

Maggie came from the lighted kitchen, carrying some rough woollen towels. Cliff introduced her to his crew and she curtsied. She said, "Food is ready, men," They caught the whiff of fried spuds and boiled meat, and Sis Johnson grinned, rubbing his ear.

"I'm hungry as all hell, men," he said.

FOUR

This was the last day of the *fiesta*. Don Alfredo slept late and when he awoke at noon, the celebrants were turning toward the Plaza, where the bullfight would be held. He ate and went to the arena.

Linda met him on State Street, tucked her hand under his arm, and said, "I'm going with you, papa."

"Where is Maria?"

"She goes with Don Martino."

"A new beau," growled the old don. "Sometimes I wish that girl would get married. Always a new beau." He regarded his elder daughter solemnly. "Why don't you get a male friend, Linda?"

"With you to go with," she said, smiling. "Humph, do you think I need a beau, when I have you?"

"Oh heavens," said Don Alfredo. "What are you

telling me, *hija?*" Yet he was smiling as they entered the grandstand. They took a seat high on the rim, the elderly don nodding to people he knew. He had no use for bullfights. He thought them cruel, unnecessary, and inhuman. He wanted to go home; his three days in Santa Barbara had worn him out.

"There's Maria," said Linda.

"Where is Don Miguel?"

"He is over there, papa, with Jeff Garland. Over by the bullpen, see?"

Don Alfredo saw that his son was a little drunk. He and Jeff Garland were seated on the top rail of the bullpen. Garland's foreman, Pedro Martinez, crouched beside the Big Circle owner, a red-haired Mexican with blue eyes strangely incongruous to his swarthy skin. He was about thirty and he was was a tough hand, Don Alfredo realized.

"Did you see the *Tejano, Senor* Blanton?" asked the don.

Linda said, "I talked to him, father."

He smiled. "You are a brazen hussy, Linda. What did you talk about, *senorita?*"

"This trouble. I do not want you in it. You cannot win, papa. Things have changed, and if you don't change—and if Jeff Garland doesn't change—then there will be gunfights. And the side of the law is with *Senor* Blanton too."

He said, "I can handle my own affairs, Linda."

"I am sorry, *senor*," she said quietly. "Come, let's watch the bullfight. See, the bull is coming out."

He got to his feet. "I couldn't watch it," he said flatly. "I am going to the hotel. Are you coming with me, or aren't you?"

"I go with you."

They went down the steps and walked up State

Street to the Santa Rosa hotel, where they were staying. Don Alfredo got a bottle of wine and poured its redness into a goblet, turning it in the light. He handed it to Linda.

She drank. "That was good," she said. She was thinking, strangely, of the *Tejano,* Cliff Blanton. He would have cold-eyed men with him, men who had gone through cattle-wars and who had driven cattle over long trails through dust-storms and blizzards. They would have guns.

He said, "Then you don't want me to fight for what is ours—what has been ours for centuries?"

"The land is not ours, now."

He said, slowly, "But what right has *Yanqui* law to order us around, to take apart our *ranchos,* to parcel them out to *Yanquis?* We are not *Americanos;* we are Mexicans. Yet, *Yanqui* law came in; it took over. A handful of bandits under Fremont, and other renegades, took over *Californio,* and made it part of their United States. Why did they want it? Gold. *Yanquis* are mad for it. So, to get it, they took the whole territory, turned it into one of their own states."

"What did we have under Mexican rule?" asked Linda suddenly.

"We had our land. We had our *ranchos.*"

"*Si,* we did that. And what else did we have? We had terrible taxes to pay; so high that they drained the country of its wealth, shipping it to Mexico City, thousands of miles distant. And what do the dandies of Mexico City care for us here in California? Not a whit, outside of our tax money—our unjust taxes. Do we have that under the *Americanos?*"

"No, you are right there."

"I am right in other points, papa. You know this system is wrong; you know that, down deep in your heart. You are a good man, a kind man. Yet, on the Santa Isabella you had retainers, poor people. Because of the high taxation, you could not take care of them as you wanted. You know that?"

He nodded slowly.

"Now they have little plots of their own. They are getting ahead much better. This thing has to be stopped, papa, or else men will die. If you listen to Jeff Garland—

"You have never liked him, have you?"

"A renegade *Tejano*! Him with his guns, his hardness. Sure, he knows how to run cattle, but he knows how to fight too. and he likes to fight; I would not turn my back to him!"

"Come," said Don Alfredo, "let us talk of pleasant things."

They heard shouts at the arena.

"One bull gone." remarked the don scowling.

A black-haired woman, rawboned and gaunt, came in, sat beside Linda. "Maria is at the bullfight," she said. "I am tired of this, Don Alfredo. My, I hope we never have another *fiesta,* for my feet are killing me. When do we leave for home?

"After the street-dance, tonight."

"Have some wine, *Tia*?" asked Linda.

Her aunt poured some wine, drank quickly and lowered her glass. *Senora* de la Mesa had been dead almost ten years; she had been killed by a runaway team. Her sister, *Tia* Tompita, had taken over the de la Mesa household and children. When she made up her mind, only death could change it.

Don Alfredo groaned softly.

"I was talking with *Dona* Morales," said *Tia* Tompita. "She said that that no-good husband of hers, who has been supported by the county for years, is riding out of town to show this *Tejano,* Cliff Blanton, the boundaries of his property. If those *Tejanos* are met with power, *senor,* there will be guns talking. What are you going to do, Don Alfredo?"

"Why do you ask?"

The bony aunt puffed her cheeks suddenly. "Why do I ask? Why, it is my business, is it not? For ten years, I have headed your household; I have raised your family. Yet you ask me if it is any of my business if you go out and commit suicide?"

Don Alfredo said, testily, "This is *fiesta,* a time of friendship, of gaiety. Do not pick an argument with me, I warn you."

Dona Tompita shrugged.

Linda realized she had a powerful friend in her aunt. While she appealed to her father through love, her aunt appealed through respect and, she guessed, a little fear. For Don Alfredo was a peace-loving man.

Finally, the bull-fights were over. The matadors, gaudy with many colours, rode up the street, picadors behind them.

Don Alfredo herded his two women into the dining-room. While she was eating, *Tia* Tompita, of course, had to remain silent; he was glad of that. Maria came in with a young *Californio,* who bowed all around, drawing a scowl to Don Alfredo's forehead.

"We do not stay for the entire dance," said Don Alfredo. "We have our buggy leave town at nine o'clock, Maria."

"That is early, papa."

"There will be dancing some other time," stated the don. "Do not wear yourself out in one season." He returned to his lobster. The meal completed, they went to the barn where the *mozo* drove out the buckskins hooked to the two-seated buggy. Don Alfredo helped Maria and *Tia* Tompita into the back seat, while he and Linda took the front seat.

"Here is Miguel," said Linda.

Don Miguel and Jeff Garland came out of the barn. His son said, "I shall be home later, papa."

"When?"

"In two hours." Anger roiled the dandy's voice. "I am a man, now; I am responsible only to myself."

"Take it easy, fellow," said Jeff Garland. He looked up at Don Alfredo. "I'll see that he stays clear of trouble." He grinned crookedly. "There ain't no stray *Tejanos* in town, anyway."

"Two hours," said Don Alfredo.

He cracked his buggy whip and the buckskins broke into a quick trot. Morning would be with them when they reached the *hacienda* on Alios Creek. They would needs climb San Marcos Pass, then go down into the Santa Ynez valley. The team knew the road. When the horses reached the foothill grades, the weight of the rig slowed them to a walk. Don Alfredo slumped in the seat, the reins in his hands.

"You had better put on your coat," said Linda. She laid the bearskin overcoat across his shoulders and he smiled at her. "*Gracias, hija.*"

Maria said, "I didn't want to leave so early!"

"One needs only to look at your face," said Don Alfredo, "to see that, *hija*. You need not put it into words."

On San Marcos Pass, the land unrolled and to the east were the badlands. From here on, it would be down-grade; the buckskins braced their rumps against the breeching. *Tia* Tompita said, "Drive slower, Don

Alfredo! You almost lost us back here!"

"Three women," he said. "And one lone man."

Santa Ynez river was almost dry as the buckskins rattled across the bridge. The Mission lay in darkness, the scattered adobe huts around it also without lights.

"A rider over there," said Linda, and pointed to the east.

Don Alfredo looked, said, "He is that Garland man, Pinto White."

Pinto White rode into an *arroyo* and the hills hid him. The sun was over the Sierra Madres when the buckskins trotted into the *hacienda* of the Santa Isabella *rancho*. Roosters were crowing and Linda's fox terrier came barking and dancing.

Breakfast was waiting in the big living-room. Fire danced in the fireplace and the *cocinera,* a heavy Campo squaw, bustled around, handing warm coffee to them.

After breakfast, the women went to their rooms to sleep, but Don Alfredo sat beside the fire. He heard a rider come into the yard; it was Don Miguel.

"You drove fast, papa."

Don Alfredo nodded, silently.

Don Miguel asked: "This *gringo,* this Cliff Blanton. I rode out with Jeff Garland; we saw Pinto White. Pinto had been over on the Upper Cuyama; he saw the *gringo's* cattle come in. He has them penned on the Point, and the upper part blockaded. He is waiting for Pablo Morales to come and survey his boundaries. We have Horseshoe cattle ranging on the land this *gringo* devil claims; he will drive them off that grass."

"That is his right."

Don Miguel was silent. His face, young, grave, was a study in bronze lighted by flame.

"Then you surrender this land, our land, papa? You

refuse to fight for what your fathers have handed down to you over the centuries? You are to abide by *Yanqui* law, *gringo* law?"

"It is too big to fight, son."

Don Miguel said, very slowly, "I do not think that, *senor*."

FIVE

Cliff Blanton and his men slept late the next morning. They had decided to leave the cattle on the Point until boundaries were established for the new Box N ranch. Cliff stood last guard, watching the sun rise higher.

Maggie beat the buggy spring hung in the *patio*. Cowpunchers dressed, washed, and trooped in for breakfast, spurs jangling. Cliff left the herd and rode to the *hacienda*. There would need be no guard posted during the daytime. The Point could be seen from the *hacienda*. He ate slowly. A good night of rest had put lots of energy into the tired crew. They and the cows could recuperate fast from their long drive.

"What day is this?" asked Shorty.

"Saturday," replied Sis Johnson.

The sun was already warm. But the night had been chilly. The altitude was rather high here, and the Sierra Madres cut off the ocean breeze. Cliff and Shorty went to the barn, saddled and rode out, their horses pulling at the bits.

"Scout the lay of the *rancho*," said Cliff.

They rode at a walk, neither man saying much. The long drive was over, the cattle were here—one phase of it had ended; now, the other phase was ahead.

"Cattle over around that spring," grunted Shorty.

These were Big Circle cattle, mostly cows. They were in good shape but rather wild. Shorty Nolan's homely face bore a wide grin. "Wild cattle, Cliff. By the way, where do they peddle their beef from this range?"

"Goes both ways, north and south. Some to Los Angeles—that's south of here, a port town, I guess. They don't take much of it, I understand; a small town, some 'dobe huts. 'Course, it goes out of there for the Orient on clipper. But most of it is trailed north to 'Frisco and Sacramento and the gold camps. In two years' time we'll prob'ly peddle some two-year-old steers. Fact is, we might have to; I've got enough cash to run this outfit for two years, but then we have to sell some stock."

"These cows'll pick up beef fast," stated Shorty. "Some of them might not calve; we might have to get rid of them."

They found other cattle, too: Horseshoe cattle. Shorty looked inquiringly at his boss. "We'll have to get those cows of our grass, Cliff."

"They might come after them," said Cliff slowly. "Garland and Don Alfredo might send some of their men over to work our range of their stuff."

"Let's hope they do," murmured Shorty. "But if

they don't?"

"We'll round them up, pen them on the Point. According to law, I can make them pay for the work we did and also a stray-pen fee for holding them."

Shorty considered. "They wouldn't like that, Cliff."

"They'll probably drive them off our range."

Using the rough map, they found Dripping Springs. Here cold water dripped out of igneous boulders set flatly against the mountain. Ferns and rushes grew around the small pond of cold water. They swung north, going toward the Cuyama River.

"Rider on our range," murmured Shorty.

They loped over, holding their right hands high in the Indian sign of peace. The man rode a Big Circle bronc. Cliff said, shortly, "You're on my Bar N range, fellow."

"Lookin' for Big Circle cattle," said the man calmly. "The name is Pinto White."

Cliff introduced himself and Shorty. "You're aimin' to drive these Big Circle cattle west to Big Circle range, I take it?"

White's sunken eyes were calm. He was thin, young, with red hair. He had a fixed gaze. "No, can't say I was, Blanton," he said slowly.

Cliff spoke clearly. "I don't want any trouble with the Big Circle, White. Your boss, Garland, crossed me in Santa Barbara, night before last. We had our say out, and Garland didn't like it. Get this straight, fellow: if you and Big Circle riders—and Garland—come on Box N graze to haze your cattle, you're welcome. But we don't want Big Circle cattle—or Big Circle Men—on our grass."

"What'd you aim to do?" asked Pinto White.

Cliff told him that if neither the Big Circle nor the Santa Isabella Horseshoe iron did not round-up their cattle on his soil, he would bunch them for the two outfits, hold them for pen-fees.

"Think you could get away with it, Blanton?"

"That's the law."

"Might be a hard law to enforce," allowed White. "One thing for the fat boys in Washington an Sacramento to make a law an' it's another thing to enforce it. Well, I'll tell Jeff Garland what you said; he's the boss, not me." White rode off.

He acted peaceful," said Shorty spitting.

Cliff smiled. "Now let's see what Don Alfredo will say, huh?"

They met Don Miguel, riding toward the Big Circle, back in the Sierra Madres.

Cliff asked, "You remember me, I guess."

The youth sat his hand-carved saddle, the wind rustling his silk shirt. His hat was of finest hand-plucked beaver and his boots of brown calf-skin with hand-forged, silver-mounted spurs. He sat a big palomino.

"*Si*, I do."

Cliff told him about the Horseshoe cattle on Box N range, and how he had warned Pinto White. He asked him to get Horseshoe stock home.

"I shall tell my father," said Don Miguel.

They heard hoofs and Maria loped up, her black horse lathered. "*Tia* Tompita was watching me closely, *hermano,* but I sneaked out to ride with you." Cliff did not exist, apparently, to her. Shorty Nolan, seeing her disregard for his boss, allowed himself a smile. "Maybe we oughta introduce ourselves, Cliff?"

Cliff smiled. He said, "We've met before, Shorty.

Miss Maria, my foreman, Shorty Nolan."

She studied the short cowpuncher. "He forgot to grow," she said clearly. "All right, brother, the day is getting short."

They rode off. Shorty shoved back his hat, whistling softly. "What a hell-cat she is, huh? About twenty, I reckon.

"Wonder if that dandy button will inform his father as to what you said?"

"We'll see," said Cliff.

They dropped into Santa Ynez on the way home, making some purchases requested by Maggie, and getting some tobacco and papers for the crew. Dusk found them pushing across their new range. They came in, ate a late supper, and Cliff dispatched the night's guards. He himself took the early morning shift. Sunday's rising sun found him watching the shadows come across the mountains and disappear.

Again, he let his men sleep late. He ate breakfast first, making the meal before Maggie could arise. Oatmeal bubbled on the big wood range and the sharp tang of coffee was good.

Maggie said "This is my job, *senor*."

"Not on Sunday," corrected Cliff. "That's your day off. I suppose you want to go to the Santa Ynez Mission, *senora?*"

"If you please, at noon Mass."

Shorty and Cliff drove the elderly woman in with the buckboard. Horses stood at hitchrails and rigs lined the tie-racks in front of the adobe Mission that lay at the foot of the Sierra Madres. *Rancheros* and wives and families were going into the Mission.

"You will come in, *senor?*" asked Maggie.

Cliff smiled. "I wouldn't know how to act, been so long since I've been in a church. No, Shorty and me'll wait for you."

Her aged eyes were bird-sharp. "I saw the horses of the Big Circle riders at the *cantina* as we passed by."

She went into the Mission and Cliff turned the rig, driving down Santa Ynez' hoofpacked main street.

Two men stood in front of the *cantina*. One was Pinto White; the other, Jeff Garland. Cliff glanced at Shorty, who said, "The big jigger, I take it, is Jeff Garland?"

Cliff nodded.

"He's seen trails," murmured Shorty. "And some he didn't see, 'cause he rode them in the night. So he holds down two jobs, huh? Rangeboss for the Santa Isabella Horseshoe and runs his own Big Circle iron."

They went into a small *cantina* set at one end of the street, half a block away from where Garland and White were.

Both were hungry; the food was good. Suddenly Cliff lowered his fork. "Garland and White comin'," he said.

The Big Circle men came in, stopped. Jeff Garland's eyes were the colour of chipped agate and Pinto White stared at them unwinkingly.

Garland said clearly, "So you're orderin' Big Circle riders off your graze, huh, Blanton?"

Cliff shoved back his chair. "There's one exception, Garland. That is, if they are on the job shoving Big Circle cattle onto your range and off mine. Then your hands can ride across my graze as long as they are busy on that job."

"Cattle drift," reminded Jeff Garland. "They might wander back on that range of yours, Blanton."

Cliff clipped his words. "You've got riders, Garland. Put them to ridin' boundary. Clear my range of your stock in three days, or I pen them and hold them for stray-fees."

"There are two kinds of pay for a job like that," growled Pinto White.

Cliff knew what the rider meant. One was in money; the other, in gunsmoke. He felt anger touch him. "Three days, Garland," he reminded. "Then, if they're not off by then, my men start working on them. That goes for Horseshoe cattle too." He looked at Pinto White suddenly. "And as for you, fellow, cross me again and I'll—"

Pinto White was drawing then, his gun coming up. Commotion took hold of the *cantina*. The portly proprietor was hollering for his wife and *muchachitas* to run—the *Americanos* were going gun-crazy. Shorty Nolan's chair was crashing to the floor, with the runty foreman coming up, gun flashing. The smash of the chair blended with that of Cliff Blanton's gun. Pinto White dropped his unfired weapon, laid his hand across his belly, and fell limply.

Cliff turned his gun on Jeff Garland, but Garland had pulled his hand back empty, and his eyes were thick with uncertainty.

Cliff said, *"Gracias,* Shorty," and holstered his piece. The proprietor was wringing his hands and calling for the doctor. Cliff backed up against the wall, his hand on his holstered gun, Shorty Nolan with him, gun out and ready. Cliff recognized Big Circle riders in the group of townsmen now in the *cantina.*

He said, "He pulled first," and was silent.

Jeff Garland knelt beside Pinto White, and turned him over. White was dead. Cliff had not meant to kill the man; the shooting had been fast, though, and he had placed his bullet too high.

Cliff asked, "Is the *Californio* ranger in town?"

A heavy man replied. "No, he isn't. I'm marshal, Blanton." The man looked sharply at Shorty Nolan. "What do you say, man?"

"He pulled first. It was self-defence."

The marshal looked at the *cantina's* proprietor. The fat man said, "I saw it, *senor,* saw it all. *Si, Senor* White he reached for the gun first."

The marshal nodded, said, "Take him down to my store, and I will call the undertaker." He looked at Cliff. "The ranger—Peter Burnett—he might want to talk to you about this, *senor.*"

"I'll be at my ranch," said Cliff.

He told the marshal about the Big Circle and Horseshoe cattle on his grass, and that if they weren't rounded-up, he'd hold them for pen-fees.

"You would be right, in the law," stated the marshal.

They went out, two men carrying Pinto White, with Garland looking long at Cliff before stepping into the street. When they went outside, Mass was over and people were coming out of the Mission. Word went through them of Pinto White's death.

Maggie came, face pale, and got into the buggy. Cliff and Shorty were already in the seat and Cliff turned the team, taking the east road. When they reached the end of the street, the de la Mesa family were taking seats in the surrey.

Cliff drew in his team.

"Tomorrow, *senor,* my men will ride to your place, and we will start gathering our Horseshoe cattle."

Cliff said, "Thank you, sir." Don Alfredo sat and looked at him slowly, measuring him carefully. The woman beside him sat silent and straight. Maria was seemingly unaware of him, and Don Miguel was silent, dark eyes sharp. Linda looked at him, her eyes slow and thoughtful, and she smiled a little.

Cliff turned his team, and drove away.

SIX

They carried Pinto White into the store, went through it into the back room, where they laid him on a pine table.

Garland stood, his riders around him. The marshal said, "This means war, I suppose, Garland. Pete Burnett will have his hands full. My jurisdiction does not run beyond Santa Ynez town."

Leo Edwards adjusted the patch on his right eye. "That's the geezer who buffaloed me the other mornin', Jeff. That was him, that Cliff Blanton."

They got their horses and headed south toward the Big Circle on South Fork. They got to the hills and they could see the buckboards and riders below them on the valley. Cliff Blanton and his rig were to the east, threading into the hills, and to the west was the surrey of the de la Mesas going toward the *hacienda* on Aliso Creek.

"He can handle a gun," murmured Martinez.

Garland glanced sharply at his foreman, nodded. An hour later they came into the Big Circle, tough men on tough horses.

They went to the ranch-house while Edwards and Gordo Garcia went to the bunk-house. Later they stepped up on fresh horses, and rode east toward the main range of the Sierra Madres.

Dusk was claiming this land when they rode into a mountain park set between two peaks. A rider came out of the buckbrush. He had a rifle and he lowered it.

"How goes the work, Ike?" asked Jeff Garland.

"Almost got that herd re-branded."

They came to a clearing. Cattle were moving and Garland caught the sharp stench of burning cowhide. Here four Big Circle riders were working a small band of cattle, about two hundred head.

Garland rode to the men who were branding a big steer beside the small fire of pine knots.

"Couple more steers unbranded in there," he said.

A man wiped the sweat from his forehead. "Thought you'd bring out some help, Jeff. We've had quite a chore working over this stock. These are big steers, and it takes four men to handle one."

"We were in Santa Ynez," said Garland. "We left Edwards and Garcia to watch the home ranch."

"Where's Pinto White? His hands ain't too good to handle a rope."

Garland told them. They looked at each other, knowing full well what White's death meant. He also told them about Cliff Blanton demanding they move Big Circle cattle from his Box N grass.

216

"An' are you, Jeff?"

Garland shook his head slowly. "We aren't, men. We'll let Blanton gather our stock; then we hit it, take it back. Maybe Blanton might stop lead." Garland hesitated, face bleak. "All right, get to work, *rancheros*. Finish branding this stock, an' we get them on the move. Come mornin', they'll be up around Arroyo Grande, loading on a boat for 'Frisco. Martinez, head across country and check on that boat."

Martinez loped off. Jeff Garland watched his men rebrand the de la Mesa Horseshoe cattle, running a wide band on the bottom of the Horseshoe, changing it to a Big Circle. The dusk was heavy when he checked the herd. Every steer bore his iron now.

"Head them north, men."

The cattle trotted past him, heading down the gulch. The steers would win top money from the renegade cow-buyer who bought stolen stock at lower prices for the San Francisco market.

They pushed the cattle at a trot, heading across the Wilderness country. They came down on the Cuyama west of the Box N.

Now the cattle, having reached the north side, were pushed into a thin line, riders staked out on either side. The Cuyama valley was behind; caution was not with them.

Ten miles farther, deep in the hills, Pedro Martinez rode down a side-hill, his horse laced with lather.

"Where is the buyer?" asked Garland.

"He's in Carrizo Pass."

"Get the word up and down the line," ordered Garland. The moon was bright now, too bright for a cow-thief. He was on edge, a sharp edge. They were playing a wide-open game, and Don Alfredo so far had held the sack. Now Cliff Blanton had come in, his cattle strung along the upper Cuyama. That had changed the complexion of the whole thing.

Either Don Alfredo trusted him, or the old Spaniard had no suspicions towards him. This was a good game, a profitable game. For two years, he had carried it on; he had cut, little by little, into the Horseshoe herds. Of course, Don Alfredo seldom rode his range, but his son—a handsome youth, arrogant, but not ignorant. Was there danger in him?

He played the game close. Always, he rebranded the Horseshoe steers turning them into his own Big Circle iron.

And the Santa Isabella Horseshoe was still a big *rancho;* a few hundred head of steers driven off now and then would not make too big a dent in the Horseshoe herds. Of course, his being range-boss for Don Alfredo also helped. One of his duties was to run a yearly tally on Horseshoe stock. He had doctored his tallies the last few years, making up for the shortage.

He would have to break Blanton, or get rid of him. There was room for himself and the Horseshoe on this Cuyama range, because the Horseshoe helped him. But there would be no aid from the Box N. The Box N had cattle, true, but they were thin, trail-worn cows and a few bulls, of small value to a San Francisco buyer.

Pedro Martinez rode back, said "They're up ahead, in a park." Jeff Garland nodded and Martinez rode back, telling the tired riders the end of the push was at hand. Carlos nursed his swollen, broken lips in sullen stubborn silence. The cattle were tired, too. They had covered thirty miles, at the least, and now they were deep in the rocky, gravel-strewn San Luis Obispo hills.

They came to the clearing and the buyer, a big husky man mouthing a black cigar, watched the cattle walk by. Jeff Garland did not know his name. He paid for his cattle in raw gold and that was good enough.

"Fair stock," he said.

Garland corrected, "Good stock."

They dismounted to settle under a overhanging boulder, dark shadows in the moonlight.

"They'll lose some weight by the time they reach my slaughter pens," said the buyer. He named his price.

Garland considered, nodded.

The buyer stripped off his moneybelt and counted the money out on the ground. "I took count as the herd came in," he said. "Two hundred and eleven head."

The buyer mounted, turned his bronc, asked, "When?"

Garland considered. "Two nights from now. Same place."

"All right."

Garland asked, "Would you buy some cows, fellow? Thin, but pretty-good stock. They've been on the trail for some time."

"I'll buy anything. The market is red-hot on the gold camps; they'd eat burro meat, they're that gaunt. Bring them on, fellow."

"Next time," said Garland.

The buyer rode off, his men taking charge of the herd. Big Circle riders settled beside Jeff Garland who counted the money into piles, placing it in front of each man. "Handier'n gold," he said. "Good old American foldin' paper."

They got their horses and headed north. They cut across the land, driving at an angle to the south-west.

When they reached the south bank of the Cuyama Pedro Martinez rode close. "Garland, these cattle—the next bunch we deliver—Box N cattle?"

"Who else around here has trail g'ant stock?"

Martinez' blue eyes were dim with thoughts. "Might be trouble," he volunteered.

Garland laughed quickly. His mouth clipped shut. "Might not be, too. We'll work it." Silence held him, pulling his face into stern lines. "There ain't that much room here, Martinez. There's no other way. We'll run them off, or draw them to a gunfight. We got to get rid of them, *sabe*?" His voice was low.

Martinez turned, looked at the Sierra Madres.

"Two ways, Jeff, two ways."

They came to the fork. Here one trail ran west, leading to the Santa Isabella Horseshoe—a trail that twisted through sagebrush and across alkali flats.

"I'm ridin' to the Horseshoe, men," Garland said.

Martinez said, "We'll ride straight in to the Big Circle."

Garland pulled to one side as they rode past. They came at a lope, the dust rising, and then the draw hid them. He turned his horse toward the Santa Isabella Horseshoe.

SEVEN

The wheels of the buckboard sang in the sandy dust. Don Alfredo drove slowly. The killing of Pinto White, back in Santa Ynez, had shattered the quiet Sunday.

"He is a killer," declared Maria. "He should be in jail!"

"Pinto White tried to kill him," said Linda quietly.

Maria looked at her sister, eyes flashing. "Are you in love with him, *hermana?* Is that why you stick up for him?" She did not wait for an answer. "I still say he is a killer—a *Tejas* killer."

Tia Tompita finally spoke. "Well, Don Alfredo, what are you going to do? Here you have a wild *Tejano* in our midst. Even now he has killed a man!"

Don Alfredo smiled slowly. "It seems to me, my

good woman, that your father, grandfather to my children, also killed a man or two in his lifetime."

"They were Indians, not white men!"

Don Alfredo said, "I beg to correct you. Walter Smith was no Indian, and your father killed him—a street-brawl, I believe, in Santa Maria. Ah, woman, you are like the rest of mankind. The generation— the young generation—is never as good as your generation to hear you speak. If I were in *Senor* Blanton's boots, I would have protected myself, too."

Don Miguel asked, "And our cattle, the ones on his range? You really intend to round them up and take them on our grass?"

"I send a crew over tomorrow morning."

Don Miguel scoffed. "Jeff Garland will not head them. You'll have to send somebody else as foreman."

Don Alfredo's dark face showed his thoughts. "Jeff Garland does not work for the Horseshoe any longer," he finally said. "I don't want this trouble, son. Jeff Garland pulled me into it against Cliff Blanton down in Santa Barbara the other night, but *Senor* Blanton has legal right to his land under our present law."

"*Yanqui* law!" snapped the youth. "Not Spanish law, damn, Yankee law!"

The aged don looked back at his son, marking the sternness of his young, handsome features. "My son, you cannot move against the law . . . and win. Think as your father thinks. We have range for our cattle."

"He runs on our range," reiterated Don Miguel.

Don Alfredo fell to silence and the bitterness of his thoughts. They came into the Horseshoe and the don and his son helped the women from the buckboard.

His riders had already come from Mass—those that had gone—and they loafed around the bunkhouse now, enjoying the warm sun. Don Alfredo squatted, his back against the wall, returned their nods, and went into silence.

Finally he said, "Jocko, you are the foreman, now."

The man looked up, a swarthy, heavy man of late middle-age. He asked, "What about Jeff Garland?"

"Garland is out, and you take his place."

The men exchanged glances. They were, for the most part, Mexicans who had ridden for him for years. A few were *Americanos* though.

Jocko shrugged. "You're the boss, *senor.*"

Don Alfredo settled lower, said, "Tomorrow morning take a crew—say five, six riders—and go to the Box N *rancho*. Get all Horseshoe cattle off the *Americano's* land and turn them west across his boundary on Dripping Springs. Work with his men, and do the job without trouble."

"Jeff Garland will fight," a man said slowly. "Him an' the Big Circle will run against this *Tejano*, I figure."

Don Alfredo went to the house, where *Tia* Tompita had some sugar rolls and coffee. Maria and Linda had evidently gone to their rooms; Don Miguel was playing cards in the bunk-house. He and the maiden aunt ate in the kitchen. The slim don got to his feet, went to the barn.

Here he saddled a big pinto. He turned the black-and-grey horse to the east, toward the hills. Cattle were grazing on the sidehills, his Horseshoe cattle.

From this high point, he saw a rider miles away, going toward the south. He could recognize him despite the distance; Don Miguel. The big palomino horse disclosed its rider's identity.

The youth had waited until his father had left, then he had saddled the palomino. He had thought this over for days—and he had made his decision.

The palomino was a young horse, and easy-riding. Two hours later, he loped into the high ranch of the Big Circle. Don Miguel stepped down. Leo Edwards, the black patch of his eye-guard conspicuous against his lighter skin, came around the corner, carrying his rifle.

"Howdy, Miguel," he said.

Don Miguel returned the salutation, scowling slightly. He turned and watched Gordo Garcia come from the high buckbrush bordering the wagon-road that led into the Big Circle *hacienda*. Garcia also carried a rifle.

He settle down, back against the house, and regarded the Horseshoe man through dark, flat eyes. "You look for Jeff Garland, huh? Well, he not here, Miguel."

"Where is he?"

"He get horse and ride out with his *hombres*. Right after we come out of town at afternoon." He regarded Leo Edwards with unblinking eyes. "Where did they go, Edwards?"

"Riding the Cuyama bog holes," replied Edwards. "Just what did you want to see Jeff about, Miguel?"

Don Miguel turned the palomino. "Jeff's through on the Horseshoe. The old man just made Jocko Jones range-boss. He didn't like what Jeff and Pinto White pulled down in Santa Ynez."

"That won't break Jeff Garland's heart, I don't figure. Fact is, us men can't see why he held that job anyway, him havin' this good range of his here."

"The old don?" asked Gordo Garcia. "He fight with thees Texan, Cleef Blanton, no?"

"The old man," said Miguel, "has run out; no, he won't fight. Come morning, he's sending Jocko and some Horseshoe men over to help the Box N get Horseshoe stock off Box N range."

Garcia thumbed his bottom lip slowly. "Jeff, heem fight," he said.

"I hope so," stated Don Miguel positively. "I'd be glad to see some man with enough spine to fight for his territory."

He touched the palomino and rode north, heading for the Cuyama river. He'd find Jeff Garland and talk to him, then swing back west to the Horseshoe *rancho*. Enrique Verde, the goat-herd, had his flock along the hills, while he dozed in the waning sun.

"You are lazy." stated Don Miguel.

Verde smiled. "Not lazy, *senor;* sensible. There is plenty of time in this world. Other men work themselves to the sod, driven by ambition and greed. There is the good air and some goat's milk and some clothes to keep out the chill, and a roof to turn the rain."

"You have seen Jeff Garland?"

"No, not today."

Don Miguel frowned, a gesture fitting his handsomely dark face. "Jeff Garland and his riders are to be along the Cuyama, riding the bog holes to see no cattle are mired."

"I have not seen them, *senor*. Only one man have I seen in the last hour, and he was your father, Don Alfredo."

"Where did he ride?"

Enrique Verde pointed toward the east. "He went

that way, *senor*, toward the *rancho* of the *gringo*."

Surely there was something amiss here. Edwards had told him Garland rode the bog-holes and this goat-herd had not seen Garland or a Big Circle rider. He would see Garland later.

Enrique Verde had been right; no Garland riders—nor Garland—patrolled this ground. And, what was more, none of them had been here this day, either. For Don Miguel heard the plaintive bawl of a bogged cow. He found the animal, sunken deep in the mud along the edge of the marsh.

Caked mud had dried on the animal's shaggy back. This animal had been in this bog for hours.

Don Miguel untied his *riata*, swung the loop cleanly a few times, and it landed around the bogged animal. He took dallies around his thick saddle-horn and the palomino braced, muscles bunched. Saddle-leather creaked and double-cinchas tightened; the animal was pulled from the bog.

Once on hard soil, the cow got to her feet. Don Miguel loosened the rope, letting it fall to the ground. The cow, angry and muddy, snorted, lowered her wide horns, lunged at the palomino. But the big horse, nimble and quick, jumped to one side. Don Miguel pummelled the cow across the rump with his double lariat and drove her into the hills.

Ungrateful fool, he thought. Pull her out of trouble, and she turns against you. He saw a rider loping west. He rode forward, his hand high. The rider was Don Alfredo.

"What do you do here, *hijo?*"

"I had nothing to do at the *rancho*," replied Don Miguel. "So I rode the bog-holes. A cow had gotten into the mud."

"Horseshoe cow?"

"No, Big Circle. There are few Horseshoe cows on this end of the range, it seems."

"I've noticed that," said Don Alfredo. "They must stay farther west; perhaps Jeff Garland turns them back toward our *hacienda*. But it is a long way to home, and dusk is rushing in on us."

EIGHT

The rest had put new life into Box N men and Box N horses. That morning at breakfast Cliff Blanton outlined his plans for the roundup. They would work the eastern end of the new range, pushing Horseshoe and Big Circle cattle east. Then, when this area was cleared, they would haze Box N stock on this land, corralling Big Circle cattle on the Point and holding them.

"What if Garland sends over riders?" asked Gene Creston.

"We'll work with them," assured Cliff.

Sis Johnson said, "They won't be over." He considered briefly. "They might, at that. Pinto White's kickin' the bucket might've brought a little brains into Jeff Garland's skull."

They were sitting broncs on the hoof-packed patio when Pete Burnett rode in—a big man on a big black gelding—and asked Cliff about the killing of Pinto White. Cliff told him the truth.

"Word came from the Santa Ynez marshal," said the ranger. "I haven't seen Jeff Garland yet to get his side of the picture. Pablo Morales is riding out this way today to survey your boundaries for you. He should be in sometime around noon chuck, I'd say. What do you intend to do with Horseshoe and Big Circle on your grass, Blanton?"

Cliff told him.

"If Garland don't send over riders, and if you corral his stock and hold them for pen-fees, he might move against you, Blanton. Glad to hear Don Alfredo was over to see you. This was a peaceful range until the last few days, Blanton."

Cliff said, stoney-faced, "They pushed me first, Burnett. Don Alfredo read his mistake, changed tactics. But if Garland puts pressure on me or my men, we're going against him, with guns or without, whichever is the most logical and what Garland wants."

Burnett said, "Fair enough, Cliff." He watched the Box N men ride east.

Maggie faced him, arms akimbo. "What will happen here, *Senor Rangero?*"

Pete Burnett's sandy eyes were grated sand. "There are two men here, tough men. The way they are leading, they'll clash. They have guns." The hardness ran out of his eyes. "That's the way it goes. I've seen it before, *senora,* too many times." He got to his feet. *"Gracias para el cafe."*

Riders were coming into the patio, and Burnett

stood beside his big black, watching them. They bunched and Don Alfredo rode to him, Jocko Jones with him. Pete Burnett told them that Cliff Blanton and his men had already ridden south. Jones turned and led the men at a lope toward Ventucopa Pass.

Burnett said, "I'm glad you're workin' with this *Tejano*, Don Alfredo. I was wonderin' about you for awhile."

Burnett stepped up, turned the black. "Some grow old and never get sense. Look at Jeff Garland. Smart enough, but smart along the wrong lines. Those daughters of yours, Don Alfredo. I saw them at the *fiesta*. They make a man mourn for his youth."

Don Alfredo sat his horse, watching the ranger ride out. Pete Burnett loped the black, strong in the saddle. He ran the horse south and east, heading for the upper reaches of South Fork and the Big Circle *hacienda*.

Two hours later, he came down the hill to where Enrique Verde ranged his goats.

The goat-herd recognized him and he squatted, watching the ranger ride up and stop.

"There will be trouble, Pete?"

Burnett nodded shortly: "It's already started, Enrique. When Pinto White was killed yesterday, the nail was driven in."

"I do not like this," declared the goat-herd suddenly. "Somebody, they will get the suspicious of me, and then we will shoot at each other."

Burnett stroked his thick nose. "What do you know about cattle?"

"Last night, in the darkness, I heard cattle, *Senor* Burnett. This morning I found their tracks down on the Cuyama, where they had crossed."

"But you didn't see anybody, huh?"

"I did not even find the herd. The sounds went away and I could not find them again."

Burnett scowled, reining in his black. Finally he said, "If you find anything, come to me in Santa Barbara." He shoved back his hat, scratched his red thatch. "I'll be on MacPherson mountain, Enrique, camped up by Don Cabezas Spring if you need me."

The sun was past noon when Pete Burnett rode into the Big Circle *rancho*. Garland and his riders were filing out of the bunk-house. When he saw the ranger, Jeff Garland said, shortly, "Step down, Burnett, and rest your horse."

Despite Garland's hospitality, his eyes were the colour of chipped onyx. Pete Burnett followed the *ranchero* into the cook-shack where Garland himself filled the ranger's plate with boiled beef and spuds.

Garland waited, cold and silent. Burnett said, "You're walkin' into it, Garland."

"Your opinion, sir."

Burnett looked at Jeff Garland. "Those are Texas men, Garland, and they've seen guns light the night. What's more, they're in the right. Funny thing, Garland. The man armed with the right, although he doesn't look as strong, almost always wins."

"I don't think they're right," said Garland.

"You're buckin' California law, fellow."

Garland shoved back his chair. "To hell with the law, Burnett. We've got too much of it now; somebody should rebel against it. I'm runnin' my stock on Box N range; they stay there. I have to expand, not grow smaller. If that damn' *gringo* had any brains, he'd sell to me. This way, I'll take his land, free."

Silence grew.

Garland said, "Well?"

Burnett changed his subject. "The Santa Ynez marshal told me about Pinto White's death. I talked with Cliff Blanton. He claims self-defence. Was it self-defence?"

Garland considered: "Yes, it was."

Burnett let his shoulders slack slightly. Garland saw this, and thought the man had held a touch of fear; that this had suddenly left him. Had he known that Burnett was tired instead, he would not have made his sudden error on the man's character.

"What's Blanton doin' now?"

Burnett said, "He and his men are gathering your stock. Don Alfredo and Jocko Jones and some Horseshoe men rode in when I was there. They came to gather Horseshoe cattle."

Garland smiled. "Don Alfredo booted me, yesterday."

Burnett finished eating. "Then you won't change your mind, huh? Hell, Garland, sooner or later, if there's any shootin', some evidence will point to you. They'll hang you down on the beach below Santa Barbara."

"When they hang me," said Garland huskily, "you can be damned sure of this, Burnett: there'll be some dead *Tejanos,* and Cliff Blanton will be one of them."

Garland went out. Burnett shoved back his plate and went to the bunkhouse. He slept about two hours. When he awoke, the sun was falling lower. He got his black and rode out, saying to the *mozo,* "Long ride to Santa Barbara, *amigo.*"

A rider sat a horse in the sandstones. Pete Burnett lifted his flat black hat. "How do you do, *Senorita* Maria?"

Maria was riding side-saddle, her dark skirt spilled

across her and showing only her feet with their hand-stamped riding-boots and silver-inlaid spurs. She said, "Hello, Mr Ranger."

Burnett pulled in, said, "You shouldn't ride these hills alone, *senorita.*"

Maria called, "Linda," and Linda rode over the ridge, and smiled.

"Everywhere she goes, *Senor* Ranger, she finds a man."

They were pretty, these two: One with a dark, brittle quickness, the other with a dark, slow deliberateness. There was over twenty years between them and himself, and for once he was dissatisfied with time.

"I was telling Maria, *Senorita* Linda, that she should not ride this wilderness area, and now I say the same to you."

"The *Tejano*?" asked Maria quickly. Linda said, "*Senor* Blanton is a gentleman, Maria; do not talk like that." Her voice was a little rough.

"She is in love with the *Tejano*," said Maria. "He has spoken two or three words to her, and she dreams of him."

Linda said, angrily, "How you talk!"

Pete Burnett tactfully changed the subject. "I saw your father at the Box N, and I am glad he is going to work with Cliff Blanton, instead of against." He had his gaze flatly on Maria. "You have some influence, I would say, with Jeff Garland. Why don't you talk him into working with your father and Blanton."

Maria lifted her tanned small hand, grabbed the wind. "I cannot hold that," she said suggestively. She added, "And maybe I do not want to, do not care to." She shrugged quickly. "What is Jeff Garland to me? Nothing, *senor.l* A man to talk with, to flirt slyly with . . . Men are not smart when a pretty woman smiles at them."

Pete Burnett smiled. The ageless pattern was repeating itself again. "The *senorita* has made a great discovery," he said. "But she must remember that other women have discovered the same, and that some men have been touched with it and become immune. Good day, *amigas*."

NINE

Jeff Garland sat with his back against a boulder, heavy Pedro Martinez squatting beside him, tie-down strings of his holster dangling.

"They've got a few head," murmured Garland. He handed the field-glasses to his *segundo,* who focused them on the riders below that marked the broad expanse of the Cuyama valley.

Martinez lowered the glasses. "Horseshoe riders are shovin' their day's gather over west to the Horseshoe range. They're holdin' your Big Circle herd in that box canyon, I guess. Over behind them, grazing on the range they've already worked, they aim to hold Box N stock."

Garland nodded briefly. "Looks that way to me, too."

Martinez settled back, closing his eyes, sucking on his *cigaro*. Garland sat cross-legged, watching this panorama below, and building a plan to fit into its structure.

The Horseshoe had found about two hundred or so odd head on Box N grass. These were now going west; riders would haze them across Dripping Springs deadline and let them run free on Horseshoe grass. Box N men were taking his Big Circle cattle out of the box canyon and pushing them toward the Point. They got them in the narrow neck that jutted out into the river, and then they closed the barrier that held them there.

Again, Garland's gaze went to the east. Box N cattle were spreading out across that *rancho's* grazing land.

There would be about a week's work ridding the Box N range of Horseshoe and Big Circle cattle. Garland was sleepy and tired; night rides had sapped him. He prodded Martinez awake and said, "All right, Pedro, let's find saddles and get out of here."

Martinez came up, stocky in the dusk. "When do we hit them—and where do we hit?" he wanted to know.

Garland's smile was bleak. "Ol' Pedro," he murmured, "always up an at 'em . . . Tomorrow there'll be a buyer north in the San Luis Obispo hills. Tomorrow night, the stage will be set." He had built his plan and now he outlined it. As he talked, he watched the Mexican's dark face, seeking the man's reaction to various points. The Mexican frowned.

"I would not do it that way, Jeff." Pedro Martinez spoke in quick Spanish. Garland considered, balancing his plan against the red-headed Mexican's. There was danger in both, but his seemed the more logical. The Mexican dropped his thick shoulders and murmured, "You are the boss, Jeff." He looked across the hills. "There is that goat-herd, Enrique Verde."

Garland looked at the small campfire there under the rocks. "Let's talk to him." Verde squatted beside the small fire warming a *tortilla* in a pan. His goats were bedded down, settled for the night under the rim of the hill. His dog came out, barking, and he ordered him back. They exchanged greetings.

"Stay off Big Circle range," Garland said suddenly.

Verde said, "But *Senor* Garland, I have paid you—"

"Just stay off, from now on," ordered Garland.

"I am on Box N range," said Verde.

"At the present, yes. But me, I don't figure the Box N will be in business long. This is no country for goats. Goats would range better on the other side of Ventucopa Pass, in the grass of the Ojai Valley."

They rode on. A mile or so farther, Pedro Martinez said, "He is harmless, Jeff. An' ol' loco man an' his crazy dog an' stinkin' goats. Maybe it's the Irish in me, but I'm not Mex enough to like a goat."

Garland shook his head. "He's got eyes, Pedro, an' he ranges this country wide. He might see something; if he does, he's dead."

They loped into the Big Circle, left their broncs with the *mozo*. Garland inquired about Pete Burnett; the ranger had ridden back toward Santa Barbara. Garland saw no danger. Riders were coming in, drifting across the hills. This *rancho* with the whale-oil lamps, set in the windows, was a magnet, promising warmth and hot grub for saddle-tired men.

That evening, Don Miguel rode in.

Garland was in his office, a pinelog building set aside. He did not get to his feet. "Take a chair," he said.

Don Miguel said, "I was here yesterday, and you were gone." The youth was silent for some time, his dark face showing conflicting thoughts. "You are to fight the Box N, *no es verdad*, Jeff Garland?"

Garland nodded.

"My father has drawn back," said the youth. He got to his feet, walked to the window. Garland was quiet, his face graven. Don Miguel turned, hands behind his back. Garland didn't like him. He was a dandy, an only son; Don Alfredo should have whaled him hard, sometime in his boyhood. Garland thought, *I can use him, though. Don Alfredo has pulled out on me, showing the wrong feather—I might be able to break him with this son of his* . . . So he said, quietly, "You want to ride with me, is that it, Don Miguel."

"I don't run," said the youth, "and I cannot fight him alone."

Garland played his cards slowly. "But if Don Alfredo finds out you work with me—He's proud, Miguel."

"I only ask to help you, Garland. I don't ask you to pass criticism on my father, or his attitude toward me."

"All right, Miguel. Be here tomorrow night, right at sundown." He added, "Don't forget your gun, either."

"I am no fool, *Senor* Garland."

Garland got to his feet, his voice hearty. "You'll do, Miguel, you'll do."

Don Miguel went out and Garland, standing there, heard the rattle of the dandy's horse-hoofs, heading out into the night. Pedro Martinez came in and

Garland told him about their conversation. Pedro Martinez settled on his haunches laughing, and then he sobered.

"But if that punk gets wounded—or killed—I don't know about it, Garland. Don Alfredo will go wild, in that case—he'll move against the Big Circle with his men."

Garland said, "Pedro, use your head. We drive out this *Tejano;* we still have the Santa Isabella Horseshoe left. This way, we lead Don Alfredo, making him bring the war to us, and if it did get into court—"

Martinez nodded, blue eyes sharp.

Next morning, three strangers rode into the *patio*. Jeff Garland left the mess-hall, reading their characters as he walked up to them.

One of them said, "We were talkin' with a cow-buyer up at Livermore. He allowed as if there was a ridin' job down here. The pay, he said, is a hundred an' fifty *pesos* a month."

The average pay for a cowhand was thirty *pesos*. Garland looked at them, reading them as renegades, and he looked at their guns, pouched and tied.

"The buyer was wrong," he said.

They made to turn. "Sorry," the man murmured.

Jeff Garland's next words stopped them. The pay isn't one-fifty; it's two hundred. And not by the month, by every two weeks. You start today. Light and rest and eat."

They rode to the barn.

Pedro Martinez came out of the tool-shed carrying a rifle. "Brands from three sections on those horses, Jeff," he murmured. "The Rockin' Six, Arizona territory; the Slash Bar Nine, New Mexico Territory: the Rafter X, from Nevada."

Garland looked at the rifle. He ran a slow gaze toward the tool-shed. From there, hidden, had trouble started, Martinez could have stopped it, his rifle talking fast and straight. "You take no chances," murmured Garland.

"I'm almost fifty years old," said Pedro Martinez. His blue eyes were sharp again, dead, emotionless. "If I took chances, there'd be a grave back yonder somewhere, an' Pedro Martinez would be in it . . . "

The *mozo* had their horses saddled. Garland's spurs hit a long lope. A pace behind, Pedro Martinez sat a solid saddle, his black moving ahead.

They came in at dusk.

While Martinez unsaddled their broncs, putting their hulls on fresh horses, Garland went to the bunkhouse. Evening chuck was over and the men lounged on bunks or played cards. Garland said, sharply, "We ride in half an hour. Get ready." He looked at the three new riders, "You get an early start, fellows."

"We're on your payroll," said one.

Garland turned and went towards the cook-shack. Pedro Martinez came up with, "We got fresh horses, Jeff," and Garland nodded and asked, "Black horses?"

"Blacks," agreed Martinez. The cook dished out some grub. They ate unhurriedly, without talk; finally Martinez spoke. "Don Miguel just rode in, Jeff." He added, "I gave him a fresh horse. He was on that long-legged palomino. Gawd, a man could see that horse a mile away on a dark night."

"What did he have to say?"

"Don Alfredo and his Horseshoe riders are staying at the Box N until the roundup is over. That means, Jeff, there'll be no more guns than those of the Box N. They have us outnumbered a little."

"We'll have the big boost, though. We'll have surprise on our side."

They finished eating, went outside, found stirrups. The men were grouped around the patio, sitting idle horses, *cigaros* and cigarettes glowing. They gathered around Martinez and Jeff Garland, seemingly indifferent to the task ahead.

Garland spoke rapidly. "Gordo, you got the dynamite!"

"*Si, senor*. Three sticks."

Garland ran a hard glance over them. He asked how many had had experience with powder; four volunteered. He selected three of these and Gordo gave them each a stick of dynamite.

"They'll expect us to hit for our Big Circle cattle," said Garland. "All right, we will. You three with the dynamite, that's your job. Martinez will ride with you; he's boss, his word goes."

These men would sneak in on the Point and let the dynamite roar in the willows and brush. This would scare the Big Circle cattle penned there into the stampede. And, while the Box N—and the Horseshoe riders, too—were trying to stop this, the rest of the Big Circle men would cut the Box N herd, shove the cows across the river and into the San Luis Obispo hills where the buyer waited.

Garland said, "Let's ride." Don Miguel came up to him. "You ride close to me, Miguel."

"*Si, senor*."

TEN

The Box N men, aided by Horseshoe riders, hazed the last of the Big Circle cattle in on the Point, and Cliff Blanton had his riders put up the barricade, penning the Garland cattle on the point. He rode to the *hacienda*.

He leaned from saddle. "Maggie," he called.

Maggie came to the door. Cliff told her that the Horseshoe men were staying till the roundup was finished, and one of Don Alfredo's men would help her. "He used to be a cook."

"Humph," she said, and went back inside.

Cliff smiled, turning his horse. Sis Johnson, shivering a little, unsaddled his bronc. "Cold, just as soon as the sun goes down."

Cliff nodded. Gene Creston rode up, stud lathered, and said, "We swing out guards tonight, I reckon."

Again, Cliff nodded.

Maggie beat on the steel with a spoon. All of the Horseshoe men had not gone with Don Alfredo to haze the herd on Horseshoe territory. They trooped into the mess-shack, found places, turned over their plates and went to work. Shorty Nolan said to Cliff, "There might be trouble, Cliff."

"There might be," murmured Cliff. They went outside into the darkness. He and Shorty hunkered beside the bunkhouse, backs to the warm adobe, and watched the men go into the building. Sis Johnson, young face tired, hunkered, said, "Well, we did some work today, huh?"

"More to do," grunted Shorty.

"Doesn't a man ever catch up?" asked Sis, grinning. "Is it this way all his life? Does he always have work to do?"

"If he didn't work," philosophied Shorty, "he'd think too much. Then he'd get disgusted and hang hisself."

Sis grinned, said to Cliff: "He's a cheerful ol' saddle-blanket." He looked at the riders coming into the yard. "Here comes the Horseshoe men back."

Don Alfredo came down, leaving his reins dragging. He settled beside Cliff, and they drew up their nightguard list.

Cliff and the old don talked, sitting in the shadows. An hour went by; then another. Cliff said, "I'm going to look around a little, Don Alfredo, before I hit the sougans."

The old man nodded.

Cliff got his night-horse, a dark bay gelding. The Big Circle cattle on the Point suddenly took up a new bawling, and Cliff thought he detected a note of fear in the sound. He reined in, scowling, then decided that one of the new night-guards had unexpectedly ridden on some cattle. He started forward as the dynamite exploded.

A red, ugly flare, accompanied by a smashing noise, rocked skyward at the far end of the point, just along the water-line. Cliff's horse was rearing, fighting the bit, as the red flame, illuminating the country clearly, suddenly died. Already cattle were moving, fear deep in them. Then another flare, great as the first, rocked the country and, hard on its explosion, came another.

Cattle were stampeding from the Point. Cliff heard the sodden smash of six-shooters, coming hard through the roar of hoofs. Somewhere timber smashed; he knew the barrier had popped. Men were hollering back at the Box N *hacienda*. He swung west, skirting the herd of mad Big Circle stock.

They came thundering by, slobber hanging from their jaws. Cows, calves, steers, bulls. A rider came by, sweeping hard against the night and Cliff hollered, "Cliff Blanton talking! Box N man."

The rider drew down, swung close "They dynamited the damn' herd, Cliff! Swum the river, got on the point, an' busted loose with powder. We had a gun-ruckus—there's a Horseshoe man down back yonder. What'll we do with these cattle?"

"Let 'em run," snapped Cliff. "Don Alfredo and the boys at the house will trail them down! Lead me to the spot, Gene!"

Gene Creston laid home spurs, and they loped ahead. All was quiet now on the point. Cliff's horse shied suddenly: a steer lay dead. Here was a calf, fore-legs broken, bawling plaintively in the night. Sympathy tugged at Cliff and mingled with it was a hard anger.

"Garland's behind this," growled Gene Creston.

Cliff swung his horse around, stood still. Gunfire was crackling, talking, somewhere to the south. The sound registered, then died; the sounds of the running mad herd killing the minor sound.

Probably usin' powder to turn that stampedin' herd," hollered Gene Creston.

Cliff nodded. Sometimes, if you shoot the leaders, piling them up, a stampede can be broken, for then the stock starts to mill. A horse ran by, stirrups flapping, and Gene Creston caught his hackamore rope, stopping him. Cliff saw that he was a Horseshoe horse and he remembered that a Santa Isabella rider named Concho had taken him out on night-guard.

"Concho," he hollered.

The answer came, "*Aqui, senor*. Here I am, een these weellows."

Concho sat with his back against the bank. He had not been shot. A rock had blasted against his leg, and his leg had a hole in it.

"You recognize any of them raiders?" asked Cliff.

Concho shook his dark head, said painfully, "That I could not do, *senor*. I saw one on hees horse, but could not make out his face. They swam across the reever, I guess, planted their powder, then swam back to the other side."

Cliff looked across the Cuyama . Water gurgled and sucked against the bank; he could not see the other shore. The raiders had made good their escape. He could hear no sounds of running cattle. Evidently Don Alfredo and his riders had checked the stampede.

"You stay here, Concho. Gene, you stay with him. I'll get somebody with a lantern and we'll get a team on a rig to take you into the *hacienda*."

Cliff rode at a lope, a hardness in him. Jeff Garland had made the first move—a surprise move. Cliff knew now the man's character was what he had suspected: tough, giving no quarter, asking none. Garland's surprise move had hit hard, clean, concise—though Cliff could not see much sense in it. Garland had dynamited his own cattle; he'd run them south. Now Don Alfredo and his men had them corralled, and they were still on Box N land. Had Garland expected them to run all the way to his Big Circle grass?

And his riders, after dynamiting the cattle, had headed back across the Cuyama. Why hadn't he sent over more riders and made a fight out of it to get his cattle back? These and other thoughts puzzled Cliff.

Cattle were coming toward him, heading back toward the Point. Cliff rode to one side, and Don Alfredo rode up, curbing his horse hard. He said, shortly, "He played a fast game, Blanton. While most of us worked on this herd, he and his men hit your cattle."

Cliff asked, "What good would that do him?"

"They scattered them," said the don. "There was some shooting, too. One of your men is hurt. He's back of the herd—"

Cliff waited no longer. Shorty Nolan had his weight on one stirrup, his horse close to the wounded man's and Cliff saw that Sis Johnson rode doubled in saddle.

Shorty Nolan was swearing suddenly, swearing terribly. Cliff had never heard his wiry range-boss swear like that. "Somebody shot him through the belly, right below the ribs. The bullet went straight through. I'll kill that man, Cliff."

"If I don't beat you to him," growled Cliff. "You see who shot you, Sis?"

Sis Johnson spoke slowly. "Too dark, Cliff. They

249

came fast . . . when the dynamite exploded."

"He's lost a lot of blood," said Shorty Nolan. "I got my undershirt tied around his belly. A Horseshoe man rode for Santa Ynez. Don Alfredo said there was a *medico* there. We've got to get him to bed."

"Why would they hit my herd?" asked Cliff.

"Just a damn nuisance stampede," growled Shorty. "Want to make some hell an' work for us! We oughta ride over to the Big Circle an' take that joint down in sections—an' then burn it!"

Cliff grinned. "I'd like to do just that, Shorty, but we can't. Pete Burnett's the law here; we ain't. And if we aim to stay here, we got to get off on the right foot."

They could not ride faster than a walk. The Big Circle cattle, their run gone, plodded through the night. Don Alfredo came up, said, "We put them on the Point again, *no es verdad*?"

Cliff nodded. "Only place we can hold them, *senor*. Double the guard, 'though I hardly think they'll come back again tonight."

Cliff and Shorty, steadying Sis Johnson between them, rode to the bunkhouse. Word had gone ahead and Maggie had towels and hot-water ready. Sis Johnson put his arm around her and kissed her rough cheek. She had tears in her eyes.

"We'll pull through, Maggie," promised the youth.

The ancient eyes glistened. *"Si senor,* God will help us. *Dios* is good to us poor foolish mortals. Here, let me help you, *senor* Cliff."

They undressed the youth and got him on the bed, his wound lying dark and exposed. With Cliff and Shorty assisting, Maggie went to work with the warm water and a clean cloth. Shorty had been right: the bullet had gone straight through. Sis Johnson lay with his eyes closed, chest rising to his rapid breathing. Cliff felt his pulse. His heart was wild and Cliff felt a touch of naked fear.

They stood there, two silent men, watching the aged woman work. She knew her business, for she had seen similar incidents before. She bound the wounds, the linens clean across Sis Johnson's belly, and then she put a light blanket over him. He opened his eyes. "*Gracias, senora*," he murmured.

"I will stay with you, my son," she said.

Cliff and Shorty went outside into the dark night. Riders were moving across the night, and cattle bawled, low and heavy. But the thing was settling down. Now a rider came in, called, "Blanton."

"Here," said Cliff.

The man stepped down, hunkered. "I was over on the south range. We talked this over, the men an' me who were out there, an' Panco Carlos says he is sure he hit one of the raiders."

"Pete Burnett will check the Big Circle for us," said Cliff.

Shorty asked, "What will we do, Cliff?

Cliff was silent for ten seconds. "We can't move against the Big Circle, Shorty, unless we have evidence. So far, we haven't got any; nothing we know would hold up in court."

Shorty tapped his holster suggestively. "There's the law on the grass, Cliff." His tone was savage.

Cliff said, almost mildly, "What if we rode against the Big Circle? We'd lose men; too many men. Grass and cattle—yes, and a man's principles—are not worth that many deaths. We'll solve this, Shorty. But don't let anger run you into anything."

Shorty went into the bunk-house, checking on Sis

Johnson. He came out now, settled beside Cliff, and said, very quietly, "He's dead, Cliff, he's dead."

Cliff was stony-faced. He heard Maggie crying softly, a sound that hammered against him, putting steel into him.

He said, "They'll pay, Shorty."

ELEVEN

Ahead, a gun talked, its flame stabbing darkness, Don Miguel, curbing his rearing horse, felt a pang of unrest, the pull of fear. A rider came by, hard on his stirrups. He put the gun on him, lowered it.

"Get these cattle movin', fellow!"

Don Miguel recognized Jeff Garland. "What the hell went wrong, Garland?"

Garland's voice was savage. "They've staked guards out with this herd, fellow; we never expected that!" He twisted in leather. Far to the north, another roar—the second flash of exploding dynamite—smashed across the night. "There'll be another shot! There it is!"

Cattle were moving in the darkness. Box N cattle, dead on the run. Garland Big Circle riders were yipping, and more gun-talk came. A man swept by and Jeff Garland's gun was talking, cutting the night. Don Miguel saw the man fall, slip from horse and hit the prairie sod. And Jeff Garland was spurring ahead, Don Miguel on his hoofs.

"You knocked that man out of saddle," said the dandy.

Garland turned, snarled: "What of it, Miguel! This is war, man—there's no quarter! They kill you—or you kill them! Swing these cattle, we're on our way!"

Don Miguel turned, circled the herd. Hoofs were pounding earth and horns clashing as the Texas long-horns took the trail. They had work ahead, and they had best do it as fast as possible. For if the moon came up . . . He felt a little sick.

He thought, *I bargained for this. I got it.* They had the cows on the lope, going down into a steep declivity. Here a creek boiled down from Peak Mountain, and they got the cattle into this water. Lassoes pounded hard across bony backs. Big Jeff Garland rode back, dark in the night.

"Run 'em harder," he said. "They don't even know we got off with this herd. They prob'ly figure we just aimed to stampede the big herd, not chisel this small bunch out of it an' steal 'em.

"How many head we got?" asked Don Miguel.

"Aroun' two hundred, I'd reckon. We'll hit the Cuyama in five-, six miles—hand tight, *muchachito*! Your voice don't sound none too tough. Well, after you do this a couple of times, you'll toughen down."

They came to the Cuyama, and the leaders took the water. They were swimming then, a dark sea of backs against the lighter backdrop of the river. He had a powerful horse that knew how to swim. The horse swam high, taking long strokes. He heard gravel ring under the shod hoofs, and the horse pulled himself out of the water.

This was a long, wide draw that twisted for miles into the San Luis Obispo hills. Here on this gravel cattle left no tracks, therefore trailing would be impossible. Garland rode up and asked, "You seen anything of Pedro Martinez, Don Miguel, or of the men who went on the Point with the dynamite?"

Don Miguel said he hadn't seen them. "Sure hope nothing went wrong back on the Point," said Garland suddenly.

Don Miguel knew what the Big Circle men meant. If one or more were killed, the body would identify the raiders as Big Circle men. And if Pete Burnett could prove anything—

"Riders coming," said Don Miguel.

Minutes later, three riders came out of the darkness; Pedro Martinez and two of the volunteers. The third man was tied across his horse, looking like a huge sack filled with grain.

Garland jabbed a thumb at the man across the saddle. "Gordo?" he asked.

Martinez snarled, "Who t'hell would it be but Garcia—the rest of us are here."

Garland lifted his horse with spurs, turned him. "Herd deep in the hills by now. They didn't even know we run any off, I guess. Night too dark an' they figured we just aimed to stampede them. You did wise by taking Garcia's body with you."

"I'm no fool," growled Martinez.

They rode at a lope, one man beating the horse that carried the dead cow-thief. Don Miguel was silent, nursing his thoughts. Martinez was on edge, sharp with anger. Don Miguel thought, suddenly, of his bed, back at the Horseshoe *hacienda*. This had happened too suddenly, too sharply. An hour ago, Gordo Garcia had been alive—a fat, big-bellied Mexican, dark-eyed and smiling. Now his corpse hung across a saddle, tied fast by ropes around ankles and wrists.

If Jeff Garland could steal Box N cattle and sell them, he could steal Horseshoe cattle even easier, for great sections of the Horseshoe range were seldom ridden over, and a Horseshoe brand could be easily run ino the Big Circle.

The moon was up now, dappling the earth. Don Miguel figured they were three hours away from the Box N. A man came riding back. "Garland, we're almost there," he said.

Garland said, 'You boys push the drags," and he loped off, Pedro Martinez with him. They rode for a couple more miles, and then word came back. The cattle were bunched; the buyer rode around then, talking with Garland. Don Miguel could not see him clearly because his hat shaded his face.

Garland and the buyer drew rein and talked for ten minutes. Finally, Miguel saw money change hands. The buyer waved his men in, gave brittle instructions. His riders started the tired cattle north.

Big Circle men rode in, Don Miguel with them. They went down and squatted, with Garland splitting the money. Don Miguel shook his head. "I don't want any, *senor,*" he said.

They looked at him, doubting their ears.

"You're not meanin' that?" asked Garland.

The dandy said, angrily, "You have ears, *senor*; you can hear." Somebody said, "Too good to pack cow-thief money, huh?" and a man laughed. Don Miguel went up to him, reached up and grabbed the man by the shirt, twisting the cloth and pulling him forward. Jeff Garland broke it up.

"You two straighten out!" His forearm pounded down, breaking Miguel's grip.

"All right, Miguel, if you won't take a cut, so much the more for us."

Pedro Martinez asked, "What about Gordo?"

The tension was broken. Men settled back, taking their hands from their guns; Jeff Garland looked up at the overhang of the cutback, some fifteen feet overhead. He studied it carefully, eyes alert and eyes contemplative.

"Right here," he said.

They untied the dead man, placed him on his back, putting his pistol across his chest.

Garland said, "Four of you go around and get on top. Get your boots braced and push that overhang down."

The Big Circle men and Don Miguel drew back, leaving the body alone. The riders gained the top and put their bootheels into the sod, pushing. The earth offered resistance; they broke this, the overhang started sliding down. Tons of earth came down slowly, sighing a little, and it settled over the dead man who lay there. It covered him, buried him deep, hid him forever.

They got their broncs and went up. Don Miguel was a little pale. Death, to him, had been far away; he was still young, and his blood was hot. Now, it was close; he too, would die someday.

Jeff Garland rode close. "Well, Don Miguel, what's the thoughts?"

"The *gringo*," replied the dandy. "He is the one that counts. Far better than he should be buried back there than simple Gordo."

Garland grinned. "Luck, that's all. Luck determines it all. Maybe luck'll turn against Blanton. Well, you've stolen your first cow, huh?"

"But not my last."

Garland considered that, face grave. He had glimpsed this change in Don Miguel, had caught its significance.

Up till now, he had been Jeff Garland's superior, for he was Don Alfredo's son, and Don Alfredo had hired Garland as Horseshoe range-boss. But now, Garland was not working for the Horseshoe; a de la Mesa was not his boss, now. Don Miguel knew he could never back out now. For if he did—or if he tried—Garland would kill him.

"There'll be more," said Garland.

They hit the Cuyama below the bogs where the river ran narrow but deep. They came out into the false-dawn, grouped close and with wet saddles. Dawn found them deep into the Sierra Madres. The light came with brightness, showing the fresh snow on McPherson and Peak mountains.

They reached Swallow Fork. Don Miguel pulled to one side, the Big Circle riders going by to the south. Pedro Martinez and Jeff Garland pulled in, too.

"When?" asked Don Miguel.

Garland considered. "We'll let you know."

"Don't forget to keep your mouth closed," said Pedro Martinez.

Don Miguel was angry. 'Damn you, man! Who could I talk to, what good would it do? My father would kill me—his son, a cowthief! I've picked my way, and don't shove me, you illegitimate son of an Irishman!"

Martinez's face pulled down, his hand went to his gun. Jeff Garland cut in with, "You got a sharp tongue, Miguel. Pedro, he's just talkin'."

Don Miguel turned, taking a trail to the Horseshoe. He remembered he was riding a Big Circle mount. The hour was early, maybe nobody would see him ride in. But he was mistaken.

Linda saw him ride into the barn. She stood beside her window and watched, and her dark eyes were thoughtful.

TWELVE

Dawn found Cliff Blanton and Shorty Nolan riding the south range and checking the Box N cattle. "There are some missin'," said Shorty. "I'd say about two hundred head."

"Might be back in the hills," said Cliff.

"Who in his right mind would steal trailga'nt cows, Cliff? And where would they take them?"

"We must be wrong," said Cliff.

They took a tally-count of the Box N cows. They had about eighteen hundred head grazing on the salt grass. But Shorty was right. They were about two hundred head short.

"I savvy the deal now," murmured Cliff.

Shorty stabbed a glance at him. "Yeah?"

"First, they jumped their herd—down on the Point.

That was to make us believe they'd come to get back their own cattle. And during the ruckus and the excitement, they got off with some of our stock. The gold camps are in need of beef bad. By now, them cows are probably headin' north toward 'Frisco."

They looked for tracks, but the ground was cut up with hoof-prints

Cliff drew in, thoughtful. Anger beat against him. "Too many creeks to run them down and hide their hoof-prints."

"There's the Mex goat-herd," murmured Shorty.

Enrique Verde had his goats foraging on a sunlit sidehill. "There was noise last night," he said, "and it scared my goats."

Cliff grinned, told him about the gun-ruckus. He saw the dark Latin face grow quiet, stern. "The senor rangero—thees Pete Burnett—he should be told of this, no?"

Cliff nodded.

"He is tough man," grunted Enrique Verde.

They had Horseshoe and Box N men out, working the range under the direction of Don Alfredo and Jocko Jones. There would be no rest from now on here on the Box N. Cliff Blanton was quiet, deep in saddle. Back yonder, at the *hacienda*, lay Sis Johnson, limp on a table, cold and silent. If he could find out who had killed Sis, he would kill that man.

The *medico*'s buckboard stood in the *patio* when they came to the *hacienda*. They went into the adobe house where Concho, the Horseshoe rider, lay on the bed.

The doctor had just finished with his job. "He will come through all right," he told Cliff. "But he had best stay off his leg for some days. Four days, at least."

"We'll keep him in bed," Cliff promised.

"The other man?" asked the doctor. "Did he die?"

Cliff nodded. "He is in the next room."

The doctor sighed and started washing his hands in the basin of hot water brought in by Maggie. "My unpleasant duties require that I be the local undertaker too. I suppose you will want to bury him from the Mission?"

"He'd like that," said Shorty Nolan. He added, "He was a fine young man." He did not speak again, for his throat was too husky.

"The funeral had best be day after tomorrow," said the doctor. "I shall take his body into town with me, and I shall be back in three days to look at Concho." "Now, if you will help me load the body?"

They wrapped Sis Johnson's body firmly in a heavy blanket and carried him out and laid him on a hair-mattress on the floor of the buggy. The doctor climbed into the seat and took his whip from its socket. "There will be great need for my services on this range," he said slowly. "I had hopes, along with the rest of our people, that peace would continue, *Senor* Blanton."

"Talk to Jeff Garland, doctor. Tell him to call off his wolves, and there'll be peace. But he has gone too far now. That boy in there came with us from the Pocos. When I find out who killed him, I'm killing that man."

Don Alfredo rode into the *patio*. He looked at Cliff, then at the doctor's retreating buggy. He asked, "And how is Concho?"

Cliff told him.

The Don said, "Me and my men put over three hundred head of our cattle across Dripping Springs this morning. Another two days, and your range should be

263

clear of Horseshoe cattle."

"Many Big Circle cows?"

"About four hundred head, I guess. We put them on the Point. Grass is growing thin, there, though."

Cliff considered. "Only logical place we can hold them, Don Alfredo." He roped a fresh horse and he and the Don rode across the sweep of the river bottom, heading toward the men who were working cattle against the rise of the foothills.

They split up, with Don Alfredo riding to the west. Cliff took the back circle, running deep into the Sierra Madres. Cattle were wild, for the dynamite and the night of excitement, of gun-flares, had quickened them, making them spooky. Cliff rode to head them off. A herd was gathering on the alkali flat at the foot of Tongue Gorge. A year from now his cows would be this sleek, this pretty. That warmed him a little.

He turned some cattle north, noticing the Horseshoe iron on their ribs. A rider was coming toward him, sliding his horse down a declivity.

Pete Burnett said, "You had trouble last night, Blanton?" and his eyes were pinsharp.

Cliff told him what had happened.

"That goat-herd, Enrique Verde, told me they used dynamite against you. I was down in Santa Ynez when the doctor came back with Johnson's body. Did you actually recognize them?"

"No," said Cliff.

The California *rangero* stroked his blocky jaw idly. "You ain't got a shred of evidence against Garland, then. Nothing that will stand up in court. What else do you know?"

Cliff told him that one of the raiders had been dropped from horse, back there on the Point. Burnett nodded sombrely, storing this in his mind.

"We saw a mess of blood on the sand, where a man had lain. But they evidently had toted him off so we couldn't find the body. Garland's got brains; he uses them."

"That's something, though," admitted Pete Burnett.

The *rangero* swung his horse, riding away. He drew up, turned, said, "Listen, Cliff. That goat-herd—Enrique Verde—he's been payin' Garland for lettin' his goats run on this graze. Of course, it's your grass, now. But Garland don't figure so, he's ordered Verde to leave, *sabe*? Get off *your* range, saying he'd own it soon."

Cliff grinned. "Where do I fit in, Pete?"

Burnett smiled, rubbing his whiskers. "I sorta like that cuss, Cliff. 'Sides, he's a square fellow. Keep an eye on him for me, will you?"

Cliff nodded.

Pete Burnett lifted his hand, loped toward the north. Cliff went back to working cattle. An hour later, he saw a rider come from he west, from the Horseshoe. It was Maria, riding side saddle on a calico horse.

"My father?" she asked. "Where is he?"

Cliff waved a hand toward a rider below them. "That's him down there, miss."

She said, "Oh," and turned the calico. Cliff rode close, said, "I'll go with you. The day is almost done. You've ridden a long ways, *senorita*."

Her eyes were dark, quiet. She was serious for once. "*Si*, I guess I have. We got word you had your trouble last night, *Senor* Cliff. I want to tell you how sorry I am about *Senor* Johnson." She was sobbing then, weeping silently. Cliff let her cry for a while. She looked up, then, smiling, dabbing her eyes with her handkerchief.

When they came to Don Alfredo, the man's dark eyes swept across her. "You are a long ways from home, Maria. What is wrong with that brother of yours? Is he too proud to ride with his sister, that he makes her go on long rides alone? Where is Linda?"

"Miguel was sleeping; he was in Santa Ynez last night, I guess. Linda is working on her crocheting; she has no time for me. And besides, I wanted to see Magdalena Cortez."

"She won't have a peaceful moment with you around," grumbled the wiry Don. The three of them rode toward the Box N *hacienda*, Maria between them. She was chattering now, bird-like and bright. Cliff remembered, suddenly, her quick, responsive tears.

She had not wept for Sis Johnson alone; she had also wept for somebody living. Was she in love with Jeff Garland?

That thought was not pleasant. For if it were true, she would be bound to be hurt.

They rode into the *patio*.

THIRTEEN

Pete Burnett rode across Box N grass, a tight feeling across his spine. This web was weaving itself. The end was in sight, the loom would be shattered. Don Alfredo was working cattle on the benchland that tongued into the Cuyama plain, and Pete Burnett lifted his right hand.

"What do you know, *senor*?"

The wiry Don shrugged, "They were not Horseshoe raiders, you may bet on that, *Rangero*."

Pete Burnett smiled. "We know that, Don Alfredo." He looked across the mountains toward the Big Circle. Two eagles were wheeling around the cone of McPherson, dim and distant and minor dots. "Garland riders, Don Alfredo . . . But there's no evidence, nothing to act on. Somebody'll have to kill

Garland, and that would hurt Maria, your daughter."

Don Alfredo was stony.

"Sorry," murmured Pete Burnett.

"There is no need of apology. Yes, that is the truth, *senor*. She is young, though, and the wound will heal. Two things are his: a rope or a bullet. Let us hope it is a bullet; that would be easier on this girl of mine."

"Why not send her to 'Frisco or Los Angeles? She'll meet young men there; she'll have a chance to forget . . ."

The don nodded.

Burnett turned his horse, said, "*Adios amigo*," and rode west, heading toward across the range on a lope, big in the sunshine. *No business of yours, Pete Burnett,* he thought. *She's not your daughter.* A rider came over the horizon. *There she is now, big as life, and as pretty.*

"A pretty girl, Maria, on a good horse. A sight for any lonesome man's eyes." He was smiling rakishly, quickly aware of the years. "Your father is back yonder, and Cliff Blanton will be glad to see you."

She responded to his barb. "I did not ride this long way to see *Senor* Blanton. Your tongue is quick, Pete Burnett."

Burnett said stiffly, "Yes, *senorita*, and it is sharp, too. Last night, Blanton's herd was raided; Sis Johnson was killed, a Horseshoe man wounded."

"Garland did it, you think?"

He sighed. "Who else on this range, Maria? Garland will show a spot and I'll close in. Or if I don't find it, Blanton will. What will that do to you, girl?"

She bit her lip, white teeth on carmine. "Is it that apparent, *senor*?"

Burnett leaned back against the rim. "Maybe I can see too deep," he said at length. "Maria, he doesn't care. He's older; he's seen more. He's tasted women, he knows them. Oh, don't tell me he hasn't! Watch yourself, girl, and use your head, not your heart." He leaned and put his hand over hers. "I speak this from my heart; I do it for you. "You'll take it that way, *senorita*?"

She said "*Gracias à tu, senor*," and she kissed him on the cheek. The gesture was that of a bewildered little girl. The warmness stirred him.

He watched her ride away, then he rode for the Cuyama. Here cattle had moved, but the gravel was deceptive, hiding hoof-marks on its hardness.

Darkness found him riding into the Big Circle ranch.

The men squatted by a cabin. Jeff Garland said, "Over here, Burnett," but the ranger only nodded to the Big Circle owner and Pedro Martinez, smoking there in the dark. Lights were dim in the bunkhouse and cook-shack. The cook eyed the ranger with dubious uncertainty.

"You hungry?" he asked.

"I could eat," said Burnett.

The Big Circle men lounged in the bunkhouse, some reading, some sleeping, some playing cards. Burnett nodded at various men. One was missing. Finally, he saw that Gordo Garcia was not there. He asked about the fat Mexican and got only grunts and nothing intelligent.

He went outside, squatted beside Jeff Garland. "Where's Martinez?"

"He probably needs sleep."

Garland let that ride. He was waiting for Pete Burnett to talk about the raid on the Box N. Instead, Burnett said, "Why not leave the girl alone, Garland? She doesn't mean anything to you."

Garland said, "Who you talkin' about?"

"Maria de la Mesa."

Garland smiled. "One time, I thought I might marry the Horseshoe *rancho*. Then Don Alfredo, guessing my game, let it be known that his worthless son, Miguel, would get the spread after he kicked off. But what business is that of yours?"

Burnett stirred, said, "If it gets too big, it will hurt her."

"T'hell with her."

Pete Burnett got to his feet. He looked toward the rising moon. "Well, my horse has had a little rest, and I guess I'll push on." Suddenly he said, "Where's Gordo Garcia?"

Garland was silent.

Burnett repeated, "Where is he?"

"I fired him," said Garland. "He rode out sometime yesterday. Is it your business, *rangero*, whether I can a man or not? I'm footin' my payroll; you ain't!"

Burnett said, tough, "Hang onto yourself, Garland. Don't rush into your death! I can't tie this raid onto you; neither can Cliff Blanton, or Don Alfredo. One man was killed last night, the Box N reports. You sure it wasn't Gordo Garcia?"

The moonlight showed Garland's seamed, angry face. "What the hell can you prove, *rangero*?"

Burnett holstered his weapon.

"You're right there, Garland," he admitted.

Burnett lifted his thickness between horn and rim and rode into the moonlight, his back big and broad. Garland looked at the rangero's back, and he had his hand on his pistol. But no, he would wait and see how things went. If they tightened and threatened, mayhap Pete Burnett would inhabit a lonely, badland grave, hidden in the Wilderness.

Garland was quick now, his lassitude gone. He glanced at the moon and hurried toward the barn. He saddled a dark sorrel and stuck a rifle in the boot and went up. He rode out the back door, heading for the timbered reaches.

He rode the plateau, keeping Burnett ahead of him and below him. Garland was puzzled; Burnett did not ride south toward Santa Barbara. He pushed east, heading across the head of the Sisquoc river, running toward McPherson Peak. Garland saw Burnett was never far from this range. Anything that passed, he wanted to see. And, if he did not see it, then he would have eyes posted to watch.

Somewhere, a goat bleated. Garland thought, *He's close to Verde's goats,* and he saw Pete Burnett ride into a clearing, leave his horse and enter the goat-herd's skin tent.

Garland got down, pulled a strand of hair from his horse's tail, tied this around his nostrils to keep the bronc from nickering. He settled on his spurs, watching the hut below.

Thirty minutes later, Pete Burnett left the goat-herd, riding south-east. Garland followed. They were almost a mile high, and Burnett rode at a walk. Garland was tired, and he thought: *I guess I was doomed to live in a saddle. Maybe I'm doomed to die in one, too.*

Now Burnett was riding across a high mountain park, the grass tall against his horse's legs. Garland drew in and watched.

So this is where he is hiding out, huh?

Garland rode back toward the Big Circle. The ride had been long, but it had had good results. From this high vantage, Pete Burnett could sit with field-glasses, the Cuyama range spread out map-like in its true greatness. Men could ride below him; he could see them, perhaps recognize them. What had the *rangero* seen already? Reason said that Burnett had no conclusive proof, otherwise the *rangero* would move against him. He had not acted yet. That meant he had no evidence to act upon.

Now he was on the slope above Enrique Verde's goats and the skin-tent. So Verde was the eyes of Pete Burnett . . . . Big Jeff Garland had a mental note-book in his memory. Penned in it were the names of men on this range. Now he drew a mental pen across one name.

He rode toward the Big Circle.

FOURTEEN

Don Miguel de la Mesa awoke about noon, a wry dullness in him. His mind went back over the night and its doings; that dullness became sharpened with momentary regret. He dressed, aware of his hunger. *Tia* Tompita was working in her garden. Linda was in the kitchen.

"You slept late, *hermano*," she said.

He stretched. *Si*, I was tired." She poured hot water from the tea kettle into the wash-basin, then went back to the stove.

"Where is Maria?" he asked.

"She went to the Box N." Linda added, "She left this morning."

"Is she falling in love with the *gringo?*"

"Would that be a crime?"

"Linda, girl," he said. "Don't give yourself away! Control your eyes!"

"Oh, hell," she snapped. "Close your mouth!"

Something was wrong with her; he guessed what it was. Word of the midnight raid on Box N cattle had reached the Santa Isabella Horseshoe. He would feign surprise.

"What bothers you, sister?"

Don Miguel sat down and started to eat.

Finally Linda told him about the raid on Box N herds, about the death of Sis Johnson. Don Miguel listened. "Garland's raiders, of course. I hope they drive that *gringo* out of the Cuyama! What does Pete Burnett say, *hermana*?"

"What can he do? Raiders hit in the darkness, were unrecognized." She turned, her back against the cupboard, and looked at him steadily. "What have you got to say about it, Miguel?" He heard a trembling in her voice. Panic struck through him; he put it aside.

"What do you mean by that?"

She said, clearly now, "I saw you leave the *rancho* last night. You rode Smokey, your palomino. I followed you a ways. You rode toward the Big Circle *rancho!* at daybreak I was awake; I saw you sneak in! You were not riding Smokey. You were riding a Big Circle horse, a dark horse."

"Then you think I rode with Garland?"

"*Si!* Smokey is light-coloured; you could see him in the night. The horse you rode in on—nobody could see him, Miguel!" She had tears in the corners of her eyes.

He said, "Yes, I was with the Big Circle. Now, I know I did wrong, Linda." He got to his feet, crossed the room, and held her arm. "I didn't know it was that

274

hard—or that savage. They stole Box N cattle. Yes, I helped. They took them across the river—sold them."

"Hush, not so loud."

He sat down again. "Yes, they stole Box N cattle. Everything was arranged: the buyer was there, right on the spot, he had the money. You know what that means, don't you?"

"They could steal our cattle, just as easily?"

He nodded quickly. "That's what it means, Linda. They could steal our cattle, our Horseshoe cattle. Oh, I've suspected it for some time. *Padre* does not know it; he does not ride the range enough. Then, he was trusting of Jeff Garland. But why did Garland let me ride with them? Now I know what he and his men do."

"That is a simple answer."

He got to his feet. "He'd kill me, sis, if word got out. Then, too, I guess he wants to hit at *papa*. I fell for the trap; I let hate for this gringo—this losing our land—I let it pull me on, drawing me in with Garland. If I break with him, he'll kill me. If I work with him, he'll have me as a lever over *papa*. What can I do?."

"I don't know."

"What about Maria?" he asked.

She said, almost savagely, "Maria is going to her cousins in Sacramento. We have talked it over, aunty and I. She will have to go!"

He considered. "That is best. You will not tell *papa?* About me, that is?"

"I am your sister, Miguel. We played together, years ago. Sometimes I am cross. Maybe I am an old maid, as sometimes you accuse me. No, this is our secret. We shall find an answer."

He kissed her, the darkness lifting. "That *Tejano*—that *gringo*—he has eyes for you. He will not let you

275

become an old maid, not if he has his way!"

"Miguel!"

He said, thoughtfully, "Maybe I have him wrong." He remembered Sis Johnson falling from saddle, smashed by Jeff Garland's angry lead. Only he—and Garland—knew who had killed Johnson. Now Johnson would be in Santa Ynez—cold on the slab. Sis Johnson was about his age.

He had the idea, suddenly, that he was marked from here out. In one reckless, swift moment, he had made a wrong decision—if he backed out now, Jeff Garland would kill him. No, he would have to play with Garland, wait for the break to come—

He walked through the dazzling sunshine to the bunkhouse. Linda watched him go. They had this secret—this terrible, living secret—between them.

She hung up her dish-towel.

Linda galloped toward the upper reaches of the Cuyama. Trouble and danger moved back, falling into the distance—the day was good, with warmth and sunshine. Two hours later, when she reached the foothills, she saw Enrique Verde, the goat-herd, ranging his goats close to the hills above the Box N *hacienda*.

"You do not go far in the hills, *senor,* and you carry a rifle. Do you need a rifle to herd goats?"

"He has ordered me out of this range," said the Mexican.

She guessed. "Jeff Garland?"

Verde nodded, eyes glistening.

"He must think he is *el* Dios, *senor*. You are on Box N grass, not his grass."

"But he claims this, too."

She considered. "Be careful," she advised. "He is afraid, maybe, that you will see something your eyes are not supposed to see."

"But what would that be, *senorita*?"

Linda almost smiled at his bland appearance. He was a fox—an old dog-fox—with the fox's wisdom. "I just said that, *senor*, to have conversation. You have seen my father, I suppose, and my sister, Maria?"

She did not ride to see her father, nor did she ride toward the *hacienda*. She found Cliff Blanton turning cattle out of the brush.

"Maria is at the *hacienda* with Maggie," he said. He felt a tightness across his chest. He remembered her slow smile that day in Santa Ynez.

She was a little breathless. "You have had some trouble, I understand?"

He nodded.

"I am sorry," she said softly.

Cliff and Linda spent the afternoon running cattle from the brush. She was a good rider, fast with her spur, and Pipo was a good cutting-horse. They sent the cattle north to where the herd grew on the flat land. Some of the Box N riders were putting the Horsehoe cattle in a bunch to the west, preparatory to shoving them onto Horsehoe grass. The Big Circle cattle were kept in a bunch.

Linda looked at the Big Circle herd. "These cattle go in on the Point?" Cliff assured her they would be held there.

She shook her head, dark eyes serious. "I do not know if that is a wise move. Sooner or later, Jeff Garland and his men will come for them—he will not pay a rent-fee."

"I don't think he will," agreed Cliff.

Her eyes were on him in quiet study. "You know what that means, do you not, *Senor* Cliff?"

"It means guns," he said quietly. His horse was close to hers. He put his arm around her and held her and kissed her on the mouth. Their horses moved apart; he surrendered her. She had that slow look in her eyes, that quietness he had noticed in Santa Ynez.

"Cliff!" she said.

FIFTEEN

Don Alfredo de la Mesa faced his two daughters in the big living-room of the Box N *hacienda*. The past days had rubbed his nerves raw. He did not want them to see his mental jumpiness.

Linda sat deep in the big armchair, looking into the fire. Maria curled in her chair, spineless and dark.

Don Alfredo said, "Then that is settled, Maria. You get the stage in Santa Ynez, tomorrow, and you go to Sacramento."

"My dear cousins in Sacramento," said Maria, scoffingly. "What a good time I'll have!"

Linda smiled.

"But the trip," said Don Alfredo. "And besides, you need to get away for a while. When did you last take a trip?"

"Just a year ago, *padre*. Then, I went to San Diego. How about Linda? She hasn't been any farther than Santa Barbara for four or five years. No, it isn't the trip you are thinking about. You want me to get away from Jeff Garland."

Don Alfredo studied her sharply. The longer he lived, he decided, the less he knew about women.

She smiled then, her face bright. "Don't worry about me, *papa*. Oh *si*, I felt that way toward Garland, a little—but pshaw—I wonder if there are any good-looking young men in Sacramento?"

Don Alfredo raised his hand. "I put it this way, Maria *mia*. You may go or you may stay. For myself, I believe the trip would do you good."

"But *padre*, you need me!"

Don Alfredo paused, stood silent. He knew what she meant. "This will smooth over, Maria," he assured. "No, if you care to go, that is your privilege."

"I'm not going."

"But Jeff Garland."

Maria said, clearly, "To hell with Garland! I won't see him any. Of course, I can't close my eyes if he comes down the street toward me."

Don Alfredo sat down, lips grim.

Maria looked at Linda. "I am going to take the *gringo*—the *Tejano*—away from Linda, *papa*."

Don Alfredo knew they were poking fun at him, but at such a time, and in such a place . . . . "Then you will stay, I understand."

Don Alfredo sat down and laughed. "Both of you are the same as your mother. *Dios*, when I was a young man, and I was courting her—oh, did she make my life miserable!" A sudden gust of wind moved across the stake-roof. "There is rain in that, *senoritas*."

He was correct. The rain came in a sudden, spitting squall.

After Maggie had come in and taken his daughters to their bedroom, Don Alfredo stood beside the fireplace, warming his back and listening to the rain. Maggie came in and said, "Here is a slicker for you, Don Alfredo," and she put the oilskin raincoat around his thin shoulders. "It used to belong to my husband."

"Magdalena," he said slowly, "we are both lonely people."

"You have your son and your daughters," said the old woman. "I have my memories. Hush, Don Alfredo, we shall be gone soon; we shall be with them." He saw the tears in her deep eyes.

"You are a brave, good woman," he said.

She was standing there, shapeless and ageless, when he went into the rain. Riders were stirring through the mist, dark shapes on dark horses. Cliff Blanton stood inside the barn, Shorty Nolan beside him.

Cliff asked, "How long will this last, Don Alfredo?"

"This rain is a month early, at least. I don't think it will last long, *senor*."

"Mud things up quite a bit," declared Shorty.

The don knew what the runty range-boss meant. On a night like this, the Garland riders could stage a successful raid perhaps.

"We're riding double-guard tonight," said Cliff.

Don Alfredo saddled a big black gelding. Other riders were going out, cursing the rain. The don went up and said,

"*Hasta luega, amigos,*" and pushed the black into the night. Soon the water trickled down from his hat-brim and the black was sopping wet.

This would be hard on the tired crew, the don realized. These men had spent long hours in the saddle. Now, through driving rain, they would have to stand night-guard; there was so much range to cover and the crew was small. Men had to be stationed at the Point, too, in addition to the southern range.

Don Alfredo rode the Point. He did not go in when the shift changed. He was tired, but there would be no sleep for him. He was cold, too, but Maggie's slicker turned the rain. He had the slicker unbuttoned in front so he could reach the pistol he had stuck under his *sarape*. But he did not use the pistol that night, for, when morning came, the rain was still falling; the night had passed without mishap. Now a grey, swirling mist covered the earth.

They held a conference in the bunk-house after breakfast. They were burying Sis Johnson this rain-soaked day in the mission graveyard at Santa Ynez.

Don Alfredo spoke. "He was your companion of the trail, *senores*. While we Horseshoe men hold the herds, you men must ride into Santa Ynez."

Cliff said, *"Gracias, senor."*

They let it stand that way. Only Horseshoe men would ride on Box N range. Maggie and Linda and Maria had a good breakfast—oatmeal, hotcakes, bacon and hot coffee. Cliff caught Linda's eye. She smiled at him, the gesture slow, happy.

The Box N men saddled fresh horses. They rode west toward Santa Ynez. The rain came in sudden, bursting squalls. The Cuyama river had risen quite a bit. The creeks were muddy with gushing water.

Cliff said, finally, "This will bust pretty soon."

"And when it does," declared Shorty, "there'll be

282

ell to pay. This thing'll be done up fine, I can tell you. One thing is, we're mighty lucky that the Horsehoe witched to our side. It'd been a chore for the four of us."

When they came into Santa Ynez, the clouds had arted a little, letting rays of sunlight dance across the wet *chamiso*. Few horses were at the hitch-racks and none of them wore the Big Circle iron. They left their roncs with the Mexican at the livery and went to the *antina*. The whiskey was hot—homemade drink—nd it warmed them. The doctor came in, said to Cliff: "I saw you ride in, *senor*. They are ready at the Mission."

They buried Sis Johnson in the graveyard that had the mighty Sierra Madres as a backdrop that showed through the thin rain.

After the ceremony, Cliff went with Father O'Donell to the Mission. The Father said, "I have received word that Pedro Martinez is in town."

Cliff's men had gone to the *cantina* with the doctor. Cliff said, "Thank you, Father," and went into the rain, walking the short distance to the big adobe town. He saw a Big Circle horse—a grey—tied in front of the restaurant. He got his men and they rode down the mainstreet. Suddenly Shorty Nolan saw the Big Circle grey.

He pulled in. "A Garland horse, Cliff," he murmured.

Cliff said, "All right, what about it? Let's ride on."

But Nolan was already going down. He said, "I an't forget Sis, out there in the rain; they're putting dirt over him now."

They stepped down, all of them. They left their roncs there. Shorty Nolan came into the cafe first. Pedro Martinez was sitting at a table and his eyes showed something, Cliff saw.

"There are four of you," he reminded them hurriedly.

Shorty said, "It only takes one," and went up to him. Cliff and Gene Creston and Mack Dunn stood at the door, and Cliff had his gun out. He said clearly, "Let them handle this; nobody interferes, *sabe?*"

There was a silence. The girl waitress stood beside Cliff, pale under her dark, olive skin, her hand at her throat. The obese owner said, whiningly, "They will break up my place, *senor?*"

"We'll pay for it," said Cliff.

Shorty lifted his hand, slapped Pedro Martinez across the jowl. The slap drove the blood out of his cheek.

Martinez got to his feet, eyes thick with anger.

Shorty Nolan gritted, "You got a gun, Mexican!"

"No, no," said Martinez.

Shorty said, "Then use your fists!" and he drove a sharp right against the man. Martinez went back and Cliff saw the gun in his sarape. Martinez was afraid of a gunfight. The Big Circle *segundo* steadied himself and came toward Shorty fists up.

Cliff had seen Shorty in action before, but never had he seen the small man move with such machine-like precision. The blocks were just right, his forearms took Martinez' mauling blows. Those his forearms missed, he took with his shoulders. He knocked Martinez across a table, spilling it with crashing dishes. Martinez got to his feet, fighting hard. Shorty's right almost lifted Martinez, despite his bulk. His left smashed the man, turning him slightly. The right came again. The knuckles fitted under Martinez' jaw. The Big Circle *segundo* went down, and he didn't move.

Shorty stepped back, a thin, tight smile on his lips as he looked at Cliff. "Didn't break too much furniture, did I?"

"Guess not," said Cliff. He looked at the proprietor. *Cauntos?* How much?"

"Get out quick, please! He will come with his shootin' gon, *senor*! The damage, she ees not moch!"

"He won't come to for some time," corrected Shorty.

They rode out of Santa Ynez. The small man was chuckling. "He had a gun, the dog, and he was afraid to use it! Afraid to pull it!"

"He'll meet you with a gun the next time," said Mack Dunn.

SIXTEEN

When the clouds had pulled apart, Don Miguel de la Mesa squatted on a hill, watching the terrain below with field-glasses. He saw the Box N men—the four of them—riding east toward the *rancho* on the upper Cuyama. Now another rider came out of Santa Ynez, heading at a lope across the flat toward the Sierra Madres. Don Miguel saw he was Pedro Martinez.

Evidently he had been in a fight, for his face was swollen. Don Miguel lowered the glasses, smiling a little. He rode into the Big Circle an hour later.

The *rancho* was almost deserted. Pedro Martinez came out of the bunkhouse, a rifle under his arm.

"What happened to your face?" asked Don Miguel.

"What t'hell difference does it make to you!" snapped Martinez. His right eye was black and his jaw was swollen.

Don Miguel smiled, a hardness in the gesture. "You're touchy, fellow," he murmured. "Where's Jeff Garland?"

"Out on the range—somewhere."

"And the Big Circle *vaqueros?*"

"With Jeff, I guess."

The young *Californio* turned his horse. "Probably be over tomorrow sometime," he said. "Don't let another bronc kick you, Pedro. You're homely as hell as it is, without that!"

Pedro Martinez watched the young don ride into the Sierra Madres, but Don Miguel did not ride to the Santa Isabella Horseshoe *rancho*. Unrest was a seething, pushing force inside of him. He had nobody to blame but himself, he thought. He had worked into Jeff Garland plans; now Garland held a club over him.

Now, the Big Circle riders, along with Jeff Garland, were missing from the *rancho*. He remembered, suddenly, the day he had ridden into the Big Circle, then to also find the hands gone. He had been told they were riding the Cuyama bog-holes, but there had been no riders along the river. They had lied to him to throw him off the track. He felt sure, now, that Garland was stealing Horseshoe cattle. He had seen how readily, how easily, Jeff Garland had disposed of Cliff Blanton's Box N cows, poor and meatless as they were.

He put his bronc up a steep slope and, when on its summit, he settled under outcropping boulders and watched the Big Circle buildings, below and to the south.

He did not have to wait many minutes. Pedro Martinez, astraddle a fresh bay horse, left the *rancho*, turning east in the mountains. Don Miguel stepped up and followed, riding the ground higher than the Big Circle range-boss.

Don Miguel pulled in, a wariness whispering in him. With four hours of riding behind him, he was some forty miles from the Santa Isabella Horseshoe, almost straight south of Dripping Springs.

Don Miguel swung around a mountain-side, the sharp wind bitter against him. He left his horse, hiding the lathered beast in the high rocks, and he climbed an outcropping, squatting there with his glasses. Below him, riding out on a high mountain park, was Pedro Martinez. And, also on the park, a group of men were working some cattle.

Eyes puckered against the wind, the young don saw the winding stem of smoke that proclaimed a branding fire. Down there on the park, the high mountains covered with timber, broke the wind. The smoke lifted lazily, grey against the thin air.

Two men tended the fire. Now two riders, roping head and hind-legs, caught a big steer, dragged him unceremoniously to the branding fire. One of the branding-men ran out and branded the steer. While he squatted on the beast's head, the other untied the lassoes, turning the beast loose. The steer trotted away, switching his tail in pain, and the riders hazed him into a separate bunch of cattle.

The glasses showed them clearly. He saw Jeff Garland, wearing a sheepskin coat, on a big horse, doing the head-roping. Another man, also a Big Circle man, roped the hind-legs. Don Miguel lowered his glasses, scowling a little.

He could make out the brands on the cattle Garland's men had just ironed. They bore the Big Circle, of course. But he could not make out the brands of the cattle yet to be rebranded at the far end of the park.

Twenty minutes later, he was close enough. He studied the brands through his field-glasses. He lowered them, face torn by emotion. These were Don Alfredo's Horseshoe cattle! Jeff Garland was turning the Horseshoe brand into a Big Circle!

He had openly rebelled against Garland using a Big Circle brand, but the state brand-commissioner had sanctioned use of the iron on this range.

He saw that Garland was working it cleverly. He had bought five thousand head; he was branding more than that. And when he drove these cattle out to sell them—and if he were stopped—he could claim they were part of the original five thousand head he had bought.

Don Miguel settled back, raking the brush with his glasses. Logic told him that a guard would probably be posted in the gully that led to this mountain branding-ground. Luck had ridden with him. Had he followed directly behind Martinez, he might have blundered in on the guard.

Then he saw Enrique Verde below him. Frowning, he watched the goat-herd come up the mountain. Evidently Verde had been close to the stolen cattle.

If he called to the goat-herd, the Big Circle men below would hear. Don Miguel watched him climb the peak, and then, suddenly, he saw another man.

This man followed Verde, trailing him by a good quarter-mile. Don Miguel, a cold band around his heart, realized that the guard had caught sight of Verde. The goat-herd was doomed to die. For the Big Circle men could not afford to let him live. He had seen their hideout, had seen them brand stolen cattle.

Don Miguel moved upward, working his way around the mountain. Always, he kept Enrique Verde ahead of him.

They were circling the mountain, three men, silent men. Verde, the goat-herd, who did not know he was being followed and the Big Circle guard, who did not know that Don Miguel was above him. A twisted, thin smile pulled at the lips of Don Maguel.

Now the mountain, rearing solidly behind them, separated them from the mountain park where Jeff Garland even now was stealing Horseshoe cattle. With this bulwark shielding them, the wind fell back. Don Miguel watched the guard wondering why he did not act. Then the answer came to him. On this side of the mountain the sound would not travel against the wind to scare the cattle.

Don Miguel's smile grew tighter. He settled on one knee. The guard would have to act soon, or Verde would be in the thick, dense brush below.

A man would be hard to see down there. Don Miguel raised his rifle, centering it on the guard. For the man had stopped, fallen to one knee. He had raised his rifle, put the sight on Verde, some two hundred yards away and in a clearing.

Miguel had never shot a man before. But he had to act fast. Suddenly, he remembered seeing Jeff Garland's gun roar, the bullets pounding ruthlessly into Sis Johnson, killing him and dropping him from his running horse. He found his sights, squeezed the trigger.

The rifle leaped, steadied. The guard below stiffened, dropped his rifle, then broke in the waist, falling on his face. The sound had not drifted to the rustler's camp. Enrique Verde heard it, though, for he fell prone suddenly, belly-down on the wet mountain grass. The guard lay silent. Don Miguel got to his feet, waving his rifle.

The goat-herd got to his feet, waved back. He was standing there, undetermined and trembling, when Don Miguel came to him, carrying his rifle.

"You shot at me, Don Miguel?"

"Did you hear a bullet?" snapped the young don. "Do you think I would miss at this close distance? No, I shot at the man—the Big Circle guard—who was lifting his rifle to kill you!"

"Guard—kill me!"

"Where are your eyes, *senor*? Surely they must be in the soles of your boots!" They walked back to the fallen guard.

"I owe my life to you, *senor*."

Don Miguel rolled the man over, the rifle falling from limp fingers. A whiskery, sallow face looked up, the scar and the black patch over the eye identifying Leo Edwards. He was dead, his heart silent.

Don Miguel got to his feet. "The end of a wasted life," he murmured. "Come, we must get my horse, and take this body out of here. Soon Jeff Garland might look for him."

"You hurry for your horse," stated Enrique Verde. "I wait here, beside this dead coward, with my rifle. This time, my eyes will be open, Don Miguel."

SEVENTEEN

Cliff Blanton left his Box N riders on the Dripping Springs deadline. "Going into the hills, Shorty," he said. "You're the boss on the Box N until I return. I'll be back come sundown."

Shorty asked, "What's in the wind?"

"Pete Burnett," said Cliff.

Shorty nodded. "I'll rod the spread, Cliff."

Cliff put his horse to the south. He headed for the direction of Pete Burnett's camp on McPherson Mountain. He had the swift impression that certain events, hidden from the human eye, were moving in sequence across the Cuyama range. Pete Burnett might have some information for him.

When you ride through the brush, and you expect a bullet any time in your back, the suspense builds up and gains great weight. This was riding on Cliff now. Pedro Martinez had been in Santa Ynez . . . . and he had been alone. Was he a spy for Jeff Garland?

That seemed illogical, though. If he had ridden to Santa Ynez to keep track of Box N men, why had he not hidden his horse instead of tying the animal openly on the street? Cliff mulled that over. He decided that after all, didn't Pedro Martinez have a right in Santa Ynez?

Cliff took his field-glasses from their case on his saddle-skirts. With these, the Point seemed to come closer; Big Circle cattle still grazed there. And Horseshoe *vaqueros* were riding Box N graze, in pairs as they worked cattle out of the rough country.

He put his bronc up a steep mountain. Yonder, cutting across the base of the hills, was a goat-herd, Enrique Verde. He watched him, wandering where the man's goats were; he could not see them, Evidently, from what Pete Burnett had said, Verde worked with him.

Verde was riding a rat-tailed black horse. Cliff watched him move into distance to the west, lost him in the *ocotillo* and *chamiso* and *manzanita*. He got his own horse, pointed him south. He was sitting his bronc in wild rose-bushes, the animal hidden by the high bush, when he saw Enrique Verde again.

He had circled the base of the mountain Cliff was on. Now, below Cliff, he was dismounting, tying his horse in the *chamiso*. Cliff saw the man climb the slope opposite him, then duck over a ridge and disappear from sight.

Cliff was silent in his saddle. Plainly Verde was on the trail of something . . . . or somebody. Cliff waited, patient and quiet.

Finally, the goat-herd returned, still clinging to the

protection of the buckbrush. Below Cliff, the panorama spread out, clear, bright. Behind Verde, he saw Leo Edwards, and he identified the man through his field-glasses.

A third man moved into the play. The field-glasses told him that this man was Don Miguel de la Mesa. The don carried his rifle, he was on foot. The solution came to him with a quick jolt.

Verde had found some evidence against Garland. Edwards was trailing him, intending to kill him. But where did Don Miguel fit into the game? Was he on the side of Leo Edwards? Jeff thought of proud, thin old Don Alfredo, of Linda, of Maria. If Don Miguel rode with Garland—

Leo Edwards went to one knee, rifle rising. Cliff found his sights, laid them against the man who aimed at Enrique Verde. The goat-herd was in a clearing. The distance was far, too far; yet Cliff's bullet might drive Leo Edwards off balance if it missed. But before Cliff could shoot, Edwards was falling ahead, smashed to the grass by Don Miguel's rifle-ball.

Cliff lowered his rifle, eyes puckered. By shooting Edwards, Don Miguel had bought chips in this poker-game of death—chips on the side of Enrique Verde. Cliff stuck his rifle in its saddle-boot and rode down the mountain.

Don Miguel said, "You're off your range, Blanton."

"I could say the same about you, too," murmured Cliff. He looked down at Leo Edwards and spoke to Enrique Verde. "Pete Burnett was telling me to keep an eye on you. I saw you heading across country and I got curious. What's on the other side of this mountain?"

Verde shrugged, evading the question.

Cliff said, quietly, "I heard a cow bawl over there. You just came from there, too, Don Miguel?"

Don Miguel spoke to Cliff, telling him about the stolen herd, how Garland was rebranding Horseshoe cattle with his Big Circle iron. He did not tell that he had ridden with the Garland riders on the Box N raid.

Cliff was silent, adding all this up. The break he wanted, and the opening sought by *rangero* Pete Burnett, was ahead. Now he would gather his Box N men and they, coupled with Burnett and Don Alfredo's Horseshoe riders, would wipe out Garland and his rustlers. This was like a huge sack. Day by day, the drawstrings came closer, gradually closing the sack's mouth. The opening was very small, now. One sudden, quick pull—a short snap—and the sack would be closed.

But they had to get out of this canyon. Three of them were no match for the Garland gunmen. With the goat-herd bouncing behind Don Miguel, they rode from the gully, Cliff leading the old horse that carried Leo Edwards' body. They had kicked sand over the blood where Edwards had fallen. Garland would never know what became of his guard.

They pushed up on the higher levels, working toward McPherson mountain. An hour later, the chill of snow in the air, they met Pete Burnett.

The big *rangero* sat a tough sorrel. "Saw you through my glasses." He looked at Cliff sharply. "What happened?"

Cliff told him.

Pete Burnett rubbed his thick jaw, a smile pulling the seamed corners of his eyes. "Well," he said slowly, "we found the evidence we need. You did wise by taking Edwards' body away from there. Had Garland found his guard dead, he'd 've been suspicious and he might've pulled stakes. We better plant this fellow somewhere."

Pete Burnett's cabin was a mile away. They got a shovel there and they buried Leo Edwards on a mountain meadow. Burnett had hot coffee in his cabin and they settled around the table, drinking the warm fluid. Don Miguel was quiet, young face serious.

He said, slowly, "I have made a mistake, *Senor* Blanton, and I ask your apologies. Blame it on my youth." He was smiling, boyishly.

Cliff said, grinning, "We'll get along, Miguel."

Enrique said, "I was close to the stolen cattles where Garland is branding. He did not have one half of the cattles branded and tomorrow night he should be done, *no es verdad?* He will move them north in the light of the bright moon . . . ."

Pete Burnett asked, "What do you say, Cliff?"

"We'll post guards and watch the hangout and the cattle. Maybe Garland, after he misses Edwards, will leave the cattle, maybe he won't."

Don Miguel shrugged. "He will miss Edwards, of course. I know Edwards pretty well; he wanted to leave, he said. He told other men that, too. Now, perhaps Garland will just figure he left, and he won't come back."

"But his horse?" asked Enrique Verde. "He ees leave his horse behind? He would be on foot in the mountains?"

"Ever since Cliff bent his six-shooter over his head—and Pinto White got killed in Santa Ynez— Edwards has had chilly boots. But he figured that Garland would try to kill him if he pulled out. Garland can't afford to have his men leave him . . . . with what they know. Edwards would take that chance, even on foot, I think."

"We'll see," said Pete Burnett.

Cliff said, "I'll go back to the Box N and we'll work cattle, the same as usual. Pete, you and Enrique watch that hidden brandin' ground. Like Enrique says, tomorrow night they should leave with the herd. All right, we jump them then, down on the level ground. You bring word to us at the Box N if he starts the herd through during daylight, or if the fact that Edwards is missing drives him away from those stolen cattle."

They sat there for an hour, making plans. The dusk was thick when Cliff and Don Miguel went out, and mounted.

He and Cliff rode into the evening, back to the camp. Shorty Nolan rode up.

"Everything okay here, Cliff."

Cliff said, "I'll see you later, Shorty." Don Alfredo rode out, looked at his son. "Glad to see you with us, *hijo.*"

"Glad to be here," said Don Miguel. He and Cliff had agreed not to tell about the stolen herd until morning. The tension in this camp was high enough now. The three of them—Cliff, Don Alfredo, Don Miguel—rode into the *patio* there at the Box N *hacienda*.

"We were waiting for you, Cliff," said Linda. "You've been gone a long time, and you must be hungry."

Cliff smiled. "I could stand some food."

EIGHTEEN

Pedro Martinez rode into the hidden branding-grounds, unmindful of the fact that Don Miguel was trailing him. He was in an angry, sullen mood.

"Boss has been waitin' for you," said Leo Edwards.

Martinez looked at the man with the patch over his eye. "Why don't you get outa my sight," he snapped. "I'm tired of lookin' at you!"

Edwards had his hand on his pistol. "Your face ain't nothin' purty to look at, 'specially since that jassax has kicked you." He added, "But you said more than you figure, Pedro."

Jeff Garland looked at Pedro Martinez's black eyes and swollen face. "Was it a sorrel or a bay that kicked you?"

"Shorty Nolan," said Martinez. "Down in Santa

Ynez. Damn it, don't ask too many questions." A grin twisted his thick lips. "They buried Sis Johnson, then rode toward the Box N. Not a Horsehoe man in town. They must've stayed with the herd."

Garland nodded. "I had a man out, scoutin' the Box N. But there were too many Horseshoe riders there to hit at the daytime. We'll let Cliff Blanton and Don Alfredo hold that Big Circle herd for a few days out there on the Point. We got another day's work here an' then we shove these cattle north across the Cuyama."

Pedro Martinez looked at the stolen Horseshoe cattle. "Best stock ol' Don Alfredo's got, huh, Jeff? We take them through tomorrow night, huh?"

"If we finish branding them by then. Uncoil your lass-rope and build a loop."

"Why not drive them through with the Horsehoe on them? That'll save the time rebrandin' them. Nobody but a cow-thief ever drives cattle by the light of the moon, Jeff."

"You talk like a lazy fool!" Garland's voice was husky. "What if we accidentally meet that damned *rangero*? We're drivin' my Big Circle cattle, not Horsehoe! He can't do a thing, 'though he might have his suspicions."

Martinez considered, stroking his black eye gingerly. "Don Miguel was over to see you at the ranch, today."

Jeff Garland studied him. "Yeah. What did you tell him?"

Pedro Martinez told him that he had said they were out working range. Garland grinned slowly, crookedly. "What he don't know won't hurt him, Pedro. We'll use him again—when we hit the cattle on the Point. Where did he go?"

"Turned back toward the Horsehoe again."

They spent the rest of the short afternoon cutting the herd and roping. Garland and Martinez roped in a team. They were old hands at this work and their loops seldom missed.

Jeff Garland roped with cold precision. He was cold inside, tight with danger. Every fibre of his big body was keened to a tenseness. Although he had a guard at the neck of the canyon, caution rode his big shoulders. This was a deadly game, a rich game—and, if it went amiss, guns would talk. Not that he was afraid of death; every man had to die sometime. But why rush the chore?

He knew the game had run its length, the rope was reaching its end. Sooner or later, this hidden mountain retreat would be found, and then hell would pop on Cuyama range. He'd make a few more raids, then call it quits. He had his take made: he had a fine ranch. He could settle back now, for the goal was almost here. He'd drive Cliff Blanton from the Cuyama. Then, with Blanton gone, he would have Don Alfredo de la Mesa where he wanted him.

That thought was pleasant.

But a number of men were dangerous on this range. Blanton was one; Pete Burnett was another. Garland weighed the *rangero's* danger to him. Well, when the time was ripe, he'd put Burnett out of the way.

He rode up to a runty, long-faced man. "Tony, ride out and take Leo Edwards' guard, will you? I'll send Carl out to relieve you in a coupla hours."

"*Si, Senor* Jeff."

Garland returned to his roping. Dusk was resting on the mountain grass. The wind was cold, touched by high snow on Peak and McPherson. A rider came up.

"*Senor* Edwards, he ees gone," said the runty Mexican.

Garland said, "Explain yourself."

Tony shrugged, spead his thin hands. "I go to the guard place, there at the small spot in the canyon. *Senor* Edwards he is not there. I look for him and I find his horse, tied to the *manzanita*."

"You call for him?"

"No, I did not want to make noise. But I climb the mountain and look for him, but he is not there. I think perhaps he has left, *no es verdad?* He talk sometimes, in bunk-house, about pulling out, as he calls eet."

Pedro Martinez had heard the conversation. "He was there when I came in, Jeff. Hell, he's jerked stakes. He's got that woman down in Santa Barbara; he hasn't seen her for a week or two. He's hit across country."

Garland said, quietly, "But why didn't he take his horse?"

Tony shrugged. "I ride back on guard."

Night riders were stationed in the middle of the meadow, keeping the two herds apart. Garland rolled this in his mind, seeking danger in it. Martinez felt gingerly of his black eye. Finally he said, "You won't see Leo again, Jeff. He'll get that woman, climb tonight's stage, and be in Los Angeles or San Diego in a few days. He's got his stake made; he's mentioned that a couple of times."

Garland considered that. There was meat in it. "He's close-lipped," he murmured. "But maybe something has happened. We better ride out and see."

"Dark," muttered Pedro Martinez.

Garland snarled, "The moon'll be up soon! And that moon is clear—a man can almost read by it . . . ."

They rode to where Tony squatted in the brush, a cold *cigarro* in his lips, his rifle across his knees as he watched the trail. They went down and settled beside him. Garland was tired, sapped by these night rides, and yet he was rawhide. He thought of Texas, and the trouble he had seen there; this was the land, and here he would stay. When he had seen this range, seen the Cuyama valley unfolding below him, running and rising in hills and stretching out into meadows, he had told himself, *This is the spot . . . the ride is over.* Here, a man could spread out, he could send his roots deep into this soil.

Martinez stirred. "The moon, Jeff."

"Light enough to trail," Garland said.

Martinez grumbled, "Hell of a night chore. He's left, I tell you; he's gone to Santa Barbara."

Garland took one side of the canyon, Martinez took the other.

An hour went by, then another. Finally, on a sandy stretch, he saw some tracks—man tracks. He knelt, eyes on them. Riding-boots, trailing spurs. The tracks ran south, then went into the brush, following a trail carved by wild creatures. He found the boot marks on this trail, and then the trail lifted to the pass. Walking slowly, feeling the night's freshness, he returned to Tony, who had his rifle on him as he walked in.

"Watch that trigger, Tony," he murmured.

"My eyes ain't what they used to be."

Garland hunkered, smiled. "Been lookin' at those Santa Ynez girls too close," he said.

Tony chuckled, then raised the rifle again. Pedro Martinez came in, lay on the ground. "I find nothin'," he grunted. "Me, I looked good—there is none." He

303

shook his shaggy head slowly.

Garland told about the tracks he had found. "There is no danger in his leaving, *senor*. He would not talk. He is too smart."

Martinez was right. For, if Leo Edwards did tell about the raids, he would only incriminate himself.

Squatting there, Garland ran over his men, judging them in his mind. Only one, he realized, held any danger toward him. He thought about Don Miguel and decided to wait and see how the youth responded to the next raid. If he showed signs of breaking, a bullet in the back would stop him. You could bury a man out in the rough country and they'd never find him.

Still, he did not like the fact that Edwards had disappeared. Surely the killer—if there had been a gunfight—would have taken Edwards' horse, making it look like the man had ridden out?

"Double the guard, Martinez," he ordered. "Me, I'm goin' up on the mountain, an' take over."

Grumbling, Martinez went to his horse. Carrying his rifle, Jeff Garland again climbed the mountainside. From where he sat under a boulder, he could see the terrain for miles.

The wind could not hit him here. He dozed, his head on his chest. Yet, inwardly, he was razor-sharp; a rat scurried the dry soil, bringing him quickly alert.

Dawn came.

Garland watched it touch the land with its magic fingers, and he marvelled at its beauty. Far to the north, black dots were moving out of the Box N *hacienda*, going like ants in each direction. He counted them and mentally added the number of men in the Horseshoe and Box N crews. They were all below him, he figured. He compared them in number to his crew. They were about of equal strength.

The sun was gaining height and warmth. He had lost his weariness and he was wide awake. He went down the mountain, sliding now and then in shale, carrying his rifle. One of the newcomers was on guard. Garland nodded to him, got his bronc, and rode into the meadow where the men were branding cattle. He got chuck, eating beside the small fire. Pedro Martinez came up, said, "We'll have this herd worked by tonight, Jeff."

"We move them tonight, Pedro."

NINETEEN

That day the three of them—Pete Burnett, Don Miguel and Cliff Blanton—watched from a distant mountain, field-glasses on the men who toiled with rope and branding iron, some three miles away. They said little. Pete Burnett sat cross-legged and Don Miguel leaned his weight on his thighs, his face inscrutable as he watched. He lowered his glasses.

"They'll probably move them tonight, *Senor* Cliff."

"What time is it?" asked Cliff.

Pete Burnett consulted his big watch. "Three," he said. He pocketed the watch and looked at Cliff. "You two had better ride, I'd say."

There was one logical trail to drive the cattle along, as they hurried toward the Cuyama river:

through Estrella Canyon.

"Miguel's right," murmured Pete Burnett. "Anyway, if I was stealin' those cattle, that's the way I'd drive them."

Pete Burnett would stay behind, watching the cow-thieves. When the herd started to move he would ride ahead of it, coming to warn the Box N and Horseshoe crews. Then the two cow-outfits could build their trap and let the Big Circle raiders blunder into it.

Cliff and Don Miguel rode down toward the foothills, keeping the bulk of the mountain between themselves and the Big Circle men. Don Miguel's darkly handsome face was worried.

He said slowly, "I'll have to tell you this, Cliff. I was with Jeff Garland—I rode with the Big Circle— the night they jumped you and ran off your cattle." He was silent for a long moment. "This is hard to put into words, Cliff. But I was angry and it looked like Dad was wrong."

Cliff looked at him.

"Garland got off with about two hundred head of your cattle. We trailed them across the Cuyama into the San Luis Obispo hills. Garland sold them there. The deal was quick; it had been done before."

Cliff asked, "Who killed Sis Johnson?"

Don Miguel temporarily evaded that question. "Gordo Garcia got killed, down there on the Point. They packed him out and we buried him in the hills. But that deal went over so fast, and I got suspicious."

"Who else knows about this but me?"

"They do, of course. The Garland men . . . Then Linda. She saw me ride in early, on a Garland horse. I told her. Now you know."

Cliff asked again, "Who killed Sis Johnson?"

"Jeff Garland. Yes, I saw it. Johnson came up, riding hard, and Garland dropped him from saddle." The scene was still clear in his mind—too clear. The lines were sharp, for the savagery of the scene had etched them deep. "Should I tell my father?"

Cliff shook his head. "No, don't do that. He's proud and hot-headed, Miguel. Linda won't tell, I'm sure. I won't."

"Garland and his men know. They'll spread the word, and it'll get to *papa*."

"We'll have to chance that," said Cliff. "When this is over, either us or the Big Circle will be boss. And if it's us, there won't be any Big Circle men around, we'll see to that."

Don Miguel settled back. "I did the whole thing wrong, Cliff. Here I am—talking about protecting myself—and I'd only get what was coming to me—"

"Don't tell who shot Johnson," warned Cliff. "If Shorty Nolan heard that, he'd lose his head."

They came loping down the slope, gravel sounding under hoofs. Shorty Nolan rode up.

Cliff said, "Gather every Horsehoe and Box N man, Shorty. Every one, *sabe?* Then head for the *hacienda*."

The runty range-boss rode off, heading for a puncher on the horizon. Cliff and Don Miguel rode to the *hacienda*. Don Alfredo and a few of the men were at the bunkhouse, and the don looked at his son sharply.

"Something is bothering you, *hijo*."

Don Miguel grinned crookedly. "You are worse than an old woman, *padre*," he assured. "Yes, you are even worse than *Tia* Tompita."

Cliff told them what he knew: tension and unease

309

gripped them, held them for a long minute, and they went for rifles and cartridges, checking their gun-belts.

Maggie beat the steel with her spoon. A few of the cowboys went in to eat.

"You have not eaten, *Senor* Cliff?"

"No, *madre*."

Her eyes were bright in the glow of the whale-oil lantern. "I shall go to my room, *Senor* Cliff. I shall pray for your safety, and for the safety of these other men. Cattle and grass is not worth this, *senor*."

"They pushed trouble at me," said Cliff slowly. "I either had to fight or run, Magdalena."

She said, "Here, *hijo mio*," and he felt her press something into his hand. She was gone then, moving into the darkness, and he looked down at the golden crucifix with the small diamonds that glistened and shot facets of light against the darkness. He felt something hold his throat and he put the crucifix in his breast-pocket, buttoning the flap down to hold it.

Shorty Nolan came in, riders behind him. "So this is it, huh, Cliff?" Gene Creston murmured, and Cliff nodded.

Cliff said, to Shorty Nolan, "Hit the iron, Shorty."

The short range-boss beat the hanging steel with the butt of his pistol. Men moved out of the bunkhouse and the kitchen, carrying rifles and with their short-guns loaded. They came around Cliff who told them again what they had seen, and that cattle would move down Estrella Gorge toward the Cuyama river.

They would station men along the sides of the brushy gorge. Cliff said, "Shoot to kill, men, for when they shoot, they'll want to kill you."

"I'd like to know who killed Sis Johnson," said

Shorty Nolan quickly. "I'd like to get that man lined up on my sights."

"Forget Sis for now," said Cliff quietly. Again, he outlined the plan, making it clear in the minds of the riders. They got their horses, then, and rode out. Don Miguel rode beside Cliff.

Cliff said, "Estrella Gorge is ahead, men."

In the sandstones they pulled in, dark in the darkness of the shadows.

A Horseshoe rider, about twenty, turned a cigarette. Mack Dunn's fist came in, knocking the match from him.

"Not here," said the Texan. "A match flame carries far."

The young fellow tore the cigarette apart, and Mack Dunn put his arm around his shoulders. "You'll do to ride the river with, Ricardo," he said.

The Mexican did not understand the Texas saying. But the youth smiled quickly. "*Gracias, senor.*"

Cliff said, "Shorty, you're the boss on this side of the gorge. Don Alfredo, you and your men cover the other side. Pete Burnett'll warn us in time."

They settled back, letting themselves relax. Shorty Nolan was tight, his ears ready. Don Miguel lay beside Cliff, sprawled out and silent, his father beside him.

The minutes dragged by. Don Miguel said, "Almost two hours since we came here, Cliff."

Cliff said, "Burnett'll come. He knows where we'll be."

Another hour passed. Restlessness was settling on the crew. They wanted action, or they wanted to settle down. Shorty Nolan said quietly, "I hear cattle somewhere, men."

The restlessness passed. Cliff got to his feet, hand

311

against the boulder. Pete Burnett rode in right hand high, and they went around him and his horse.

"They're coming," said the *rangero*. "They're about three miles back, I'd say. Get your men out in places, Cliff."

Pete Burnett told him that Pedro Martinez and Jeff Garland rode point, with the rest of the Big Circle men pushing the cattle. When he had left the herd, Martinez and Garland had been about a mile ahead of the cattle, making sure that the canyon was clear.

Cliff said, "All right, listen to this. Let Martinez and Garland ride through. You men take the Big Circle riders. I'll get Garland."

Shorty said, "There's still Martinez. I ride with you, Cliff. Two to two then, not two to one."

"I go with Cliff," said Don Miguel.

Shorty said, looking at the *Californio*, "Blanton and me has rid a long ways, Miguel. What do you say, Cliff?"

Cliff knew why Don Miguel wanted to ride with him. He said, "We need you on the rim, Shorty."

"You're the boss," said Shorty Nolan.

They were riding out then, with Cliff and Don Miguel watching them. Pete Burnett said, "Hope this turns out all right, Cliff," and Cliff said, "It will, Pete." Then the ranger was riding south, hoping to catch up with Shorty. Cliff saw Don Alfredo and the Horseshoe men dipping out of sight, riding over the lip of Estrella Gorge.

Don Miguel said, "Cattle, Cliff. I can hear them."

Cliff said, "We'd better go."

They left their horses in the rocks. Carrying rifles, they went over the lip, sliding in the shale.

Cliff settled, said, "You stay here, Miguel. I'll take

the opposite side. They'll probably have men riding the rim, too, but I guess Shorty and your father will take care of them."

Cliff crossed the canyon floor, fifty feet wide at this point, and put himself on his haunches in some *chamiso*. He could see the brush behind which Don Miguel hankered, but he could not see the *Californio*. The cattle came closer, and then Jeff Garland and Pedro Martinez were riding toward them, their broncs on a running-walk. Both men, Cliff noticed, carried rifles.

Cliff and Don Miguel went out into the moonlight. Garland and Martinez had stopped some sixty feet away, and Garland said, loud and clear, "Cliff Blanton, huh? An' Miguel, too!"

Martinez said, voice sharp, "They're on to our game, Jeff!" and he was leaving his horse, hitting the ground with this rifle across the saddle and with the horse shielding him. Jeff Garland, too, was going down, and Cliff was shooting.

He was on one knee; Garland's horse was rearing, and Garland was shooting over the saddle. Cliff heard something whine into the bank behind him and he shot three times, dropping Garland's horse. Garland was on both knees, his waist buckling, and he dropped his rifle. He said something, but Cliff could not hear it clearly, and then Garland was silent, his head twisted under his shoulders as he lay face down beside his dead horse.

Cliff put his rifle toward Martinez, but the man was down. Martinez's horse ran by, wild with fear, stirrups flapping against his ribs, and disappeared down the gorge. Cliff got to his feet and looked at Don Miguel, who stood on wide, unsteady legs. To the south, rifles and pistols were talking, and already

313

cattle were running.

Cliff said, hurriedly, "You hurt, Miguel?"

"I'm all right. You?"

"We better get these men out of here—when the cattle come—"

They got Garland and Martinez up the bank a ways, putting their bodies in the rocks. The guns had quit now, and Cliff waited, the cattle coming closer. They were running wild, uncontrolled; they were like his thoughts. He saw them come, split up over the dead horse, and dust rose. This settled, and the cattle were gone, their running thin as it retreated into distance.

"They're both dead," said Don Miguel.

Cliff said, "They are." Riders were coming along the rim, calling for them, and Cliff called back. He heard Shorty's voice and he asked, "Where's Don Alfredo?"

"Them rustlers headed west," hollered Shorty. "Him an' his men were on that side, so they took after them."

Don Miguel said, suddenly, "My leg," and he slid down, with Cliff catching him. Shorty and Mack Dunn and Gene Creston came sliding down and they took the youth, and laid him on the ground. Cliff said, "They got you, huh, and you said you'd got through okay—"

"You had enough on your hands down there," said Don Miguel.

Cliff looked at Shorty. "The rest of the men."

Shorty said, slowly, "One got killed, Cliff. A Horseshoe man."

Ricardo," murmured Mack Dunn. "We never left a one of them living, 'cept those that are getting away. I don't think they'll come back."

"Riders comin'," said Gene Creston. "Both directions, Cliff. Yonder's Don Alfredo, comin' back." He counted the men who raced across the plain toward them. "They're all there, 'cept Ricardo."

Cliff walked forward, meeting Linda and Maria. Maria said, "Dad, and Miguel," and did not wait for an answer, but rode into the circle of rocks. Linda looked down and Cliff remembered her as he had first seen her than night in Santa Barbara.

She said, "Papa, and Miguel?"

Cliff said, "They are all right. Ricardo was killed. Garland and Martinez are dead, too."

She said, "Oh, God," and she came down. She was weeping then, and Cliff held her. They were dead and they would breathe no more; she wept for her enemies, she wept for mankind. Cliff caught that swift impression again: the greatness of her, the kindness, the shadows, the light. He had caught it once before, holding it for a brief second, that night when he had met her with the lights of Santa Barbara touching her. He had wanted to put his head against her dark hair then, but they had been strangers. Now, with this behind him, he lowered his head against hers, putting this face against her dark, smooth hair. Her sobs were leaving her, but still he felt the touch of her tears against his lips. He held her and let her sobs die, and she was quiet then.

DOUBLE-BARREL WESTERNS

Twice the Action —
Twice the Adventure —
Only a Fraction of the Price!

Two complete and unabridged novels in each book!

Hell to Hallelujah and **Ride to the Gun**
by Ray Hogan.

__2917-0 $3.95

Hangman's Range and **Saddle Pals**
by Lee Floren.

__2913-8 $3.95

Vengeance Valley and **Wildhorse Range**
by Allan K. Echols.

__2928-6 $3.95

LEISURE BOOKS
ATTN: Customer Service Dept.
276 5th Avenue, New York, NY 10001
Please add $1.25 for shipping and handling of the first book and $.30 for
each book thereafter. All orders shipped within 6 weeks via postal service
book rate.
Canadian orders must reflect Canadian price, when indicated, and must be
paid in U.S. dollars through a U.S. banking facility.

Name _____
Address _____
City _____ State _____ Zip _____
I have enclosed $ _____ in payment for the books checked above.
Payment <u>must</u> accompany all orders.   ❑Please send a free catalogue.

REAL WEST

The true life adventures of America's greatest frontiersmen.

THE LIFE OF KIT CARSON by John S.C. Abbott. Christopher "Kit" Carson could shoot a man at twenty paces, trap and hunt better than the most skilled Indian, and follow any trail — even in the dead of winter. His courage and strength as an Indian fighter earned him the rank of brigadier general of the U.S. Army. This is the true story of his remarkable life.

__2968-5 $2.95

THE LIFE OF BUFFALO BILL by William Cody. Strong, proud and courageous, Buffalo Bill Cody helped shape the history of the United States. Told in his own words, the real story of his life and adventures on the untamed frontier is as wild and unforgettable as any tall tale ever written about him.

__2981-2 $2.95

LEISURE BOOKS
ATTN: Customer Service Dept.
276 5th Avenue, New York, NY 10001
Please add $1.25 for shipping and handling of the first book and $.30 for each book thereafter. All orders shipped within 6 weeks via postal service book rate.

Canadian orders must reflect Canadian price, when indicated, and must be paid in U.S. dollars through a U.S. banking facility.

Name _____

Address _____

City _____ State _____ Zip _____

I have enclosed $ _____ in payment for the books checked above.

Payment <u>must</u> accompany all orders.   ❏Please send a free catalogue.

**THE RAPID-FIRE WESTERN SERIES THAT FEATURES
AUTHENTIC AUTOMATIC WEAPONS
ACTUALLY USED IN THE OLD WEST!**

GATLING

by Jack Slade

Master armorer, dead shot and expert in the art of death, Gatling tested automatic weapons from all over the world — on live bodies. At his command he had more firepower than a cavalry regiment, and more guts than a Cheyenne war party. Paid in gold for his bloody work, he was probably the single most dangerous man in the Old West.

2750-X	#1: ZUNI GOLD	$2.95
2751-8	#2: OUTLAW EMPIRE	$2.95
2807-7	#3: BORDER WAR	$2.95
2846-8	#4: SOUTH OF THE BORDER	$2.95
2873-5	#5: THE WAR WAGON	$2.95
2912-X	#6: BUTTE BLOODBATH	$2.95

LEISURE BOOKS
ATTN: Customer Service Dept.
276 5th Avenue, New York, NY 10001
Please add $1.25 for shipping and handling of the first book and $.30 for each book thereafter. All orders shipped within 6 weeks via postal service book rate.
Canadian orders must reflect Canadian price, when indicated, and must be paid in U.S. dollars through a U.S. banking facility.

Name _____
Address _____
City _____ State _____ Zip _____
I have enclosed $ _____ in payment for the books checked above.
Payment <u>must</u> accompany all orders. ❑Please send a free catalogue.

ROMER ZANE GREY

Classic Tales of action and adventure set in the Old West! Characters created by Zane Grey live again in exciting books written by his son, Romer.

THE OTHER SIDE OF THE CANYON. Laramie Nelson was a seasoned Indian fighter, cowhand, and shootist, and above all a loner. Although he was one of the most feared gunmen in the Old West, his word of honor was as good as his sharpshooting.
__2886-7 $2.95

THE LAWLESS LAND. Back on the trail, Laramie Nelson confronted an outlaw chief, performed a top-secret mission for President Grant, and tangled with a gang of blockaders aiming to start a range war.
__2945-6 $2.95

KING OF THE RANGE. The Texas Rangers needed somebody who could ride all night through a blizzard, who could track like an Indian, and who could administer justice from the barrel of a Colt .44 — they needed Buck Duane.

__2530-2 $3.50

LEISURE BOOKS
ATTN: Customer Service Dept.
276 5th Avenue, New York, NY 10001
Please add $1.25 for shipping and handling of the first book and $.30 for each book thereafter. All orders shipped within 6 weeks via postal service book rate.
Canadian orders must reflect Canadian price, when indicated, and must be paid in U.S. dollars through a U.S. banking facility.

Name _____
Address _____
City _____ State _____ Zip _____
I have enclosed $ _____in payment for the books checked above.
Payment <u>must</u> accompany all orders.   ❑Please send a free catalogue.

SPEND YOUR LEISURE MOMENTS WITH US.

Hundreds of exciting titles to choose from—something for everyone's taste in fine books: breathtaking historical romance, chilling horror, spine-tingling suspense, taut medical thrillers, involving mysteries, action-packed men's adventure and wild Westerns.

SEND FOR A FREE CATALOGUE TODAY!

Leisure Books
Attn: Customer Service Department
276 5th Avenue, New York, NY 10001